HUNGER FOR LIFE

ANDY MARR

To Anna,
With love to you and your
beautiful family.

For Seonaid.

You are forever in my thoughts.
Our past beats inside me like a second heart.

PROLOGUE

IT'S A WARM, SUMMER AFTERNOON AND I'M STANDING OUTSIDE AN enormous stone building that I will later learn is the Royal Infirmary of Edinburgh. I've never seen such a huge building before and can hardly believe the number of windows and doors that line its vast, turreted façade. Birds are singing in the branches of the giant oaks that stand to either side of me. There's a cut-grass smell in the air. I close my eyes for a moment, feel the sun's warmth against my cheeks, then look up at Dad, who's waiting patiently for me to finish taking in the scene. 'Ready?' he says. I nod my head. He ruffles a hand through my hair, touches my shoulder, and together we walk across the street and into the hospital building.

When we reach the ward, I see Mum sitting on a bed with a little bundle of blankets at her breast. She smiles broadly as I scamper over to her. 'Look, baba,' she says, moving the little bundle down towards me. 'You have a little sister.' I stand on my tiptoes to gaze into the blankets and a tiny little face looks back at me. I'm amazed; I had no idea they made people so small. Mum smiles and pats the bed next to her. 'Come on up,' she says. I'm too small to climb all that way, but Dad's there to help me. He lifts me onto the mattress and I bounce over towards Mum, desperate for another look at my sister. 'Would you like to hold her?' Mum asks. I nod so hard that my neck starts to hurt.

Mum makes me scoot up against the pillow and places the baby next to me on the bed. I place a gentle hand on her chest, and then look at Mum and Dad to check I've done everything right. Dad smiles. So does Mum. 'Oh my, what a wonderful big brother you are!' she says. My chest swells with pride.

'Can you remember her name?' Dad asks.

I scrunch up my face, searching for the name I've forgotten ten times already. Mum and Dad laugh. 'It's Emma,' Dad says. 'Can you say Emma?'

I look down once more at the little bundle, sleeping softly against my leg. She's the most beautiful thing I've ever seen. 'Emma,' I say.

Soon, my head begins to drop, and before I know it I am being shaken awake by Mum. I prise open my eyes and find myself cheek against cheek with Emma. I smile as I gaze into her face. Mum strokes my face and says, 'Time for you and Daddy to go home, sweetheart.'

I throw out my bottom lip, let it wobble a little. 'My want to stay bit longer.' But visiting time is over. Dad picks me up off the bed and plops me on the floor next to my shoes. 'Baby!' I say, starting to cry.

'Don't worry, James,' Mum says. 'Emma will be home with Mummy tomorrow. After that you can spend the whole rest of your lives together.'

I consider this. A whole lifetime together? It's a lovely thought. It's lovely enough even to stop me crying. I walk over to the bed and stand on my tiptoes, plant a kiss on Emma's face. See you tomorrow, I think. And every day after that, forever and ever.

Forever and ever. It's a long, long time.
I cannot wait for it to start.

PART I

1

'AREN'T WE THERE YET?' MUM ASKED, GLANCING RESTLESSLY at the buildings that blurred past our window.

'Be there in a jiffy,' the driver said. His answer prompted a groan from Mum; he'd said the same thing when she'd asked the question a minute earlier. And the minute before that. Perhaps he noticed Mum's reaction, because he immediately made an effort to strike up a conversation. 'You here on holiday, then?' he asked, cheerily. Then, remembering where we were headed, he pinched the bridge of his nose with his fingers and cringed. 'Ah, bollocks,' he said. 'I'm sorry, love.'

Mum said nothing, just sighed heavily and combed a hand through her hair for the hundredth time that morning. I laid a hand on her arm and, trying to keep the panic from my voice, told her everything was going to be okay.

'Oh?' Mum said, turning impatiently towards me. 'And you know that, do you?'

My eyes dropped to the floor. The truth was that no, I didn't. If I'd known for sure, I wouldn't have felt so much like puking. 'I'm sure it's just another false alarm,' I said. 'You know how much they love their false alarms.'

But Mum's attention had already strayed once more to the streets outside. 'For goodness sake,' she said, pressing her face to the window of the taxi. 'I still have no idea where we are. Damn it, I knew I should have booked a hotel closer to the hospital.'

Actually, we'd tried to do exactly that when searching for a place to stay a few weeks earlier, but our visit had coincided with the year's Wimbledon championship, and with the courts only a couple of miles from the hospital building all the nearby hotels were either completely full or charging twenty-third century rates for their rooms. Even when we'd started to look further afield, the pickings had been unbelievably slim. We'd eventually been forced to settle for a twin room in some dusty budget hotel on the outskirts of the city.

Mum was in no state to remember this fact. She'd been a bundle of nerves ever since the phone call had driven her from her bed earlier that morning. The same call had woken me, and I'd listened groggily as our latest telephone drama had played out a few feet from my pillow. 'Oh god,' I'd heard Mum say. 'And now? Is she conscious?' When the answer came she put a hand to her chest and breathed deeply, before nodding for me to start getting my shit together, which I promptly did.

Tucking the phone beneath her chin, Mum began fumbling through her suitcase for some fresh clothes, which she threw onto the floor of our tiny en-suite. 'So, what dosage did you offer her?' she wanted to know. The muscles in her jaw tightened as the answer came through. 'You bloody fools,' she said. 'Have you already forgotten how she reacted to the Prozac you gave her last month?' She picked up a towel from the edge of her bed and turned once more towards the bathroom floor. 'Listen to me,' she said. 'Don't take your eyes off her for a second. I'll be there as soon as I can.'

Mum was true to her word. Less than an hour after she hung up the phone, the cab pulled up at the front door of St Jude's. Mum handed the driver the crumpled banknote she'd been fussing with throughout the journey before clambering outside the taxi and towards the hospital.

St Jude's looked pretty much the way you'd expect it to; a collection of brutal concrete structures that were about as welcoming to patients as the symptoms that had brought them there in the first place. The building that Emma was in, the Victoria Wing, was the ugliest of all, a hideous, out-of-scale monster that had been thrown up with breath-taking clumsiness in the middle of a car park and clad in crusty grey bricks. It was deeply demoralising and barely functional, and it caused my heart to sink whenever I saw it.

Inside the building, there was none of the usual light or warmth you generally associated with hospitals. The whole place was dingy and lifeless, its walls covered in dirty scuff-marks and bits of old Blu-Tack. Emma's ward, the eating disorders ward, *did* boast a nurse's station, but the space was forever empty, and there *was* a so-called common room, but its turquoise chairs all had gashes in their vinyl covers and its television was set permanently to an obscure music channel that seemed to play the hits of Dire Straits on repeat. Put simply, the place was little more than a shithole.

Mum and I made our way along the ward's narrow main corridor, past a ghostly figure who stood with a phone to her ear, whispering desperately for her listener to take her home. A few yards further along, another waiflike girl sat huddled inside a blanket, staring emptily at the wall in front of her. By the time we reached Emma's door a moment later, we still hadn't encountered a single member of staff, so we made our way directly into the room. We found her lying beneath a heavy blanket on her bed, her gaze fixed on the ceiling above her.

'Oh, sweetheart,' Mum said. 'How are you feeling?'

Emma did not move and made no attempt to answer.

'Emma?' Mum said, more urgently this time. 'Can you hear me?'

Emma's head moved, almost imperceptibly, towards us. 'They fucked up again, Mum.' she said, weakly.

Mum and I both breathed a sigh of relief. 'Oh, my darling,' Mum said. 'Thank goodness you're alright.'

'I'm really not,' Emma said, though I think even she knew what Mum meant.

'How's your head?' Mum asked.

'It's okay.'

'Does your chest hurt? Have they checked your blood pressure?'

'Mum,' Emma said. 'You don't have to worry. The panic's over.'

'Are you sure?' I asked. 'Because you still look fucking terrible.'

'James!' Mum snapped. 'Language!' But I could see my comment had brought its desired result; the hint of a smile on Emma's lips. 'Thanks, Jamie,' she said. Then, pressing a fist to her temple, she lay back down on her pillow and closed her eyes.

Feeling suddenly bereft, I sat down on the chair by Emma's window and looked around her spare, institutionally impersonal room. For the past four months, Emma had been almost entirely confined to this poky little chamber. It contained nothing more than her bed, a battered chest of drawers, and a small television with a crack in its screen. Since she no longer had the energy to watch television and spent her whole time lying in bed, the chest of drawers was her only distraction from the thoughts that plagued her mind.

Emma's doctors back home in Scotland had never wanted to send her to London, had hoped instead to find her a room in Hope Park, the Glasgow clinic where she'd spent her first spell in hospital and where she'd shown some signs that she might eventually want to get better. But Hope Park had remained agonisingly full even as Emma's health had continued to decline, and eventually the doctors had been forced to shut their eyes and say a silent prayer as an ambulance arrived outside our home to drive Emma the four hundred miles to London.

It had been clear since Emma's first night in the hospital, when the staff had reneged on its promise to offer her one-to-one supervision after meals, that St Jude's would fail to provide her with the level of care she needed. In the weeks that followed, Emma had frequent panic attacks, but the staff regularly left her to cry on her own. She was supposed to be allowed out for fifteen minutes each day to sit on a bench in the garden outside the ward, but the nurses constantly claimed they were too busy to take her. One morning, when she was told she wasn't allowed to do her group therapy, she argued back and was locked in her room for an entire day.

Emma was terrified. Each night, she'd call home, beg us to help her escape her confinement. 'You have to get me out of here,' she'd say. 'It's such a terrible place. They're making me worse.'

'We can't do that, darling,' Mum would tell her.

'I'll try harder. I'll be good if I come home. Please, Mum. Help me, please, for fuck's sake.'

Emma had never sworn as a kid, but in the past few years she'd been confronted with the full ugliness of life and her childhood cries of *darn it* and *blooming heck* had been replaced with *fuck* and *shit* and all manner of other profanities. Mum and Dad had staged a few protests when they first heard her curse, but pretty soon they'd grown so used to it that they'd given up asking her to stop.

Not that anyone could blame Emma for swearing. Even the Edinburgh doctors were openly frustrated with her treatment. For three months, they'd forced themselves to continue working with their London counterparts, but by early summer the relationship had soured to such a degree that they began making arrangements to have Emma moved from St Jude's. It was welcome news, but there was a mountain of paperwork to clear before anything could happen, and until then there was nothing for us to do but stand by and watch Emma continue to suffer in the narrow confines of her room.

It would have helped Emma to have us around more, to offer that bit of physical affection she missed so badly. But there was no question of us making a day trip to London all the way from Scotland, and the cost of accommodation in Tooting, even at non-Wimbledon prices, made it impossible to stay in the city for longer than a few days at a time. So, reluctantly, we'd been forced to settle for our daily phone call to Emma's room and a weekend visit at the start of every month.

By the time of my fifth visit, there'd come to be a shape and character to the days I spent in London. They were strange days, now I look back on them, built entirely around the hours I spent with Emma. When I wasn't in the hospital,

I could generally be found walking restlessly around the neighbouring streets or reading books in a nearby park. Others might have found it difficult to ignore the grand museums, libraries, concerts, and the whole vast infinitude of cultural opportunities London offered, but I never once considered making use of its attractions during those trips to the city. I was there for the sole purpose of visiting Emma, and when I wasn't in her room itself, I simply wanted to remain close by, to feel my proximity to her.

Visiting times were after lunch and dinner. On Emma's better days, we listened to music and shared gossip as we flicked through the pages of her fashion magazines. On bad days, when Emma refused to rise from her bed, I lay by her side, my head touching hers, and shared whatever thoughts happened to be passing through my head at the time. I took care to make the best of every moment we spent together, though the pleasure of being with her was tempered by the thought that I'd soon be forced to abandon her once more. I tried to forget this during my visits, to remain relentlessly bright and cheery, but the plan never quite worked, and my hours in her room were pervaded by a sense of sadness and panic.

I felt this even more keenly than usual in the minutes that followed my early-morning race to the hospital with Mum. Still stoned following her most recent overprescription of anti-depressants, Emma had fallen asleep long before Mum and I caught sight of our first nurse, a large, humourless lady with thin lips and an enormous shock of grey hair. She was clearly surprised when she entered the room to find us sitting with Emma. Mum was furious. 'Where the hell have you been?' she demanded. 'Why on Earth was nobody here watching Emma?'

There was a long silence. The nurse shifted her eyes

nervously around the room, as if she half hoped to find one of her workmates waving to her from the top of Emma's telly. 'I don't know,' she said, eventually. 'My colleague must have gone on break.'

Mum exhaled impatiently. She'd been a nurse herself for longer than I'd been alive and, having spent years caring for patients on busy wards, she was painfully aware of how badly the hospital was failing Emma. 'Your colleague shouldn't have gone on break without advising anybody,' she said. When the nurse shrugged, Mum clamped her eyes shut and took a deep breath. 'Okay,' she said. 'I'd like to speak to the person in charge, please.'

The nurse sniffed. 'I'll go and get her,' she said.

'No,' Mum said. 'I'll come with you. Emma's seen enough drama already this morning.'

'I'm coming too,' I said, standing up from my chair.

Mum shook her head. 'There's no point in both of us ruining our day,' she said. As though our days weren't ruined already. 'You stay here, keep Emma company. I'll see you outside in a few minutes.'

When Mum left the room, I walked over to the edge of Emma's bed. My chest, I realised, felt heavy, though what it was heavy with – sorrow, fear, rage – wasn't immediately clear. The way the morning had gone, it might well have been all those things at once.

I knelt down beside Emma, and when I placed a hand on her bony shoulders I started to cry. At twenty years of age, she had the body of someone of eighty or more. Her once-soft skin was stretched tight over her face, her hair dull and brittle. It broke me to remember how she'd used to laugh as we played together as children, how deeply in love she'd been with life and the world. Now, lying asleep on a hospital bed hundreds of miles from home, she was too old to be young, and always would be. She'd learned the cruelty of life, and no longer had room in her heart for anything but sadness and pain.

I brought my hand to Emma's face, ran my fingers across her cold cheek. 'I'll be back to see you soon,' I said, my voice shaking. 'You'll feel better by then.' I took a deep, stuttering breath, blew it out again as the next great wave of emotion crashed against my chest. 'I'm so sorry you're feeling like this. Remember, though, we've been here before. Things will be better. It takes time, but you'll come home and we'll get over this. Until then, don't give up. Please, Emma, don't give up.'

I took in another deep lungful of air, wiped my eyes with the sleeve of my coat. Then, as quietly as I could, I kissed my baby sister on the forehead and made my way from the room.

The rain continued to beat down as Mum and I made the short walk from the hospital to breakfast at a small café on Tooting High Street. We'd made regular visits there since our first journey to London some months ago, not because the food it served was particularly good, but because we wanted to establish some kind of routine during our trips to London and a regular eating place seemed central to this plan.

The café was called Marvin's Mochas, for no good reason at all. For one thing, its owner's name was Giovanni, and for another the only coffee they sold came out of the industrial-sized bucket of Nescafé that stood behind the counter. It was a proper greasy-spoon café, the kind that cooked everything in lard and served its drinks in stained, chipped mugs. But while it was far from sophisticated, it suited our needs perfectly. Giovanni and his waitresses were polite, the screwed-to-the-floor chairs were pretty comfortable, and the food cost hardly anything at all. This final perk was of the utmost importance, as neither Mum nor I ever left St Jude's with anything close to an appetite and were reluctant to spend money on food that wouldn't be eaten.

'I'm sorry, James,' Mum said, after a silence that had lasted through our attempts to make a dent in our very full English breakfasts. 'I know this wasn't the way you planned to celebrate your graduation.'

I shrugged. 'Yeah, well. There'll be plenty of time to celebrate when Emma's out of hospital.'

Mum looked at me, sadly and with great sympathy. 'Why don't you go into the city tomorrow?' she asked. 'You could go and visit the art gallery. You like galleries. Or take a ride on that big wheel of theirs.'

'The London Eye,' I said.

Mum chuckled. 'Well, okay,' she said. 'If that's what you want to call yourself.'

I let that one go. The morning had been difficult enough already.

'Thanks,' I said. 'But I'm fine here.'

Mum looked disappointed. 'I'm happy to visit Emma on my own you know.'

'I know,' I said. 'But I want to see her.'

We fell into another silence, more awkward this time. No stranger to awkwardness, I knew the best way to shake off an unwanted silence was by pretending to text a friend, so I reached for my phone. However, my hand had barely found my pocket when Mum caught my attention with a well-timed cough. When I looked up from the table, I found her smiling sadly at me. 'James?' she said.

Oh dear. We were about to have one of our little conversations. Our little conversations always began with those sad little smiles. Sighing discreetly, I offered Mum a little smile of my own, inviting her to continue.

'Have you considered taking that little holiday now you're finished with your studies?'

'Oh, Mum,' I said, pushing my plate away from me. 'Please. Not today.'

'I know. But... have you?'

My little smile vanished, making way for an angry little frown. 'Mum, I already told you I have.'

Despite the little frown, Mum relaxed slightly in her chair. 'Good,' she said. 'That's good. Because, you know, you have a chance to really *do* something this year.'

Mum had been talking like this for some time now, talking about the possibility of my travelling in the months after I graduated. It would be good to broaden my horizons, she said, to meet a few new people, see a bit of their world. On every occasion I'd nodded thoughtfully, told her what a good idea it was. In truth, though, I had no intention of broadening my horizons any further than my own back garden.

Perhaps I could have risked a week away, but I knew Mum wasn't just talking about a weekend in Paris, or a few days in Skye; she was talking about a month in Canada, or a winter in Australia. There was no way I could do that. Canada was hours from home, Australia an entire day. That was way too far, Emma was way too sick. I'd never forgive myself if anything happened to her. There was just no way I'd forgive myself.

I don't know how long Mum had known that I was anxious, but she was certainly aware of it now. 'You don't have to worry,' she said. 'Your dad and I will look after her.'

I snickered. 'Dad will look after her, huh? Like he's looking after her now, you mean?'

Mum shook her head, but said nothing. For a long moment there was only the sound of the rain outside the window. Then, finally, she took a deep breath and leaned across the table towards me. 'James, I know things aren't easy at the moment, but you can't miss out on life because of your family. It wouldn't be right. None of us want to hold you back.'

Sighing, I inclined my head. 'Yeah, I know.'

'Especially Emma,' Mum said.

'Jesus, Mum, I *know*!'

Mum stiffened, her eyes going hard and frosty, and sat back in her chair again. Raising her eyebrows, she checked the bill that sat on the table, counted out some pound coins and dropped them onto the Formica. 'Well,' she said. 'I think we both need to go back to the hotel, get a bit of rest. Let's just drop the subject for now, shall we?'

That was fine by me. I hadn't wanted to speak about it in the first place.

12 JULY 2004

I can't stop my thoughts. I can't stop comparing myself to others. I can't stop looking at myself, both directly and in the mirror; I have to check that I'm not too fat yet. I feel bloated and when I look at myself, I feel repulsed. Still, I can't stop myself looking. Not looking makes me paranoid, so I have to check.

I'm frightened that I'll never get better. I'm scared of being trapped and confused and dictated to all my life by these FUCKING VOICES IN MY HEAD – they never cease. They're the ones who keep me going in the 'wrong' direction.

I should just give up now. There's no hope for me. I'm weak, cold, tired and starving but something inside me won't let me be free to fight. I want to go back to safety and numbness. There I was secure. I need to go back. I need to go back to be safe.

2

WE HADN'T ALWAYS BEEN LIKE THAT. WE HADN'T ALWAYS BEEN so fucked up. Actually, for many years after Emma was born, the four of us – me, Mum, Dad and Emma – had been happiest when we were all together. There'd been the usual tantrums and squabbles, of course, but we were a solid little family, and for the most part our lives together were happy and simple.

Back then, Emma had been my best friend in the world. Scrawny and a little too tall for her age, she possessed an odd combination of knock knees, light skin, and green eyes that could melt a person's heart from a hundred paces. She was two years younger than me, but if I ever noticed the gap in our ages it never troubled me. In those days, before the world existed, before there were jobs and politics and clothes and exams and opinions, I wanted nothing more out of life than to be beside her, playing games and making believe in the happy confines of our home.

We'd lived in the same house then as we lived in now, a small semi-detached bungalow on the west side of Myreton, a small coastal village about twenty miles east of Edinburgh.

It was an awkward looking thing, an oversized Lego house with a flat roof and dreary pebble-dashed walls that had all the character of a Belgian landscape. But for all its lack of grandeur, it had been a wonderful place to grow up. Emma and I had filled our days with activities, building houses from dining room furniture and catching ladybirds in our garden and inventing plays based on fairy tales we both loved. In the evenings, Mum would read to us or Dad would chase us around the house on his hands and knees. A thousand times we thought we'd die laughing as he bounced us on his shoulders or tickled us under the arms.

Some nights, while the rest of the world slept, we'd creep through to one another's room and climb under our covers together. There, surrounded by darkness, our foreheads pressed together conspiratorially, we'd whisper stories of our past adventures. On and on we'd talk, whole hours disappearing as we took turns comparing and repeating our shared memories. Do you remember walking in Glen Nevis, how soft the grass was, how good it tasted to drink water from the icy mountain streams? Or that winter we sledged through snow into a gorse bush on Myreton Hill and got covered in thorns from head to foot? Remember when Billy Sutton fell off his scooter and broke his nose, how the trail of blood he left on the pavement turned brown and took months to disappear? Living among these old adventures was an incredible thing. Overwhelmed by the beauty of nostalgia, we shivered ecstatically with every story we told, and often we were forced to stuff our fists inside our mouths to stop our giggles from waking Mum and Dad.

And yet, for all the happy times we shared together, Emma was a remarkably insecure child. Even at home, in the place she felt most at ease, she always seemed awkward and constantly needed arms to cradle her. Everybody in the house was required to be warm and affectionate to one another at all times. Whenever the slightest hint of tension arrived, she would shrink deep inside of herself, oblivious to everything and everybody around her.

Away from home, things were even worse. Emma spent most of the time hiding behind Mum's leg, shrinking away from strangers and stealing restless glances at the world around her. When she began school, she was immediately consumed by a general feeling of dread. She dragged her feet through the house each morning, and constantly complained of stomach aches that magically disappeared on weekends. During playtime, I'd often see her standing head-down by a corner of the school building, as far as possible from the fun and games of the schoolyard. She always looked slightly overwhelmed, as though she was trying to figure out how her classmates managed to play so easily together, to understand why they showed no signs of the strain that was beginning to engulf her.

Seven-year-old children develop all sorts of tactics to help them cope with life, to reassure them that the world isn't such a big and scary place. Some adopt an imaginary friend. Some punch a classmate in the face. Others take a few deep breaths and make the best of their days. But Emma didn't do any of those things. Instead, she sneaked into the school toilets, stuck her first two fingers down her throat, and vomited.

Fifteen years would pass before any of us learned about Emma's puking, but I remember the period well, because it was then that she started to cough, too. It began as a simple clearing of the throat, a quiet, almost apologetic hem that Emma was always careful to conceal. Within weeks, though, it had progressed to a dry, hollow bark that came as it pleased and frequently stuck around for hours. The coughing was never violent – there were no dry heaves or gasps for breath – but it was incredibly persistent, and within weeks it had driven Emma and everyone around her to distraction.

Bedtime was the worst. Lying in the room next to Emma's, with only a thin wall separating us, not a night went by when I managed to escape her awful, seal-like bark. I often heard Mum in Emma's room, offering extra pillows and cups of hot milk to try and ease the discomfort, but nothing helped, and I'd be left to scream desperately into my pillow and kick my feet against my mattress in a muffled frenzy until finally, finally, exhaustion forced Emma to sleep and the house fell quiet.

And so it continued, day after day, week after week, month after month. Mum and Emma made frequent visits to the village doctors, but they could never quite figure out what was going on. They prescribed all kinds of syrups and sprays, but they were offered in hope more than expectation and rarely did anything to help. As time passed, Emma and I became increasingly sluggish. At school, we sat all day with our heads propped against our fists, drawing idle circles on our jotters, while at home we abandoned the usual games in favour of the living room sofa, where we lay for hours watching television and dreaming of sleep. Without really meaning to, I began to lose hope that things would ever return to the way they'd once been.

But then, just as summer was about to begin, the cough began to improve. A few weeks after that, it vanished completely. Emma had grown pale and weak since the previous winter, but now she quickly regained some of her colour and all of her energy. We began to play together again, and for the first time in months the house was filled with laughter. My parents, watching this apparent return to the good old days, took a deep breath and rejoiced.

Years later, I'd look back on this period and wonder how we could have been so naïve, how we could have missed this early clue that something was so terribly wrong. Why, on first peering into Emma's mouth after the coughing began, had we not raised a finger in the air and declared that vomiting was to blame, that the stomach acid she brought up with her lunch each day had caused the cough by destroying the lining of her throat? And Emma's sudden recovery? It seemed like a miracle at the time, but the reason for it was simple enough. After nine months of constant puking, her throat was too damaged, too sore, for her to continue the habit. So, she stopped and her throat began to heal.

I used to hate myself for failing to work that out, and I know that Mum and Dad did, too. But we were being too hard on ourselves. We always look for the signs we missed when something goes wrong. We become like the detectives you see on television, trying to solve a mystery, because maybe if we gather together the clues, we'll be given some control. We can't change what took place, of course, but if we uncover enough evidence, we can prove we could have stopped it from happening, if we'd only been a little smarter. I suppose it's easier to believe in our own stupidity than it is to believe that all the clues in the world wouldn't have changed a thing.

No longer able to find solace in the solitude of the primary school toilets, Emma was forced to try out a host of other coping mechanisms. Exercise helped a lot, as did the hundreds of small rituals that she began to follow over the course of the day. Nothing, though, did more to ease the anxiety than skipping food.

As Emma moved through her first years of high school, she began to behave less and less normally. Every morning, I'd see her fixing her hair by the bathroom mirror. She had short hair in those days, and she spent ages trying to spike it upwards. When she was done with that, she'd walk to the front door and put on her shoes, the ones with the huge heels, before leaving for school. It took me a long while to understand what she was trying to achieve – the higher up she went, the less wide she looked; the less wide she looked, the more invisible she could be.

Each night, as Mum was preparing dinner, she'd tiptoe through to the kitchen and say, 'I'm not hungry'. The two would argue, Mum sneaking an extra morsel of food onto Emma's plate and Emma removing it alongside another great spoonful back into the saucepan. At the table, she'd push the food around her plate with her fork, taking pains to keep her meal as far from her mouth as possible. Mum, Dad and I would pretend not to notice for as long as we could, but after a few minutes one of us would always crack. 'Oh wow, this is really good!' we'd say, way too enthusiastically. 'You should definitely try this!'

Emma would shake her head.

'Come on, darling,' Mum would say gently. 'You have to eat.'

But Emma would just push back her plate, looking away from the table and from our eyes. 'You don't understand me,' she'd say sadly, before rising from her chair and walking from the room.

You don't understand me. That had been Emma's constant cry throughout those early years at high school. And the thing was, it was difficult to disagree with her. So much of her life during the period made no sense. I'd see her in the school corridors every day, never once failing to notice how badly she was struggling to fit in with her friends. She always stood a little apart from everyone else, and while their talk was all of fashion and friends and music and sex, Emma's mind, I knew, was always on her next piece of homework or class test. After school, she'd rush home and make a beeline for her room, where she spent the whole night worrying over some meaningless assignment or revising for exams that were still months away. For the first time, I became fully aware that something inside of her was truly broken. I only wished I knew how to put her back together again.

In the end, it was Dad who uncovered the truth, one evening when I was around fifteen. While Mum was working and Emma was taking a shower, he walked through to Emma's room, opened the top drawer of her desk, and took out her diary. He was still sitting in the room, the diary perched open on his lap, when Emma arrived back from the bathroom.

I missed the first part of what followed, the house's walls just thick enough to hide the drama that was unfolding in Emma's room. Slowly, though, their voices rose, and I began to catch certain words, and then phrases, and then, eventually, every single thing they said.

'Promise me you won't do it again.'

'Daddy, please stop crying.'

'Promise me, Emma.'

'I promise! But please, *please* stop crying.'

'Oh, my girl,' Dad said. 'My darling baby girl.'

A few minutes later Dad came back through to the living room and threw himself down on the sofa, his bloodshot eyes fixed determinedly on the television screen. I could hardly believe his tears. I'd never seen him cry before that night, not even as we'd stood together and watched Granny Barnes being lowered into her grave ten years earlier. I sat next to him, motionless, trying not to cry myself. Then, suddenly, his eyes were on me, no longer sad but angry, as he demanded, 'Did you hear any of that?'

I nodded.

'Did you know?'

I shook my head.

When Mum got home from work later that evening, Dad was waiting for her in the living room. I'd sneaked off to bed an hour earlier, where I'd laid in shocked silence the entire time. As soon as I heard Mum's keys turning in our front door, I grabbed my Walkman from my drawer, laid a pillow over my head, and pressed play. I couldn't bear to hear anything more. I needed to shut everything out until everything got better.

I waited. For years I waited, hope never quite dead, for the situation to improve. *In time*, I told myself. *Be patient*, I told myself. *It'll happen*, I told myself.

It didn't.

3
———

By the time Mum and I made our visit to London in the late summer of 2004, seven years had passed since Dad's fateful journey through to Emma's bedroom. I was now twenty-two years old, recently graduated from Edinburgh University with a degree in history, and with no idea where to go from there. Mum and Dad were confused by my uncertainty, but the subject of my future was not one I'd given much thought to during my four years in Edinburgh. I had a vague notion that I wanted to do something meaningful with my life, that I wanted to be some kind of success, but those things would have to wait until Emma had staged her amazing recovery. This, clearly, was still quite some way off.

At least the hospital's most recent pharmaceutical fuckup hadn't had any long-term effect on Emma's condition. Or at least that's what Mum was told when she called St John's a few hours after our terrifying race to Emma's ward. Emma was out of bed, the nurse said, and enjoying some time alone in her room. She was still rather tired, though. Would it be possible for us to postpone any further visits until the following day?

'Nonsense,' Mum said, when the nurse finished speaking. 'You're talking nonsense. We both know Emma hasn't enjoyed a single thing since she was admitted to your ward. And that's hardly likely to change if she spends another day alone in her room. Still, if you insist we give her some extra time to recover, then fine. Just make sure you keep an eye on her until tomorrow. And I mean it.'

By the following day, Mum and I were both desperate to see Emma, and all too aware that it was the last time we'd see her before leaving for home. We arrived in the early afternoon to find the ward as depressing as ever. I was a nervous wreck by the time we reached Emma's door, but experience had made me an expert in these situations; without even thinking, I threw on a counterfeit smile and stepped inside.

'Hey, Sister Christa,' I said. We'd got that name from *The Big Hungry Caterpillar*. We'd had the book when we were little, and Emma had always chosen it when Mum offered to read to us. The book was dedicated to Sister Christa, and for some reason Dad had adopted the name for Emma, which had always made us laugh. Twenty years later, we were still using the name, though by then it was about as funny as chlamydia.

Emma was crouched on her bed, her arms wrapped around her knees, her head turned away from the door and resting against the wall. 'God, it's lovely and warm in here,' I said. My voice was so cheery, I was practically singing. 'We've been walking around the grounds for an hour waiting for lunchtime to finish.'

'How *was* lunch?' Mum asked, with equally false cheer. 'What flavour did you have today?'

This was one of Mum's favourite jokes. The only nutrition Emma had received over the past four months had been a tasteless gloop that was syringed down the tube that hung from her nose. Emma must have smiled at the joke once or twice for Mum to have repeated it so many times, but she was in no mood for teasing today. She looked down towards her knees and said, 'They forgot to bring it to me.'

Mum's smile fell away. 'Again?'

Emma nodded miserably. Usually, she took extreme care to point out the failures of the hospital staff in the hope that, taken together, they might speed up her release from St Jude's. On this occasion, though, she knew she was effectively obliging herself to accept the meal that, had Mum and I not been there, she'd have been proud to avoid.

Mum was furious. 'It's ridiculous,' she said, as she rang the bell by the bedroom door. 'It's bloody ridiculous. How can they... That's the second time this week, is it not?'

Emma dropped her eyes to the ground. 'It's the fifth, actually,' she admitted shyly.

Mum's mouth started to speak, but her brain decided it didn't have anything to say yet and shut it again. To save her the trouble, I leaned over and rang the bell a second time.

'Take me with you,' Emma said. She took a step towards Mum, then reached out and touched her hand. 'Please, take me home. I promise I'll try harder.'

Emma's caresses were a rare thing, and all the more precious for that. Despite everything, Mum visibly relaxed in the second Emma's hand touched her own. She sighed heavily and lifted her chin, meeting Emma's eyes without flinching. 'Believe me, darling, I would if I could. And you know the Edinburgh team are working hard to change things for you. But it's going to take a while.'

Emma blinked once. 'And what am I supposed to do till then?'

'You'll just have to sit tight.'

Emma snickered. 'That's easy for you to say.'

Mum clearly had something to say to that, but we were too close to flying home to get into an argument, so she let it go. 'Try not to panic, Emma,' she said, eventually. 'We'll be back to see you in four weeks.'

'For fuck's sake, Mum!' Emma shouted. 'I can't wait another month. I can't stay here another *day*. Please, you have to take me with you. You *have* to. This place is killing me!'

'Emma!' Mum snapped. 'I *can't*. You know that. You've known that since the day they slapped the section on you.'

Emma shook her head angrily. 'It's not fair,' she said.

'No,' Mum told her, 'it's not. But that's how it is.' Sighing deeply, she pressed a hand against her forehead, before turning to face the door. 'For god's sake,' she hissed, 'does one of us have to die before they decide to grace us with their presence?' She punched a fist against Emma's bell and did not remove it again until, finally, we were joined in the room by a member of staff. The one who appeared was dressed in shiny leopard print trousers and a black cropped top.

'Hallo,' the nurse said. 'What is problem?'

Mum was staring daggers. 'I'm sorry to bother you,' she said, dryly, 'but it appears you've forgotten to feed my daughter again.'

The nurse stared back at Mum, her face steeped in confusion.

'You don't have a clue what I'm talking about, do you?' Mum asked.

The nurse glanced at me nervously, pleading for assistance. I offered none. 'It's the food?' she said, after a moment.

'Yes, of course it's the bloody food!' Mum said. 'What else *could* it be? For god's sake, you people leave her sitting in this room like a prisoner for weeks on end. The least you could do is remember to feed her.'

The nurse swallowed audibly. 'I go,' she said. 'Moment please.'

'Oh, my god,' Mum said, once the three of us were alone again. 'Where do they *find* these people? And also, what on Earth was that woman wearing?'

'She has a night out tonight.' Emma said. 'She's been talking about it all week.' She glanced quickly over her shoulder to make sure nobody was listening. 'To be honest, I think she's a bit thick. She keeps asking us all how we manage to stay so slim.'

I turned to look at Mum, who looked as shocked as I felt. 'Well, that's... not perfect,' she said, after a moment.

'It's a long, long way from perfect,' I told her.

Mum considered that. 'Yes,' she admitted, finally. 'But... Well, it does us no good just sitting here getting all down in the dumps. We've got to look on the bright side, haven't we?'

Emma gave Mum a hard stare.

'Now don't, Emma,' Mum said. 'You have plenty to be grateful for. You have us. You've got your friends...'

'Friends?' Emma said. 'Really? Like who?'

'What are you talking about?' Mum asked. 'Friends. Like Kirsty, and Isla.'

'Ah, yes. I remember them. Perhaps they'll even remember me a little when I finally get out of here.'

'That's not funny,' Mum said.

'It wasn't a joke,' Emma told her.

Mum fell silent for a moment, contemplating her next move. I had no idea why she felt a need to press on with such a disturbing subject, but she was clearly determined. 'What about the other girls on the ward?' she asked. 'Why not take the chance to make some new friends while you're here?'

Emma let out a long, weary sigh and buried her face in her hands. 'Mum, I know you're trying to help, I really do. But please, let's stop talking.'

It was then, as Emma held her hands over her eyes, that I noticed it, the flash of white beneath the sleeve of her dressing gown. At first, I guessed it was some sort of wrist warmer or long-sleeved bodysuit, which made sense, because Emma always buried herself beneath at least four layers of clothes. But then, after a moment, I looked a little harder and recognised it for what it was; a bandage.

'Oh!' I said. 'What happened to your arm?'

Emma followed my eyes to her wrist and immediately flushed. 'It's nothing,' she said, tugging guiltily at the sleeve of her gown.

'But you've hurt yourself,' I said stupidly. 'Look, it's the same on the other arm!'

'James!' Mum said, sharply. I turned to find her shaking her head in warning. I stared at her for a moment, genuinely puzzled. Then I glanced again at Emma's wrists, at the guilty expression she was wearing, and understood, with a perfect, terrible clarity, what had happened. Suddenly, my lips began to tremble, and I felt a tremendous stab of pain somewhere in my chest. I sat down heavily on Emma's seat, clamping my eyes shut and gritting my teeth, waiting for the feeling to pass. Goodness knows how long I stayed like that, but when I opened my eyes again, the nurse had reappeared with Emma's feed.

'Here is the food that you asked for is here,' she said, using too many words.

Mum rolled her eyes impatiently, then looked at her watch and, after a quick calculation, clicked her tongue. 'Well, we might as well go,' she said, turning to Emma. 'I'm sorry, darling, but our flight leaves in a few hours. We'd have had to pop off in a few minutes, anyway.'

For the past few minutes, Emma had been distractedly rearranging the few objects on top of her chest of drawers. Now, as Mum made her announcement, she darted to our side, her eyes wide with fear. 'No, please, don't go,' she cried. 'Please, take me with you. I can't wait any longer.' When Mum shook her head, Emma turned and grabbed hold of my arm. 'Please, James,' she begged. 'Make her take me. I know *you* understand, at least. Please. I can't do this anymore.' I looked into her eyes and she looked back into mine. 'Don't leave me,' she said, desperately. 'Please don't leave me.'

I swallowed hard. 'I'm sorry,' I said. And then, without looking back, I turned and made my way disconsolately from the building.

Mum joined me outside five minutes later, looking as crushed and bedraggled as I felt. As soon as she saw me, she broke into that old fake smile of hers for the hundredth time that weekend. 'She's alright,' she said, reassuringly. 'She's gone for a wee lie down.'

The lump I'd only just managed to swallow suddenly reappeared in my throat. I knew as well as Mum did that Emma was unlikely to get back out of bed before we next arrived in London.

We sat down on a bench in the hospital gardens and fell into silence. It was some moments before Mum spoke. 'James, I know this weekend was difficult,' she said. 'But I don't want you worrying too much. Emma's team's confident they'll see an improvement soon.'

'Oh, really?' I asked. 'And what team's this? Are you talking about the psychiatrist who appears once a week to fuck up Emma's medication? And the doctor she never fucking sees? Shall we include that cleaner who helps her bin her food when the nurses aren't looking? And let's not forget the nurses themselves – after all, they're the ones who left Emma that syringe to 'play with' last month, the ones who took an entire fucking week to realise she was using it to suck the food they gave her straight back out of her stomach.'

'James –'

'No, Mum,' I shouted. 'I'm serious. I don't know why we can't do as she asks and get her the fuck out of that place. Hope Park was a thousand times better than that shithole back there.'

'They've no space for her in Hope Park, James. Believe me, the Edinburgh doctors are doing everything they can to find somewhere else for her. There's just no alternative at the moment.'

Sighing deeply, I let my head fall to my chest. I desperately wanted to leave the conversation, to put the day behind me, but there was one more question I had to ask if I was going to find any peace at all. Turning again to Mum, I said, as gently as I could, 'why did Emma have those bandages on her wrists?'

Mum sighed. I noticed a tightening in her throat, a sadness come over her face. 'Your sister starts to feel a little desperate sometimes. So, she scratches her wrists to help her cope. It helps to relieve a little of the pain, she says.'

I closed my eyes tight, tried to remember how to breathe. If there was ever a time that some tiny part of this illness would start making sense to me, I wished it would hurry up and arrive.

4

BACK IN EDINBURGH AIRPORT, WE GATHERED OUR BAGS BEFORE sloshing through heavy rain to the old Corsa that awaited us in the car park. Too exhausted to drive, Mum threw her suitcase into the boot and handed me the keys before collapsing wordlessly into the passenger seat. That set the tone for the rest of the journey, which we spent in silence, listening mechanically to the spattering of rain against the roof and the fast thrumming of the wipers against the windscreen. Two or three times, Mum dozed off with her mouth open, her head lolling to one side. I had some trouble staying awake myself, though the awful weather stopped me from cracking the window to fight the tiredness.

The rain was coming down in buckets by the time Myreton came into view, but even beneath a heavy grey sky the village was unmistakably beautiful. It's a picture-postcard little place, with immaculate stone houses, charming little shops and a medieval church, whose ivy-coated ruins provide a centrepiece for the High Street. A long stretch of sand, considered to be one of the country's most beautiful, lies along the northern edge of the village, while at its southern border a final row of pretty cottages give way to miles of patchwork fields.

We lived on the east side of the village, in a small housing estate that had been thrown up in the '60s, safely away from the Victorian mansions and Edwardian villas of the Myreton nobility. The buildings within the estate were a good deal uglier and more crowded together than others in the village, but none of that mattered to me. The house was my home, my sanctuary, and, returning there after the troubles of the past three days, the panic in my chest finally began to ease.

I parked the car and we scurried down the path towards the house, our shoes splashing against the wet stone steps that led to our front door. Clambering inside, we shook the rain from our jackets before walking through to the living room, where Mum immediately slumped onto the sofa. There were deep shadows around her eyes, and folds of skin gathered around her chin as her head sagged towards her chest. She looked so old and weary, suddenly, that I thought I might cry. It must have showed, too, because when she looked up at me her expression immediately, unnaturally, brightened. 'Well,' she said, with all the sparkle of a high-school cheerleader. 'It's good to be home.'

I agreed that it was, though in fairness a month in a Chinese torture chamber would have seemed like a holiday compared to our latest trip to London.

'Do you fancy going out to see your pals for a wee bit tonight?' Mum said.

I wrinkled my nose. 'I think I'll just watch some telly and go to bed.'

'Some company might do you good,' she said.

'Some sleep might do me better.'

Mum considered that for a moment, then reached for

the Radio Times. 'Anything in particular you want to watch?' she asked, but before I could answer a familiar set of footsteps began to make their way through the garden towards the house. Mum and I turned our eyes towards the back door just in time to see Dad appear through it. If he was happy to see us, he made no effort to show it.

'Well?' he asked, turning to face me. 'How was it?'

I shook my head vaguely, as if I might have misunderstood the question, and sat down on the little tub chair next to the telly. Dad mumbled impatiently and turned to Mum. 'Mary? Tell me. How did it go?'

Mum shut her eyes for a moment, as if composing herself before she spoke. 'Nothing's changed since I spoke to you last night.'

'You didn't speak with her doctor?'

'He wasn't even working today.'

'And the head nurse? Was she on holiday too?'

'She's barely involved in Emma's treatment, John. I'll call the doctor later this week, tell him what's been going on.'

Dad looked at the ceiling and gave a frustrated sigh. 'For Christ's sake,' he said. 'If you want something done...' He shook his head, combing his hair with his fingers. I saw then how decrepit he looked. Dark circles hung heavily beneath his bloodshot eyes, and the deep wrinkles around his mouth and jaw were largely concealed by a week's worth of stubble. He was dressed in a pair of threadbare overalls, which he'd worn throughout his forty years as an electrician. Before Emma got sick, he'd been careful to replace his work clothes every six months; now it was more like every two years, by which point the material would be so stretched and worn that we'd actually hear the stitches pop as he moved around the house. Sometimes, when I was angry with Dad, I began to suspect he wore this bedraggled appearance as a sign of martyrdom, but deep down I knew it wasn't the case; he was simply in too much pain to give a single, solitary fuck about how he looked.

'I should've gone there myself,' Dad said.

Mum fixed Dad with a hard stare. 'Well, yes,' she said. 'Maybe you should have.'

Dad stared back at Mum. 'What's that supposed to mean?' he asked.

'You were very welcome to join us in London, John. I asked you more than once to come along when I booked the flights last month.'

Dad's face tightened. 'If I'd thought for a moment that Emma wanted me there...'

'What are you talking about?' Mum asked.

'She *hates* me, Mary.'

This statement was greeted with stunned silence. I looked at Mum, hoping my eyes weren't as wide as they felt, and she looked back at me, her own eyes filling with tears. 'John,' she said, turning to Dad. 'What are you talking about? Emma loves you.'

'Oh?' Dad said. 'And you know this, do you?'

'Dad,' I said. 'Mum's right. You're being silly.'

Dad glared at us for a moment, then looked away. 'Aye, well, there's no point talking about it anyway.'

Actually, we probably *could* have done with talking more, but there was no point in arguing. Dad was one of a generation of men who entirely refused to betray their emotions to anybody. There must have been things that bothered him – he was only human, after all – but I'd never once heard him talk about them. My whole life, he'd guarded himself like a secret, making a joke of everything and evading questions with expert precision.

The silence he kept hadn't really been an issue in the

days before Emma's illness took hold; back then, there'd been plenty of room for him to swallow down whatever little things were worrying him. But in the past few years so much had happened, so much had gone wrong, that his problems had overwhelmed him completely, filled every little space inside of him. There, they'd turned toxic, spread through his body like a poison, until finally the only thing he had left to show for his years of silence was a devastating sense of bitterness and confusion. This inner anguish had wrought huge changes on him. The smiling, carefree father Emma and I had known as children had been replaced by an angry stranger who struggled to find any joy in the world around him. The smallest things would send him into a closed-fist, red-faced rage, at which point he'd storm out of the house to the garage.

We called it the garage; this is what the space was originally designed as. But while it retained some of the old features, like a collection of old paint cans and an extended family of spiders, it hadn't been used for its intended purpose in the seven years since Dad had decided to sell the small electrical shop he owned in nearby Cranston and begin working from home.

Dad had inherited his shop, along with the rest of an old television repair business, in the summer of 1981, after his boss, Bob Hales, suffered a heart attack during a game of mixed doubles on Cranston golf course. Dad had tried to make a go of the store out of respect for Hales' good intentions, but he'd always been far more at home in the workshop that backed onto the shop, mending the old televisions and radios his customers brought in for repair. He finally sold up a week after his fiftieth birthday, having decided to shrink the business to such a degree that it would fit inside the old, cobwebby garage we'd spent the past twenty years ignoring.

On paper the move had seemed perfect. Dad would save a little money on bills and be spared the daily commute to and from Cranston. His hours wouldn't have to change, and when he was done working, he could simply wander across the garden to enjoy a meal and some company with his family, the way he always had done. But the workshop was hardly finished when Emma's illness was discovered. Dad did work there as planned, but as the family tensions increased, he began to visit the garage outside of his working hours, too. At first it was just for an occasional cigarette, a chance to gather his senses, but gradually his tools and cables were joined by some creature comforts; an old chair, an even older television, and enough beer and cigarettes to last a month. By the summer of 2004, the garage was as much a den as a workshop, and it wasn't uncommon for Dad to retreat to the garage after a lunchtime argument and stay there until the wee small hours of the following morning. There were periods when he was, in essence, an absent father. The only difference between him and other absent fathers was that ours, geographically at least, was only a few yards away from his family.

I felt deeply sorry for Dad, and God knows he deserved the sympathy. But I resented him too, for doing so little to help himself. Mum had begged him for years to visit a doctor, to speak with somebody, anybody, about what was going on, but he'd always scoffed at the idea. It was twenty years since he'd visited a doctor's surgery, he told her, and it would be another twenty years before he found himself there again. I could have kicked him for being so selfish, but I never did. I should have said something, yelled at him even, but I didn't do that either. None of us did. In the end, we just stuck to safe topics of conversation and did everything we could to keep the peace. And in those moments that he began to shout, when he lost his temper and stormed off to the garage, we all had our ways of shutting down and closing off.

When, following our return from London, Dad predictably refused to lay his heart and soul open in Mum's hands she decided to change tack. 'Emma loves you,' she said, gently. 'You just need to be more patient with her, that's all.'

Dad looked stung. 'I don't need any lessons in how to look after my children, Mary.'

'No, I know that,' Mum said, forcing a smile. 'I didn't mean it like that.'

Dad considered that for a moment and seemed to accept the point. Sighing deeply, he shifted his gaze distractedly around the room, bumped the wall unconsciously with his fist a couple of times. Then, without another word, he turned to leave the room.

'John,' Mum said, just loud enough to stop him in his tracks. 'Don't go back off to the garage yet. Come, stay here a while. We haven't seen you for three days.'

'Mum's right,' I said, my voice filled with false cheer. 'Stay here with us. We need you. You're the dad. You're the head of the family!'

Dad closed his eyes for a second, his hand resting on the handle of the back door. When he opened them again, his face was virtually devoid of expression. 'When was the last time we were any kind of family?' he asked. And with that, he pushed the handle of the door and made his way back outside.

5

———

THE FOLLOWING EVENING, I MET MY OLD FRIEND, HOLLY, IN the car park of the Grange Hotel. We'd arranged to meet some friends in the hotel bar, but the night was so bright and warm that we decided to postpone our journey indoors until Steve, another of our companions, arrived back from a day out in Edinburgh. We sat down on a small garden wall, and I closed my eyes and turned my face to the sun as Holly began to fill me in on what she'd been up to in the two months since we'd last seen one another. Very quickly, I began to feel lighter, unshackled, as if something I'd been carrying had just fallen away. I sensed a space clearing around me, making room for me to breathe. For the first time in weeks, I was enveloped by an odd sense of peace. And it was good.

The feeling lasted for around five minutes. Then Holly stopped talking about herself and moved the subject onto Emma and my nightmare journey to London, and suddenly my chest grew heavy all over again.

It wasn't that I minded sharing my secrets with Holly. In fact, if I'd had to choose a single person to tell my secrets to, it would have been her. For years, she'd been my confidante, someone with whom I could share my innermost thoughts. She never judged me and I knew she'd stay with me through anything. So, no, the problem wasn't telling Holly about Emma's condition – it was finding the strength simply to talk about Emma at all.

Still, I managed to remain dry-eyed as I described all that had happened during my latest visit to London. When I was finished, I turned to Holly to find her staring back at me in disbelief. 'My god,' she said, her eyes wide. 'So, where do they go from here?'

I shrugged. 'They don't tell us much,' I said. 'To be honest, I sometimes think they're just making everything up as they go along. It certainly seems that way sometimes.'

'The London doctors?'

I nodded.

'And her Edinburgh people?'

'They're fine,' I said. 'They're fine… They're…' I shut my eyes tight, rubbed my temples. 'Oh, I don't know, Hols. Can't we just stop talking about this?'

Holly shook her head impatiently. 'Sure,' she said. 'Because ignoring your problems will make them melt away into oblivion, won't it. You fucking moron.'

I'd known Holly long enough not to be offended by her insults. To look at her, with her big blue eyes and cutesy blonde hair, you'd have thought that butter wouldn't melt in her mouth. But then she'd open that mouth and begin to speak, and you'd immediately realise that she had all the grace and innocence of a used condom.

Despite this, or perhaps because of it, Holly had been one of the most popular girls in our school. Boys followed her around like puppies, jostling for her attention, asking if she'd made plans for the weekend, or seen a certain movie, or heard a particular song. There was always a part of me that wanted to add my name to Holly's list of suitors, but that part of me was incredibly stupid, and I knew it. Very few of the boys managed to hold her attention for long, and those who did all possessed the same haughty expressions and improbably clear skin. Next to them, it was impossible to imagine that she'd even look twice at me, so I contented myself with staring at her obsessively in the classes we shared and memorising the rest of her schedule so I could accidentally run into her a few times each day.

My luck finally changed during our third year at high school, when Holly was caught cheating on a test in maths class and forced from her throne at the back of the room to the seat next to me at the front. Furious at being separated from the other queen bees, she spent the rest of the class defacing the front sheet of her test paper with a compass. Then, at the end of the period, she turned her big eyes towards me and asked, 'Did you really understand all of that shit?'

I flinched visibly at the sound of her voice. 'Hnnugh?' I asked, smooth as butter.

Holly nodded towards my answer sheet. 'You actually knew some of the answers?'

'Hurhm,' I told her, with a quick nod of my head.

Holly stared angrily at her own paper. 'Well, apparently I haven't a fucking clue,' she said. When I gave no answer, she leaned in towards me, conspiratorially. 'You know, this is the point when you're supposed to offer me some much-needed help,' she said, in a stage whisper. 'Like, maybe in the library? Tomorrow lunchtime?'

Blushing wildly, I managed another little nod. Holly smiled. 'Yay,' she said. 'See you tomorrow, then.' And with a little wave of her fingers she turned and walked away.

And that's how our friendship began – with a series of maths tutorials. Though, in truth, we never managed to work more than a minute before Holly leaned back in her chair, nail file in hand, and began filling me in on the dark secrets of her closest friends. For the first few weeks, I searched desperately for some kind of spark between us. When it turned out that the sexual tension was mine alone, I settled for becoming her best friend, offering a friendly ear when she needed to tell me about all the boys she loved instead of me. It wasn't always easy, but I remained philosophical. I saw my unrequited love as a rite of passage, something all teenagers had to go through at some point or other. In a way, I was even lucky; better to get it out of the way early than spend five more years dreading its arrival.

Four years at university had more or less put an end to my infatuation, but Holly had lost none of her good looks. Whenever we walked down the street, the boys would stop and turn to stare as she breezed past them on the pavement. I sometimes thought I should feel offended for her when they did that, but in truth I understood their interest, and occasionally even shared it. Even now, as we sat together on the wall of the Grange, Holly leaning forward in anticipation of Steve's arrival, the pale flesh of her ample cleavage clearly on display, I was finding it very difficult indeed to follow our conversation. I knew I shouldn't be staring – I'd been in enough trouble with her over the years for looking where I wasn't supposed to – but still...

Holly was partway through a story about a birthday party for her gran or friend or something like that when she rolled her shoulders and looked around to me, barely giving me time to avert my eyes. 'Hey, Perv!' she shouted, snapping her fingers in front of her face. 'My head's up here.'

I looked up guiltily. 'What?' I said. 'Oh, no, I thought I saw... There was a wasp or something.'

Holly grinned. 'Strange. All I can see is a big fuckin' pile of sexual frustration.'

I waved my hand towards her, signalling that it was best not to enter into this conversation. Ironically, this same hand represented the full extent of my sexual encounters since the last time she'd broached the topic some months earlier.

'True, though,' Holly said. 'I mean, aren't you starting to wonder whether you'll ever have sex again?'

I shrugged. 'I'm still getting over the fact I even managed to do it in the first place.'

Holly grinned. 'Well, don't worry. You'll be alright.' She pressed my cheeks together and wiggled my face from side to side. 'After all, who could resist this face?'

Her grip was squeezing the tip of my tongue out of my mouth. 'You'd be thurprithed,' I said.

'Wrong attitude, Jamie,' she shouted. 'Now repeat after me; I'm a sexy little stud muffin.'

I rolled my eyes. 'I'm a thekthy little thtud muffin.'

'And I eat sixty-six scrumptious sausages for –'

'Oh, thut up,' I said, batting her hand away from my face.

Holly's laugh came from her belly, hearty, helpless and completely uncontrollable. 'Oh, boy,' she said, 'it's good to talk to you again. It's so good to be *home*. Another year at that university and I think I'd have gone mad.'

I didn't doubt that. Holly had surprised everyone when she'd decided to study in Aberdeen. She'd always felt a strong connection to her home, had always seemed completely unsuited to life in the city. Holly herself had soon realised this and had spent most of the last four years regretting the move. Now, having finally graduated, she was keen to put the experience behind her and move back to Cranston, where she'd continue to stay, probably until the day she died.

Unlike Holly, I'd never actually lived in Cranston, but the town had always been something of a second home to me. When, years earlier, Dad had owned his store on the High Street, I'd spent countless days there spinning on office chairs and eating polystyrene chips with Emma behind the reception desk. Later on, when I turned twelve, I went to Cranston High, joining the masses of other kids who travelled there by bus from the surrounding farms and villages each day. Even now, my best friends all still lived in the town, and so I continued to do most of my socialising there.

Most of this socialising took place at the Grange, which had been our regular watering hole since the summer we turned seventeen. The Grange was an entirely unremarkable small-town hotel, usually half-full of middle-aged golfer types who met once a week to discuss share prices and complain about their children. The owner was a self-important fool who simultaneously carried an air of grandeur and a heavy chip on his shoulder, while the bar staff he employed were all professionally grumpy upstarts who made no secret of their contempt for the pub and all who drank in it. We'd often dreamed of taking our custom elsewhere, but Cranston's only real alternative was The Sheep's Heid, which was essentially the local equivalent of Tehran. And so, because we all considered death by boredom to be preferable to death by stabbing, we'd continued to stay put.

It wasn't long before a familiar set of footsteps signalled the arrival of our friend, Steve. At six three, Steve was the tallest of my friends, though he rarely held himself up to his full height, something that made him look as awkward as he often felt. As usual, he was wearing an oversized shirt that emphasised his concave chest and skinny frame. He always buttoned his shirts up to the top button, as if he was going to wear a tie, which he never did.

Steve and I had been friends since our first day of high school, had sat side by side in every one of our classes, always nearest the front, always eager to curry favour with the teachers and avoid the missiles that were being launched by classmates nearer the back of the room. We'd both been way too quiet to be considered cool, but it was Steve, as the skinniest kid in our year, who'd suffered the most. He was never out-and-out persecuted, but things were far from easy for him, especially with girls. His quick wit made him popular enough with them to a point, but when it came to pushing for a girlfriend, he got the 'just good friends' speech every time.

His seemingly limitless growth spurt had ended in our senior year, and since then he'd begun to fill out a little. But the taunts of his old classmates had stayed with him, and even now, with a first-class degree, a credible goatee and a considerable band of friends to his name, he remained pretty shy. Even the sight of Holly waiting for him outside the Grange had turned his face the colour of a bad sunburn.

'Hey, Big Socks,' Holly said, when he was by our side. 'How's it hanging?'

Steve looked shyly to his middle. 'By a thread,' he said.

Holly considered this for a moment, then wrinkled her nose. 'Attractive.'

Steve shrugged. 'It's okay,' he said. 'It's not like anybody's rushing to see it anyway.'

Holly laughed, then nodded towards the front door of the hotel. 'Speaking of things nobody wants to see, what say we go inside?'

When we arrived at the pub, Dan was standing at his usual spot by the bar and halfway through telling a dirty joke to an enchanted audience. For the past year, in the absence of his old school friends, Dan had been spending the majority of his evenings with a bunch of local rugger buggers he'd met through his university friend, Will Spencer. The boys looked exactly as you'd expect them to, like television gladiators awaiting an interview. They'd stand every night in the middle of the floor with their boxer's stance, the top button of their pink shirts unbuttoned, their confident eyes roaming slowly over the bar in search of pretty girls and adoring fans. Whatever else their private schools might have taught them, they'd certainly learned how to look awesome.

At a mere five feet seven inches, Dan was a head shorter than most of the boys. His body sagged slightly where their muscles rippled, his teeth were crooked where theirs gleamed, and his brown hair was thick and unruly where theirs shone. To judge solely from appearances, it was difficult to believe he'd been accepted into this prestigious little clique. But to judge from appearances was to ignore Dan's quick wit and effortless charm. These were the characteristics that each of the boys aspired to, and the fact that Dan possessed them in such abundance was a constant source of fascination to them. No matter that he looked so freakishly average. His sense of humour and charisma were the benchmarks toward which the entire group was working, and few within the circle were held in higher esteem.

Steve, Holly and I arrived by Dan's side just in time for the punch line to his joke, which involved a female dwarf and the Pope. Dan watched his boys fall about laughing, before turning his attention towards us, grinning proudly.

'Alright, me old fruits?' he said, slapping us playfully on the cheeks. 'How's it going?'

'Oh, you know,' Holly said. 'Just glad to be here.'

'Arf arf,' Dan said, without laughing. 'How were the graduation ceremonies?'

'Like watching paint dry,' Steve said. 'In slow motion.'

Dan smiled. He always loved to hear us speak disparagingly about university, I suppose because it helped to justify his own miserable experience as a student. Like me, he'd studied in Edinburgh, but throughout his time there I'd neither heard him talk about his studies nor seen him working on them. I'd almost forgotten he was even attending the place by the time he'd gained his degree, a 2:2, which he referred to affectionately as Desmond, after the Archbishop.

'So, come on then,' Steve said to Dan. 'What are your plans now you're done pretending to study?'

'Haven't a clue,' Dan said, cheerily. 'Though I always thought prostitution might be a bit of a laugh.'

Steve grinned. 'What a whore-ibble thought.'

'At least you'd always be hard at work,' I said.

Dan smiled proudly. 'I'd call myself the *Whorenado*.'

We tried to think of another pun but couldn't, so instead Dan clapped his hands together and said, 'Come, now – a toast. To the Fab Four, who entered the dark world of further education and lived to tell the tale.' We chinked our glasses together, but before I could take a drink my phone vibrated in my pocket. It was a text from Emma:

Gemma next door cut her wrists this afternoon. They've told us she's out of danger but she still hasn't come back from the main hospital. I wish you were here. I'm so afraid. Everything here is just so terribly frightening.

Dan started to order another round of drinks, but my

heart had gone out of the evening completely. It felt wrong to be here, to be surrounded by all this laughing and joking in the same moment Emma lay trapped in her lonely hospital bed. I couldn't be with her in person, of course, but shouldn't I at least take on a share of her suffering? To be happy at all seemed unbearably selfish.

A deep sadness welled up inside of me. For some time, I stood, silent and still, by my friends' side, hoping the feeling would pass, but it only grew worse. The muscles of my chin began to tremble, and a great white noise rushed into my head, fizzing and buzzing, the way it always did when grief got the better of me. More than once, Holly tried to catch my eye, but I looked away every time. If I met her gaze, I knew I'd cry, and I didn't want that, didn't want her to see me with my defences down.

Dan was preparing another toast when Holly's patience finally ran dry. 'James?' she said. 'Whatever's the matter?'

'I'm okay,' I said, shaking my head, trying to clear the noise from my ears. By now, the group's full attention had turned to me, but there was nothing I could do to make myself appear normal. 'I'm... uh...'

'Jamie?' Holly said again. Her voice was gentle now.

'I have to leave,' I said. I wanted to offer an excuse for going, but my voice had already started to crack. Keeping my eyes firmly on the ground beneath me, I turned from my friends and was gone.

6

The following month, I took a job keeping bar at the County Hotel. The County was on a quiet section of Myreton's main street, strategically placed to attract the bare minimum of tourists, who generally liked to stay as close as possible to the golf courses that surrounded the western edge of the village. The hotel had once been grand, but the main building had been sold off to the council years ago and now all that remained was an ugly two-storey annex that housed a bar, a function room and a few outmoded bedrooms.

The bar, which was small even by village standards, was scruffy and dingy and smelled like a stale beermat. The walls were yellow from tobacco smoke, and the carpet was pocked with cigarette burns and stains that sucked at your shoes as you walked its gluey surface. There was little in the way of lighting, and the room's sole window was permanently filmed over with grime, so customers entering the bar generally had to stop and allow their eyes to adjust to the darkness before they walked inside.

The County may not have been the most attractive of

Myreton's hotels, but it was certainly the friendliest. The hotel's small band of regular customers – tradesmen or retired ex-tradesmen, mostly, who lived on the nearby housing estate – arrived each day to while away a few hours exchanging gossip and debating outrageous conspiracy theories they'd picked up from the rag mags that floated around the bar. I was always welcome to join in the conversation, but for the most part I was content simply to pour the occasional drink and hum songs in time to the flashing lights of the fruit machine.

After I took the job, my life quickly began to follow a familiar pattern. Once or twice a day, I worked a few hours at the hotel before either making my way home to sleep off some of my lethargy or setting off to meet Steve and Holly at the Grange. I tried to enjoy these visits to Cranston, to join in the laughter and conversation of my friends, but more and more I found myself tense and awkward around them, stealing anxious glances at my watch as my mind began the search for an excuse to leave.

It wasn't just the Grange. In the past few months, all these public exchanges, all the countless social dealings that made up the fabric of the day, had come to seem incredibly difficult. I tried desperately to fit in, but for the most part I was only physically present, attempting to match my facial expressions to the people around me while my mind drifted back to Emma in her hospital room.

By late autumn, Emma had been trapped in St Jude's for seven months. Throughout that time, she'd failed to gain a single ounce in weight, and she'd been entirely without counselling since her psychotherapist had quit her job two months earlier. Most importantly, she'd been able to grab half an hour of frantic after-dinner exercise every evening for the past three weeks.

'What were the staff thinking, asking the girls to manage their own after-meal supervision?' Mum asked Emma's Edinburgh doctors, when she heard of this latest controversy. 'Did they honestly think they'd turn down the chance to burn away some calories? Emma and that girl she was paired with must have clocked up more miles than Paula Radcliffe in the past bloody fortnight. It's a bloody disgrace.'

The Edinburgh team obviously agreed. They were working harder than ever to get through the tangled mess of red tape they needed to clear in order to secure Emma's release from St Jude's. But the prospect of Emma leaving London was no longer as exciting as it had been earlier in the year, for Emma would no longer be moving on to Hope Park, but rather continuing her treatment at home in Myreton. The doctors gave no clear reason for this decision, but hinted that Emma was in danger of becoming institutionalised after spending so long in her St Jude's bedroom, and that a spell at home might therefore do her some good. They still called a couple of times each week to update us on how things were going, but the progress was so slow and the news so increasingly depressing that by late summer I began to leave the room whenever the phone rang. It was cowardly, I knew, but I just couldn't bear to face the situation anymore. I needed it to go away.

I needed it all to go away.

Towards the end of November, Holly and I arrived at the Grange to find Dan and his boys hunched furtively over the side of the bar. It was obvious they were misbehaving, but we couldn't tell how until we reached their side and found them giggling over the condiments tray. When he saw us staring, Will grinned at us through a thick layer of salad cream. 'It's a competition,' he explained, as though we could have expected anything else, 'to see if we can eat all this shit before the bar staff notice.' He rifled through the tray and came up with some sachets of French mustard. Still grinning, he poured the contents into his mouth and gagged twice before forcing himself to swallow.

In the course of the next five minutes one of the boys threw up over a cheese plant after downing a cellar of salt and another poured a sachet of malt vinegar into Will's trouser pocket. When, finally, Dan accidentally sneezed some ketchup over the shirt of an American tourist, we were asked to vacate the premises. Undaunted, the boys simply moved the party onto Cranston's east beach. They'd been planning to do so anyway on account of the fact that Will had managed to get hold of some weed from a friend at the rugby club. The beach had long been the boys' favourite place for a spot of illicit drug-taking.

I always welcomed the change of pace that came when we moved to the shore. Whatever the weather, it was nice to taste the fresh sea air on my tongue rather than the unsettling fart smell that generally filled the Grange. Also, the sight and smell of the weed remained a novelty to me. I'd never encountered it until we'd made the first of our trips to the beach a couple of months earlier, and would still watch, fascinated, as Will fiddled with an assortment of papers and tobacco and resin to create his own very amateur brand of joints.

I'd never tried any drugs, hadn't even smoked a cigarette. Mum's warning that I'd drop dead where I stood if I so much as looked at an illegal substance had always been enough for me to avoid them like the plague. But on the night of the condiments controversy everybody looked so happy as they sucked on the joint that I began to wonder whether a little puff might make me happy too. And so, when it reached Dan, who was sitting next to me, I stunned everybody by asking to take part.

'No, don't!' Holly said. But Dan had already handed me the weed. I drew the smoke in, then coughed it out. 'Oh, my god!' I said. 'It fucking burns.'

Dan laughed. 'It gets easier once you've tried it a few times.'

Holly was glaring at me. 'I can't believe you did that.'

'Oh, don't be so dramatic,' I said, wiping my eyes with the sleeve of my coat. 'It's just weed. Everybody has to try it sometime.'

'But not you, James,' Holly said. 'It's just not something *you* do.'

There was a moment's tension, when all that could be heard was the gentle crashing of waves against the sand. But the rugby boys were always careful to snuff out any kind of silence as quickly as possible. Holly had barely even begun her sulk when Will clapped his hands together and said, 'Well, lads, are we all about ready for that little swim?'

That did the trick. Holly immediately turned her attention to Will. 'You're going swimming? Are you fucking crazy? It's the middle of winter, guys. You'll freeze.'

The boys said nothing, just giggled stupidly and staggered off towards the sea, leaving Holly and I alone with the joint. I let Holly take a couple of draws, then took it off her and tried one of my own. Holly looked at me, disappointed. 'As if we didn't have enough reasons to worry about you already,' she said.

'What are you talking about?' I asked. I should really have ignored the comment, but my words were out before I knew it.

'Jamie, you've been as quiet as a mouse lately. And you seem so unhappy all the time. I mean, it's not like we don't know about your sister. And we understand, you know, that it's a big deal.'

I said nothing, just stared out into the darkness.

'How *is* Emma?' Holly asked gently.

I shrugged. 'There's talk of her getting out of London in a couple of months.'

'She's coming back to Myreton, you mean?'

I nodded. 'I know, it sounds positive. But it's not. Things are far from easy when she's back home. She hardly eats, if she eats at all, and unless she's out burning calories on one of her walks, she rarely leaves her room. Her Edinburgh doctors are great, but they only visit for a few hours each week. Outside of that, there's only me and my parents to keep her safe, and there's only so much we can do. I'd love to say I'm happy she's coming back, but the truth is, I'm terrified.'

There was a moment's silence before Holly asked, with unusual hesitancy, 'Have you thought about telling her what all of this is doing to you?'

'What do you mean?'

'Just tell her it's... not *cool*. What she's doing.'

'But she's not doing anything, Hols; or anything wrong, at least. This isn't her fault. None of this is her fault. She has a disease; anorexia is a disease, like cancer or AIDS. She can't help the way she acts any more than you can help sneezing when you catch a cold.'

I watched Holly's brow furrow out of the corner of my eye. Then, after a moment, she said, 'I don't think that's completely true, Jamie.'

'What do you mean?'

Holly looked me right in the eye and gave my arm a reassuring squeeze. 'Sweetie, you're talking as though anorexia's a medical disease, but it's not. I mean, it's a mental illness, isn't it? So, strictly speaking, Emma does have at least *some* control over the way she acts.'

I blinked twice. 'No, she doesn't.'

'Yes,' Holly said, softly. 'She does.'

There was a short, but undeniably awkward, silence. 'I think I'd know,' I said. 'After all, I *have* been around Emma her whole life.'

Holly looked dubious. 'So, you're not angry with her?'

'No,' I said. 'I mean, sure, she can be an arse sometimes; a *real* arse. But even then, even when she's at her most vicious, I don't blame her. I feel sorry for her, actually. More than anything, it just breaks my heart.'

Holly thought about that for a minute. 'Well,' she said, choosing her words carefully. 'It's not an easy situation.'

I shifted uncomfortably on the sand. Some of what Holly had said was threatening to start making some sense. Before things got out of hand, I decided to change the subject by holding the joint to my face and staring at it reproachfully. 'Does this stuff actually work?' I asked. 'Shouldn't I have started giggling or something by now?'

Holly smiled. 'Just give the weed back to me.'

'I'm fine,' I said. I took a long, ambitious draw, and then coughed it all out. A moment later, I began to feel dizzy and nauseous. I lay down groggily on the sand.

'Dumbass,' Holly said, plucking the joint gently from my fingers.

For the next few minutes I lay curled up in my coat and concentrated on not being sick, while Holly sat next to me, smoking quietly. Through the darkness, it was possible to hear the boys laughing and yelling, while the occasional splashing sound confirmed that they'd somehow managed to do battle with the freezing North Sea waters. Eventually, the whooping grew louder as they raced back towards us. They were carrying their clothes in bundles under their arms but making absolutely no effort to pop them back on.

'How was the water?' I asked.

'Nice!' Dan said, though his lips had turned blue. 'You should have come in.'

I shook my head. 'Ain't no drug in the world strong enough to get me in there, buddy.'

'Ach, come oan,' said a voice, in something resembling a Glasgow accent. 'Have a wee bitty fun.' Peering through the darkness, I found Will, grinning broadly, with his dick in his hands, squeezing his foreskin into a wrinkly little mouth that spoke directly to me. 'Come oan, ya fanny,' it said. 'Gie it a try. You'll hae a fuckin' ball.'

Smiling despite myself, I shook my head again and turned to Holly. 'I should get going.'

Holly turned her eyes to me, though it had clearly taken some effort to peel them away from the assortment of genitalia that was on display. 'You really shouldn't be driving after smoking that shit, you know. Won't you stay at mine tonight?'

'I'll be okay,' I said, though in truth my legs felt heavy as I struggled to my feet.

Holly eyed me dubiously for a moment, then took my hand and squeezed it, just a little too hard. 'Okay,' she said, quietly. 'But remember, I'm always here if you need to talk. I might not be able to solve your problems, but I can promise that you won't have to face them alone. I really do give a shit about you, Jamie. You know that, don't you?'

I stared at Holly, speechless. If those weren't the kindest words that anyone had ever said to me, I didn't know what were. Nodding mechanically, I let go of her hand and set off through the darkness towards my car.

Holly needn't have worried about me driving home that night. I had no idea if the weed had been crap or if I'd smoked it all wrong, but in either case the joint had left me with nothing more than a scorched throat and a vague sense of anti-climax. It was a shame, really, because I could have used something to calm me down after my conversation with Holly.

It wasn't so much the things we'd spoken about that bothered me as the things I'd left unsaid. Because the thing was, however much I loved Emma, however protective I felt towards her, there *were* times when I got angry. There were times when I wanted to shout in her face, to push a slice of cake into her mouth and yell, 'Just fucking eat it!' There were times when I became almost blinded by rage, when an electric anger filled my body and it was all I could do not to tear the hair from my head and scream. And yet, I knew the anger was pointless, because no matter what I said Emma wouldn't change, couldn't change, not while the voice in her head was there to remind her how worthless and disgusting she was. And the sad thing was, the voice was *always* there, from the moment she woke up until the moment she fell asleep.

This last thought led me into darker territory, and by the time I climbed into bed I could already sense the first signs of panic. I'd lost count of how many times this had happened recently, how many times the thought of Emma had led my mind to places I didn't want it to go. Bedtime was always the worst. I'd lay still for hours, waiting for sleep to take hold, but every time it did, a new wave of terror would wash over me and I'd be awake once more. I was superstitious about the scenes I imagined in those moments. Whenever I pictured something terrible, I had to shake my head and count to three; it was the only way I could stop it from really happening.

I lay motionless for a few moments, trying to fend off the panic, but it showed no signs of abating. There was an aching in my chest, a tightening in my throat as my thoughts threatened to overwhelm me. I kicked off my covers and crept through to the kitchen, where I poured myself a glass of wine from the fridge. I looked at the glass with almost tearful gratitude, then swallowed down a couple of mouthfuls. I closed my eyes, leaned against the countertop as the warmth of the alcohol began to spread through my body. *Good god,* I thought. *There's nothing like it. Give me all the counselling or TLC you want, but nothing in the world will ever come close to matching the healing powers of a few soothing gulps of wine.*

Feeling calmer, I made my way through to the living room with the bottle of wine and grabbed hold of the remote. I turned on the telly and closed off my mind, switching channels whenever the thoughts came close to getting me. I wished there was some kind of remote control for my brain, that I could turn it off in the same way that I could turn off the telly. It would be so nice just to press the off switch and immediately empty my mind of all its thoughts. Leave a blank screen where the nightmares used to be.

I turned the remote to my forehead and pressed the off button. 'Beep,' I said. But nothing else happened.

An hour later, the wine bottle lay empty beside me on the couch and I felt more relaxed than I had all day. I felt a twinge of shame for drinking as much as I had, but the feeling was more than offset by the lovely feeling of emptiness inside my head. Staggering to my feet, I stumbled out to the garage and placed the empty bottle with the rest of the recycling. Squinting into the bin, I counted another four bottles, one for every night I'd run panicking from my bed in the past week. As I stared at them, the thought occurred to me that I could become an alcoholic. At that precise moment, it did not seem like an unreasonable solution to my problems.

7

EMMA RETURNED HOME IN FEBRUARY, AND IMMEDIATELY settled into the task of losing the weight she'd gained since she'd left home the previous spring. Throughout her ten months in St Jude's, she'd regarded us as compatriots in her battle against the doctors. Within a few days of her return, however, she became convinced that we were spying on her, reporting to the doctors behind her back, and we became her enemies once more. The tantrums that followed were epic. She shouted if we accidentally looked at her food. She screamed if we made plans that interfered with her schedule. She kicked, and bawled, and threw things, and punched walls, and made life hell for all of us.

'You have to eat more than one apple a day, darling,' Mum told her a week after she arrived home. Emma was already noticeably thinner than when she'd left hospital, and she'd begun to get that glazed, distant look that she got whenever her body began to shut itself down.

'Oh yes,' Emma said. 'You'd love that. You'd love to see me stuffing my face like a fucking *pig*. But I won't do it. I won't give you the satisfaction of getting one over on me.'

It made me cringe when Emma spoke to Mum like that, especially when I thought about everything Mum was doing to help her. She'd cut her hours at work so she could take care of Emma, and every evening she spent hours in Emma's room, giving her cuddles and offering the countless reassurances she needed to get through the night. I guess Emma valued the support, but she was far too wrapped up in her problems to really show any sort of appreciation for it.

The relationship between Emma and Dad was even more complicated. With Emma hiding out in her room and Dad stationed in his garage, whole days could go by when they avoided one another entirely. Mum made frequent attempts to coax Emma from her room, and more than once I heard her begging Dad to calm his temper as they argued in the kitchen. Both Emma and Dad, though, seemed determined to continue the silence that had raged between them for the past two years.

Perhaps it was just as well, because in those rare moments when fate brought Dad and Emma together in the same room, the tension within the house became unbearable. The two of them would sit in stony silence, gazing mournfully at the television, which was invariably tuned to some crappy sitcom from the seventies. Anxious to avoid any awkward silences, Mum and I would make a few increasingly desperate attempts at conversation, before falling into an awkward silence of our own and joining Emma and Dad in pretending to watch the telly. If we were lucky, we'd get through the rest of the evening without all hell breaking loose. But even in the quietest moments we all knew it was only a matter of time before we were forced into battle once more.

I hated every minute I spent at home, but I stuck around as much as I could. It seemed wrong to leave the house, to leave my family to cope without me. I wasn't sure how much good it did, but I wanted to be there, to help keep the peace in any way I could. It was only in the worst moments, when it was all I could do not to scream, that I left the house behind for a few hours.

One of these evenings arrived in early March. I was finishing eating dinner in the kitchen when Emma came through to refill her hot water bottle. Because it was the first time I'd seen her since breakfast, I decided to test the waters and try for a hug. But as soon as she felt my hand on her shoulder, she swung herself around to face me. 'James, what the fuck are you doing?'

'I'm giving you a hug,' I said. I was aware that I'd just done something terribly wrong.

'Well, don't,' Emma said. 'For fuck's sake, don't touch me.'

'Why not?'

'You just ate that burger. You haven't even washed your hands yet.'

'So, what?' I asked, smiling. But then I realised; I still had some grease on my fingers. Emma actually believed that if our skin touched, her body would absorb the calories from mine.

Suddenly, I understood how bad things had got. My shoulders slumped, and I thought I might cry in front of Emma for the first time in years. But I held myself together until she tiptoed back off to her bedroom. Then, before the tears could take hold, I grabbed my coat and made my way to the County.

Sharon's eyes were glued to the television screen when I arrived at the bar. With two years' experience under her belt, Sharon was the longest serving of all the County bar staff. As the hotel's sole barmaid, she should really have been driven screaming from the premises long ago. But throughout her time at the hotel she'd continued to move behind the bar with an incredible elegance, ducking the sexist jokes and lame attempts at protracted flirtation from the lustful clientele. In doing so she'd managed, against all odds, to maintain not only her position, but also her sanity.

'What are you watching?' I asked, after Sharon handed me the vodka and coke I'd ordered.

'*Casualty*,' she said. 'Couple of kids got hit by a van.' She clicked her tongue, as if reacting to a real-life event. 'Not sure the little one's going to make it.'

Sharon returned her attention to the TV, leaving me to settle on my stool and take a few soothing gulps of my drink. It was still early in the evening, and most of the customers had wandered off to their wives in search of dinner. The only other customer left in the bar was Gordon Ainsley. Gordon was a slovenly bastard with yellow eyes, brown teeth, and a Lego-man haircut that fell lank across his neck and forehead. In the absence of a job, he spent his days hovering around the village bars, waiting to fall into meaningless conversation with anyone clumsy enough to make eye contact with him. Fortunately, I knew better than to meet his gaze, so I held my drink in my lap and stared earnestly at the County carpet.

I was already on my third drink when *Casualty* finished. Miraculously, both children had escaped their accident with only a few broken bones and some terrible, terrible acting. Flushed with relief, Sharon turned to me. 'Thank goodness they both remembered to wear their helmets.'

Before I could answer Gordon gave a little cough at the other end of the bar. Sharon and I exchanged glances; we'd heard enough of Gordon's little coughs to know they signalled his intention to engage in conversation. Instinctively, I moved my face towards my chest, making myself as small as possible, but it was no good. Very soon, his great, clumsy footsteps began stamping towards me.

I turned around to find him standing an inch from my shoulder and wearing his village-idiot grin. There was something yellow and crusty on his chin, which I tried to ignore. 'See the football yesterday?' he asked me, in his grating monotone.

'I don't think there was any football on,' I said.

'No?' Gordon said. He scratched his chin thoughtfully, setting into motion a small avalanche of yellow crust, which floated into his glass. 'Well, you'd know better than me, I suppose. To be honest, I was never really one for the sports. Tell me, though, do you like sharks?'

I didn't, and I told him. Gordon nodded again and grabbed a handful of peanuts from the bar, which he began to chew in a way that made me want to throw up for the rest of my life. I turned to face Sharon, who appeared to be fighting off a similar urge. 'How are things?' I said, loud enough to drown out the sound of Gordon's crunching.

Sharon threw a meaningful glance towards Gordon. 'You see it all,' she said. 'And how're things with you? You been to London lately?'

'Not since Christmas,' I said.

'Aren't you due another visit?'

I shook my head. 'Emma was discharged.'

'Oh,' Sharon said. 'Well, that's great. Isn't it?'

I shifted my gaze to my knees. 'You'd think she'd have put on a bit of weight after ten months in hospital. I'm not sure she looks any better at all, though.'

Gordon, who'd run out of peanuts, decided once more to join the conversation. 'Your sister anorexic or something?' he asked. I wasn't surprised to note a complete lack of empathy in his voice. He'd spent so many years looking after number one, protecting his own interests, that not giving a fuck was almost a reflex.

When, reluctantly, I answered Gordon's question, he sucked on his bottom lip and shook his head solemnly. 'It's a terrible thing,' he said. 'A terrible thing.' I nodded politely and stared down at my drink, praying for an end to the conversation. Instead, Gordon moved a step closer to me and jabbed an elbow into my ribs. 'Here,' he whispered, conspiratorially. 'You can die of it, you know. It's what killed that Karen Carpenter.'

I was out of my chair as though catapulted, my head filled with such a sudden, powerful rage that I thought for a moment I might throw a fist into Gordon's face. 'Don't say that,' I demanded, my teeth clenched. 'Say whatever else you want around here, but don't ever let me hear you say that again.'

Gordon raised his hands submissively. 'I'm sorry, James,' he said. 'You had me thinking, that's all.'

'Think all you want, Gordon. Just don't fucking say it. Okay?'

'Okay,' Gordon said, glancing nervously towards Sharon. 'I'm sorry.'

I hardly heard Gordon's apology. My mind was already reeling from the hideous words he'd just spoken. I felt sick and exhausted to the point of dizziness. If there'd been any way at all to have the entire conversation erased from my memory, I'd have taken it right then.

That's not to say I was deluded. I wasn't. I never denied the truth. I simply chose not to face it. After all, why spend my days concentrating on the fact that Emma might drop dead at any moment? This wasn't the sort of truth that would ever set me free. It frequently made me feel terrified and defenceless and furious and sick with worry. But free? No, I never felt free. I felt like shit.

Working hard to avoid Gordon's continued attempts at apology, I bought another couple of drinks – doubles this time – and slunk off to a booth by the side of the bar. I sat back with my head against the cold, brown leather and closed my eyes. Immediately, pictures of Emma jumped through my head. I snapped my eyes open and knocked back one of my drinks in a single gulp. Within two minutes, the second glass was empty, too. Raising my hand, I signalled for Sharon to pour me another.

By midnight I was slumped low in my seat, a shot glass in one hand and a beer in the other because, fuck it, why not? Why go home now, miss out on the rare opportunity for a little *fun*? What, was there some rule now against me letting my hair down every once in a while? I put these questions, slurred these questions, to the room, mumbled angrily when I got no answer. A moment later, Sharon was by my side. 'I think it's time you thought about going home, James.'

I laughed loudly then. 'Home, James!' I said. 'Ha! You're funny.'

Sharon looked at me, confused. 'Oh, come on,' I said. 'You know, it's that old saying. *Home James, and don't spare the horses!* It's funny!' I raised my shot glass in honour of the joke, reached for it with my mouth and missed by such a distance that the entire contents poured down the front of my shirt. Sharon closed her eyes, took a deep breath. 'Ah, calm down,' I said, my head lolling badly towards my left shoulder. 'We're just having a bit of fun.'

'Who's having fun?' Sharon said. As drunk as I was, I still noted the deep look of concern on her face. That shut me up.

Sharon put a hand on my shoulder, crouched down until her eyes were level with mine. 'Just... be careful, okay?'

But I didn't want to be careful. I wanted to drink. Which I continued to do, vigorously, for the next hour. When the bell finally sounded for last orders. I shouted over to the bar for two triple measures of vodka. Sharon, sighing wearily, suggested I have a single measure instead. We compromised on a double, which I poured down my throat with reckless abandon. Then, with a wave to the empty bar, I picked my coat off the back of the chair and stumbled out into the night.

I blanked out as soon as the fresh air hit me. I remember nothing from that moment until I walked through the front door of my house and fell forward into the hallway, landing with a thump by the coat rack. I stumbled back onto all fours, but the whole world seemed to be in motion and I fell again, this time into a tiny space between two small tables. I fumbled around for some time, feeling for some way back out, but the surfaces around me kept finding surprising new angles of tilt, and soon I was completely unable to escape my narrow confines. I fell into the grip of a silent panic. *Am I expected to stay here until morning?* I asked myself. I*s this the price I have to pay for a night of revelry?* I hoped not. My back was already beginning to spasm.

Then, through the darkness, a pair of slippers landed a few inches from my face. I looked up to find Mum struggling to pull me out from my little cell into the centre of the room. Her face, still heavy with sleep, was flushed with effort.

'Oh god,' I said, struggling to help her. 'Mum, I'm so sorry. I didn't mean...'

'Hush now,' Mum said. With one final grunt, she

managed to get me seated on the carpet. 'There,' she said, blowing out her cheeks. 'That's better.'

I shook my head desperately. 'You weren't supposed to see me like this.'

'Hush now. You'll wake your sister.'

'I'm so sorry.'

'It's okay, James,' Mum said.

'It's *not* okay,' I said, hoarsely, and suddenly my chin began to tremble.

Mum clicked her tongue in sympathy. 'Oh, sweetheart,' she said. 'Don't cry. Please don't cry.' She knelt down next to me and brought my head to her shoulder, stroking my hair just like she had when I was a child.

'I'm so sorry,' I said again.

'It's okay, baby. I know. I wish I could fix this for you. Believe me, I'd do anything to take the pain away. But listen, you're going to get through this, okay? I swear it. You'll find your way through this, and you *will* come out stronger. Do you hear me?'

I nodded, wiped my eyes with the back on my hand.

'Okay then,' Mum said. 'Let's get you into bed. Things always seem easier after a good night's sleep.' Bracing herself, she lifted me upwards by the armpits, threw one of my arms across her shoulder, and helped me through to my room. Then, pulling my duvet over me, she kissed me lightly on the forehead and edged back towards the hallway. In the moment before the room turned to darkness, I looked around and saw her by the door, a finger poised on the light switch, watching me, the son who'd woken her from sleep only to stamp on her heart and leave her feeling empty and hollow. She was exhausted. She was trying not to cry. And I felt so guilty for what I'd done that it was difficult to breathe.

21 MARCH 2005

The TV's on, music's playing, and magazines are sprawled across my floor, but I'm neither watching, nor listening, nor reading. I am too busy, captivated by my own self. I bend and straighten my arms, cross and uncross my legs. The first time, I catch sight of bones and I'm filled with relief. But relief soon transforms into disgrace as the bones sink and continue to sink back into the growing sea of fat around them. I check again a thousand times, pinching and looking and prodding until bruises appear on the skin, but the result is always the same. It's disgusting. I'm disgusting.

I desperately want to put an end to the ritual, but I have to keep checking, tormenting myself, for if I gaze away, even for a second, then somehow something dreadful will happen and I won't be able to fix it. I can't let that happen, whatever 'that' is. I have to keep checking. I must keep checking...

I look in the mirror. I check myself from all angles. I turn again and again, checking and rechecking, just in case I missed something. I move about to see if the fat moves. It does. I'm ashamed.

Even then I can't stop. I look at my face. It's fat and repulsive. Hair down? Up? Which makes me look thinner? Down, I think. But who am I kidding? I can try to hide some of the fat, but it's impossible to hide it all. Try as I might, I'll never hide it all.

I'm so ashamed of the person I've become.

8

SOMETIME TOWARDS THE END OF MARCH, EMMA CAME through to the living room, her jaw set, and asked, 'Who moved the hairdryer on my dressing table?'

Mum and I looked towards Dad. Unlike us, Dad had been slow to accept that there was no quick fix to Emma's illness. He was convinced the professionals weren't acting quickly enough to help her, and this belief grew stronger with every drop in her weight. Pretty soon, he had taken it upon himself to invent an alternative treatment plan for her. The plan was based on the good old-fashioned 'cruel-to-be-kind' philosophy and consisted of a series of interventions that he hoped would snap Emma out of her old habits.

'Aye, well,' he said, when faced with Emma's question. 'I only moved it an inch or two.'

'John,' Mum said. 'You can't do that. It'll only make things worse.'

'Oh, so now it's *my* fault she's like this, is it?' Dad said.

'That's not what I meant,' Mum said.

Dad shook his head. 'Aye, aye, what a life,' he said, his voice full of bitterness and resentment. I forced myself to look at him and immediately wished I hadn't. It wasn't so much the anger that bothered me as the weariness in his eyes, the way the skin on his face had begun to sag around his cheekbones. Once some sort of hero to me, he now looked stooped and small after years of worry and fear. It had got to the point now that I could hardly bear even to glance in his direction.

'I'm sorry,' Emma said. 'I don't mean to be like this.'

'Really?' Dad said. 'Are you sure? Because, truly, sometimes I wonder whether you're not perfectly happy in that crazy little bubble of yours.'

Emma's head snapped back like she'd been slapped. 'You shouldn't say that,' she said.

'Does the truth hurt so badly?' Dad asked.

'It's not the truth,' Emma said. 'You're not allowed to say that to me.'

'I'll say whatever I want,' Dad shouted. 'This is my house.'

The argument snowballed pretty rapidly from there. Emma offered Dad a feeble apology. Dad called Emma a selfish little cow. Then Emma started to cry. Mum tried to calm the situation, but when she did Dad turned and bore his teeth at her, literally bore his teeth, like some kind of animal.

That's when I lost the plot.

'For Christ's *sake*!' I yelled, jumping to my feet. 'Would you all *shut up*! God dammit, I've had *enough* of this!'

Dad put his teeth away and Emma stopped sniffling as I barged past them and walked, head down, jaws clenched, into the cold night. Breaking into a run, I made my way down our street and across the golf course and down the dirt track that led to the shore, and when I got there I threw myself onto the sand and screamed. The scream was not one of sadness. It was not one of release, or self-pity. It was a scream of raw pain, a pain that my body simply had no other way of expressing.

I wasn't sure how much longer I could do it, how much longer I could keep sitting around and waiting for the worst to happen. The terror made me sick to my stomach. And what was worse, it never disappeared. I'd stay up half the night, listening for danger – dry retching from the toilet, the rattling of a pill bottle, the rattle of death – and spend half the next day with my head propped against my chin. I'd see an ambulance pass me on the street, its lights and sirens blaring, and immediately assume it was headed for our house. Even the briefest glimpse of Emma in her nightdress could spark off a sense of terror that left my nerves shattered for days.

Life wasn't supposed to be like this. It wasn't supposed to be so hard. As a child, I'd always felt safe in the knowledge that things would get easier, that with every passing year I'd move a little closer to the perfect life I'd always imagined for myself. Whatever I did, whatever decisions I made, everything would work out in the end. I'd overcome my problems, put everything neatly into place and everything would be fine.

But that wasn't life. That was a dream. The real world was nasty. It was cruel. It didn't care about happy endings or the way things should be. There was no such thing as saints or heroes. In the real world, bad things happened. Battles were lost. Pain was everywhere.

It was a nightmare. It was an endless fucking nightmare.

PART II

1

FOR THE PAST HOUR, DAN AND HIS BOYS HAD BEEN PLAYING dinosaurs by the bar of the Grange. Right now, they were a group of Tyrannosaurus rex, and working hard to list the struggles that T-Rex faced in the cutthroat modern world on account of their tiny little arms.

'Can't... reach... the toilet paper.'

'Watch me having a wank.'

'If you're happy and you know it... oh.'

'Could someone pass the salt, please?'

Each new problem was greeted by a great wave of laughter, but the joke had gone on rather longer than it deserved to, and I was now struggling to maintain the smile I'd nailed to my face since arriving at the bar. Steve, who'd arrived with me, looked equally uncomfortable.

Fortunately, the joke finally seemed to be drawing to a close, a fact that had left the boys increasingly anxious. After the first prolonged silence in more than an hour, there was something genuinely panicked about the way Dan threw his elbows beneath his armpits and screamed, 'Hey, Ma, I can't feel my legs!' The subsequent laughter was as hearty as ever, but the death knell had sounded on the joke and we all knew it. For the first time that evening, I dared to imagine a return to relative normality.

But then one of the boys was gripped by a sudden burst of inspiration. 'Hey,' he said, 'guess what I am?' He sucked in a big belly-full of air and let out an ear-piercing screech. The other boys threw their hands up in the air and cheered. 'Velociraptor!'

And they were off again, the T-Rex jokes replaced by an even more unsettling screechy noise, the accompanying laughter even louder than before. Smiling even more painfully now, Steve and I remained by their side long enough to hear the first complaint being raised to the hotel staff, the wandered off to the fruit machine in search of an excuse to leave.

Then, miraculously, something interesting happened; Will Spencer arrived with a couple of girls. Steve and I looked at one another, confused. This wasn't in the script. Girls were never in the script. The Grange was home to snobby golfers and stupid tourists and Dan and his rugby jocks. Everybody knew that. And yet, here was Will with two actual girls. Actual *pretty* girls. Steve and I watched in silence as he led them to the bar and introduced them to Dan. Dan made a joke and they began to giggle. I found that unfair. I wanted to make them giggle too. Immediately, I abandoned my plans to run off home and waited for a chance to talk with them. Steve did the same.

The noise at the bar had begun to settle in the moments before Will walked up to it, but the peace was shattered within seconds of his arrival. 'Hey, Will, listen to this,' Dan said. 'HEEEEEEEEK!'

'Velociraptor!' the others yelled in unison.

Will grinned. 'Alright,' he said, 'listen to *this*...

HEEEEEEEEK!' His impression sounded just like everyone else's, but everyone else laughed as though they'd never heard anything so funny.

Standing by his side, Will's guests were pretending to look impressed, but they seemed confused by what was happening. Within a couple of minutes, they'd edged away from the group and were making themselves comfortable on the chairs next to Steve and me. Then, to our amazement, they asked how we were.

I glanced towards Steve. 'Uh, good,' I said. And that, for the moment, seemed to be about the best I could do.

'How did you like Jurassic Park?' Steve asked.

Good one. I wouldn't have thought of that.

'I don't understand,' one of the girls said. 'Why were they laughing so much? Did they want us to laugh as well?'

'Mostly they just need to make noise,' I said. 'They start to doubt their existence if they fall quiet for more than a second.'

The girls giggled. Usually, it pissed me off when girls did that, because it was always so fake, but with these guys it wasn't fake at all. 'Well at least we got out of there while we could.'

I suddenly became aware of an accent. *Vile ve could*, she said. *Ve got out of there vile ve could*. 'You're not from here, are you?' I said. 'Are you German?'

'No, but you're close. We're from Austria.'

Steve and I widened our eyes and gave an impressed nod, the standard look when someone tells you where they're from. Then we introduced ourselves.

'It's nice to meet you. I'm Elisabeth. And this is Hannah.'

'Mmm, that's nice,' Steve said, which sounded creepy. Realising this, he quickly added, 'So, are you old school friends?'

Elisabeth shook her head. 'We only met six months ago, when we arrived in Scotland. We volunteer just along the road at Rose Glen.'

'You work at Rose Glen?' I asked.

Elisabeth nodded. 'That's how we know Will. He works there too. Do you know it?'

I told them I did. Rose Glen, one of Cranston's many care homes, had been a part of my life for years. I'd sung carols in its dining hall with a friend's choir for the past five Christmases. A few summers back, I'd met an ex-girlfriend for the first time by the foot of its main staircase. Also, Mum had worked there since my time at High School. When I mentioned this last connection, Elisabeth squealed. 'You're Mary Barnes' son? Oh my god, we *love* Mary Barnes!'

Already, Elisabeth was doing most of the talking. She spoke quickly and in a thick, almost comical, accent. 'But it's not my fault,' she explained, smiling. 'I'm from Vorarlberg, so I grew up around Austrian farmers. Even when I speak in German, most people outside of the region think I'm still learning the language.'

Elisabeth would soon turn twenty, but I wouldn't have guessed it. She wasn't much more than five feet tall, and the clothes she wore – a tight yellow t-shirt and skinny blue jeans – emphasised her narrow hips and small breasts. Her face was one of the friendliest I'd ever seen, and her smile, which only waned during the most serious parts of our conversation, revealed a set of teeth that should have been too big for her mouth, but which suited her perfectly. This smile, coupled with her large, brown eyes, seemed to bring a warm air of optimism to everybody she looked at. Here was a girl who was not only cheerful but whose cheer spread to everyone around her. I liked her from the moment I saw her.

Although Hannah hadn't been short of conversation, she

seemed happier to leave the talking to Elisabeth. That's not to say she was disinterested. In fact, she listened attentively to everything that was said, and observed us all closely as we continued our conversation. When she *did* speak, she looked you straight in the eye, as though she was daring you to open your heart to her right there and then.

She wasn't a great deal taller than Elisabeth, but she had a fuller build, which gave the impression that more than an inch or two separated them. Her long brown hair was pulled back into a ponytail, with a strand of hair falling down from each side of her face. Her clothes were darker and more bohemian than Elisabeth's, but she had the same kind of open, friendly face. She was really pretty, actually, and I desperately wanted to talk to her. So, when Steve and Elisabeth became locked in conversation over some topic or another, I took a deep breath and moved over to sit by her side. Hannah turned to face me and smiled.

'Hi,' I said. 'I'm James.'

'I know,' Hannah said. 'I remember.' She said this without the slightest hint of sarcasm, but I felt stupid in any case. I hoped the room was dim enough to hide the fact that I was blushing.

'How are you enjoying Scotland?' I asked, grateful, at least, I didn't stutter.

'Oh, I like it,' Hannah said. 'The people are kind and the beach is on my doorstep.'

'And you're here to stay?'

Hannah shook her head. 'I'm going home to Vienna in September for a month or two. Then, at the end of the year, I have to travel.'

'Travel where?'

'Oh, all over – Rio, Israel, New York, Vietnam, Japan, Taiwan. Some other places, too.'

'That's a long list.'

'It's a big world,' Hannah said, and grinned. 'I want to see it all. I want to die knowing I danced in Rio during Carnival, and took a ride across Route 66, and surfed in Hawaii, and watched the Northern Lights in Norway. Truly, there are so many things I need to do.'

It was a long time since I'd spoken like this to a girl. I'd forgotten how stressful it was, the job of entertaining a person without embarrassing myself completely. Not stressful in a bad way, but still, I could have done with an opportunity to recover my senses. Fortunately, Hannah's mention of rum forced my eyes towards the empty glass that she'd been playing with. Clearing my throat, I offered to buy her another drink. She nodded heartily.

Holly had arrived at the hotel with Steve and I, but we'd seen neither head nor tail of her for over an hour, since she'd tired of Dan's prehistoric adventures and wandered off to speak with an old friend from school. As soon as I reached the bar, however, she stomped over to my side. 'Jamie,' she said, '*what* are you doing with that girl?'

'I'm taking your advice,' I said. 'You told me to find one.'

'But I didn't mean *her*, Jamie. She's awful.'

'I like her, actually,' I said, grinning.

Holly narrowed her eyes towards me. 'Then you're quite obviously blind.'

I paid no attention to this. Holly's first impressions of people were rarely positive. She'd always been slow to accept new people to our group, and quite often refused to accept them at all. She seldom had anything she could genuinely hold against them. She was simply a born cynic.

I grabbed my drinks and made my way back to the table, and to my conversation with Hannah. She told me all kinds of things: how she'd travelled alone through

Germany for a week during the summer she turned sixteen; how she liked to have brief yet deep conversations with strangers she met at train stations. She told me how, thirty years earlier, her father had left home in Canada to spend a summer in Europe, only to meet her Viennese mother and settle in the city. She told me how, good or bad, she enjoyed all new experiences that came her way, and how she wanted to be a doer of good deeds on a legendary level.

She asked me all kinds of things, too: would I rather be rich or successful, handsome or clever? What was my earliest memory? Had I ever had an imaginary friend? Which song would come first on the soundtrack to my life? A hundred little questions just like those. In over three hours, we didn't stop talking for a second.

By closing time Dan and his boys were as drunk as mules, and we hadn't even left the hotel car park before they began climbing onto one another's shoulders and fighting as horses and knights. Watching them, Hannah only smiled, but Elisabeth was keen to join the game and invited Steve to act as her steed. Steve never usually involved himself in these games, but tonight, flushed with success after his evening with Elisabeth and keen to hold her attention a little longer, he readily obliged.

Unfortunately, Elisabeth was as drunk as the boys, and even more wobbly. Steve tried valiantly to hold her steady on his narrow frame, but he hadn't even joined the battle before his left leg buckled and Elisabeth disappeared over his shoulders. Elisabeth let out a howl, before bouncing off the wall of the pub and landing on her back against the kerb.

'Fuck,' I said, running towards Elisabeth. 'Are you okay?'

'I'm fine,' she slurred. 'Look everybody, I've been

rescued. Mary Barnes' son has rescued me.' And then, touching her elbow, 'Ouch.'

I stifled a smile and said, 'Okay, let me give you a lift home.'

'Uh, ja,' said Elisabeth. 'Because I hurt my ass.'

I turned to Hannah. 'You take this one,' I said, handing her Elisabeth's arm. 'I'll go fetch her majesty's horse.'

Elisabeth turned to Hannah. 'I hurt my ass,' she said.

Steve was a few yards away, looking slightly pale and leaning against the wall of the pub. I suppose, like me, he was imagining how embarrassing it would have been for him to meet, greet and hospitalise a girl all in the same evening. I walked up to him and squeezed his shoulder. 'Time to go, Tonto.'

We drove the girls to the small apartment they shared near the centre of town. At the front door, we found the courage to ask them to the cinema the following Thursday and they bobbed their heads enthusiastically. We said goodnight to them, told them we'd pick them up at eight, not to miss us too much before then ha-ha, and then swaggered back to the car feeling extremely happy with ourselves.

It was past midnight when I arrived home, so I'd expected to find the house in darkness. But as I entered the house, I saw a patch of light filtering out from beneath Emma's door. A familiar sense of panic began to fill my chest as I hurried towards the room, but as I drew closer I began to make out voices, none of which were distressed. I knocked on the door and stepped inside to find Emma and Mum in their pyjamas, sitting side by side on the edge of Emma's bed.

'Just a bad dream,' Mum said, answering the look of

concern on my face. 'But it's all better now. Isn't it, love?' She smiled reassuringly at Emma, who smiled back, though she looked exhausted. Emma had always suffered from night terrors, but in the past few years they'd grown more frequent and more aggressive. Since her return from London, nights when she hadn't woken us, screaming and thrashing her way out of bad dreams, had been rare.

'Did you have a nice time in Cranston?' Mum asked.

With disaster now averted, I was able to think back to my evening with Hannah. 'It was good,' I said. 'Fun.'

'Fun?' Mum said, genuinely puzzled. 'That doesn't sound like the Grange.'

'Yeah, well...' I said, with a nonchalant shrug. I was trying to play it cool, but my face was refusing to cooperate.

Mum narrowed her eyes into slits. 'What are you so happy about?'

'Nothing,' I said, grinning even wider.

Emma had been watching me carefully; now she broke into a little smile of her own. 'He met a girl,' she said.

Mum's head darted from me, to Emma, to me. 'No!' she said, beaming. 'Did you? Really? A girl? *Really*?'

I started to laugh. 'Jesus, Mum, is it so difficult to believe?'

'No, no,' Mum said. 'But it's just... well, it's just lovely.'

Rolling my eyes self-consciously, I turned to Emma. 'How did you know?' I asked.

Emma shrugged. 'I'm still your sister,' she said. 'Don't think I can't still read you like a book.'

And all of a sudden, I was transported back to my childhood, to a time when Emma and I were so close that I never quite knew where my thoughts ended and hers began. In those days, the understanding between us was there for everyone to see, in the glances we exchanged, in the games we played with the rules only we could understand. The familiarity was so strong, so natural, that we made the children around us look remarkably singular by comparison. Until that moment, I'd forgotten completely how it used to feel. Goodness, it was good to feel it again, if only for a second.

Unaware of the moment that had passed between her children, Mum was still revelling in thoughts of my mystery girl. 'Well, I think it's wonderful,' she said, apropos of nothing. 'Absolutely wonderful.' Then, suddenly, she was laughing, laughing out loud at this chance for me to find some new focus, and based on the tears that filled her eyes, I guessed she'd been waiting a long time for that to happen. Awkwardly, I moved in to kiss her goodnight. Like a shot, she wrapped an arm around my shoulders, pulled me close, and buried her head into my neck. She held me there for a long moment, and when she finally spoke, I could tell her words were borne of relief. 'You're doing just fine,' she said.

I stepped back from the embrace, embarrassed by the drama that had just played out in front of me. Then I looked at Emma and realised that she was grinning – actually grinning – directly at me. 'Love you, Jamie,' she said.

I fought back a sudden prickling of tears, then told her that I loved her too. And for that moment, nothing more was required. It was, in its way, perfect. I felt safe, and strangely optimistic. My worries had disappeared, like rain on summer earth. I took a deep breath, savoured the feeling for a few seconds more. Then, with a final smile, I turned from the room, secure in the knowledge that even the most difficult times contained moments that made a person feel truly alive.

2

LIFE WAS NO LESS ROSY THE FOLLOWING MORNING. I WOKE early to bright sunshine and spent the next two hours grinning stupidly at the paint on my ceiling. Lying there, I knew, as clearly as I knew I was born, that Hannah and I were going to fall in love and that it would happen sooner rather than later. I couldn't explain why, exactly; there was just something between us, some kind of connection that I'd never experienced with anyone before. It was going to be epic.

That was breakfast time. At lunch time, Steve called and dropped a bombshell. 'It's not going to happen for me with Elisabeth,' he said. 'She has a boyfriend waiting for her back home.'

'What are you talking about?' I asked, defensively. 'How do you know that?'

'She told Dan. He decided to play Poirot for us last night. Uh, did Hannah say anything about a boyfriend?'

I thought for a moment. 'No. Why would she?'

'Because she has one, apparently. Some guy called Christian. They've been together since high school.'

I sank gloomily against the wall and felt the excitement in my stomach turn to bitter disappointment. Then groaned.

'I'm sorry, buddy,' Steve said, and I could tell that he meant it. 'I suppose, given the circumstances, it would be best to call off our little date on Thursday night.'

I disagreed and told him so. I tried to convince him that he was wrong, but he stood firm, and after calling me a big child for sulking, he wished me all the best for the trip and hung up the phone.

Hannah must have been watching for my car, because she was outside her flat before I'd even finished parking. I stepped out onto the street and watched as she approached, unsure as to whether I should shake her hand or give her a hug. The dilemma was soon put to bed by Hannah, who came at me with open arms and planted a kiss on each of my cheeks.

'Where's Elisabeth?' I asked.

'They called her into work this afternoon,' Hannah said, as she made her way around the car.

'Oh. So, it's just you and me?'

Hannah nodded. 'You okay with that?'

Was I okay? Man, I was so much better than okay. I felt light-headed and reckless, like I'd won some sort of competition. I wanted to celebrate, maybe run a lap around the car park or break into a little dance. But that would look stupid, I knew, so instead I waited until Hannah climbed into the passenger seat and gleefully fist bumped the sky.

When I followed Hannah into the car, my heart was pounding and my hands trembled against the steering wheel. If Hannah noticed my excitement at all, she kept it to herself. 'So, what's the plan?' she asked. 'What are we going to see?'

'I don't know,' I said. 'I thought we could drive to the cinema and decide when we got there.'

Hannah grinned. 'I like that. Do we have any music?'

'You can turn on the radio if you like.'

Hannah leaned forward and reached for the dial. The radio hissed, shrieked and blasted a few bars of Mozart before finally settling on Radiohead's *Exit Music (for a Film)*. Hannah, delighted with her discovery, smiled and slumped back in her seat. She listened to Thom Yorke's nasally vocals in silence for a couple of verses before joining in. Singing heartily and drumming away on her knees, she was like a ball of energy, and already I felt this energy permeating my own body. I felt as fresh and as happy as I'd been in months.

Radiohead ended and became The Stone Roses, who in turn became The Killers. Finally, when they became the hourly news, Hannah rolled her eyes and turned off the radio. We arrived at the cinema soon after and bought two tickets to a film called *Somersault*. Only five others had taken their seats by the time the adverts began.

'Shame these guys bothered to turn up,' I said. 'We might have had the screen to ourselves.'

'I'll chase them away if you like,' Hannah said, then picked a piece of popcorn from the box on my lap and threw it at a couple sitting a few rows in front of us. It bounced off the shoulder of the man, who turned around and snorted at me. Hannah smiled proudly. 'You want to try?' she asked.

I looked towards our neighbour. Even in the half-darkness, I could make out the tattoos that covered his huge neck. 'Best not,' I said.

The movie, a bittersweet coming-of-age drama, suited the evening perfectly. It was the kind of patient and pretentious character study that Hannah and I both loved, and we left the cinema feeling reflective and dramatic. We talked without stopping on the drive back to Cranston, and when we arrived there Hannah invited me into her apartment.

The apartment looked entirely different to how I'd imagined it. In the hallway, a collection of prints had been hung in celebration of Cranston's rich fishing heritage, while in the living room a large cream tarpaulin covered one of the walls, presumably to represent a ship's sail. The white walls and nautical theme were hardly an unusual choice of décor for an apartment in a conservative harbour town, but they seemed at odds with the colourful city girl who stood before me. Still, the flat was clean and comfortable, and the girls had dotted it with little objects – a red ashtray, a Lautrec poster, and some coloured glass beads – to make it feel more like home. On the living room table, a large bag of weed gave a further clue that the tenants' hobbies stretched some way beyond boats. I liked the place a lot, and I told her so.

'Well, it's home, at least.' Hannah said with a smile. She led me down the narrow hallway to her room. 'It's a little messy,' she said, pushing the door open. 'But come in – there's something I want to show you.'

Hannah wasn't exaggerating when she said her room was untidy. Every inch of available space was filled with random piles of books and DVDs and souvenirs she'd collected during her time in Scotland. A pile of rocks and shells sat on top of a chest of drawers, and a large wardrobe by the door was bursting with a hundred dresses of all kinds and colours. The walls were white, I think, but they'd been covered so completely with photographs and postcards and posters and sketches that it was almost impossible to see the paint at all. Another large pile of papers covered her desk. When she saw me inspecting them, Hannah smiled.

'It's my father,' she explained. 'He worries that I miss Vienna while I'm away from home, so he cuts out interesting articles from the Austrian papers and sends them over at the beginning of every month. I never find time to read them, but I keep them anyway. It's a nice reminder of home.'

Hannah touched the papers gently, then returned to her search. A moment later, she picked out a Walkman from a box on her floor and turned triumphantly towards me. 'I want you to lie down and listen to this,' she said, handing me a pair of earphones. 'And remember,' she added, smiling, 'it's one of my favourites, so you're not allowed to hate it.'

'What is it?' I asked, as I sank into Hannah's mattress.

'It's Sigur Ros. And it's beautiful. Close your eyes. I'm going to press play.'

The song, *Njósnavélin*, was a vast, unhurried record, full of hope and sensitivity. As I listened, a sense of calm swept over my body. There was something about the song that felt different, that made *me* feel different, as though everything had slowed down just to let me breathe for a while. I could have listened to it forever.

'You liked it?' Hannah asked when I handed her back the headphones. When I nodded, she smiled and pretended to blush. I considered reaching out and touching her hand and wondered whether she might have been thinking the same. But she wasn't; seconds later, she jumped to her feet and began making plans for a midnight feast.

I stood up too. 'Actually, I'd better go.'

Hannah looked towards her feet, disappointed.

'I'm sorry, but I'm working early tomorrow. I'll see you soon though, okay?'

She nodded and I threw on my coat, smiling. With

renewed vigour, I'd begun once more to fantasise the adventures we'd share during our summer together.

The following morning, I met Holly in Zanzibar, one of the quasi-hipster joints that had recently begun to pop up along Cranston High Street to feed the town's sudden and apparently insatiable demand for Edison bulbs and single origin coffee beans. The café prided itself on its unique style, which it shared identically with a thousand other spaces around the country. Words like 'artisan' and 'bespoke' were thrown at random throughout the chalkboard menu, while the exposed brickwork was lined with quirky sixties movie posters and motivational quotes. It was all quite sickeningly pretentious.

'So, you're happy with this arrangement, are you?' Holly asked when I'd finished describing my first adventure with Hannah. We were sitting, as usual, on an ancient leather sofa by the front window of the café. 'I mean, you do realise this girl has a boyfriend, don't you?'

'So?' I asked, grinning. 'Why should that matter to me?'

'Because you *fancy* her.'

'What? No, I don't fancy her.'

'Oh my god, Jamie, that's such an obvious lie. You should see the way the two of you sit grinning at one another when you're together. It's like you've just discovered teeth.'

'So, we enjoy one another's company. That's healthy enough, isn't it?'

'For now,' Holly said. 'But you won't be smiling when she breaks your heart.'

'She won't break my heart. I'll be careful.'

'No, you won't. You never are.'

I took a sip of my coffee, turned my head to the window. Outside, a heavy rain was falling. The sky was covered over with dark, low-hanging clouds. Most of the shoppers had taken refuge from the shower in the stores and cafes. Those who remained on the street looked as though they wished they'd followed suit as they fought against the elements for control of their carrier bags and umbrellas. 'Fine, then' I said, at last. 'I promise this time. I promise I'll take things easy.'

Holly shook her head impatiently. 'James, you should know yourself better than that by now. There's no way you'll *ever* let that happen.' She gave a final, disappointed tut and wandered off to order another shot of coffee.

3
———

Scotland was enjoying an early taste of summer when I met Hannah again the following week. We'd planned to go to the cinema again, but the sun was so warm and bright when I arrived at her apartment that I asked her whether she might want to go to Myreton beach instead.

Hannah grinned. 'Is the sky blue?' she asked.

Back in Myreton, I parked the car by the foot of the hill and stepped out into the evening sun. The beach was busier than usual, playing host to families and dog-walkers who were eager to make the most of the unseasonal warmth. Against the percussion of the waves, I could hear the laughter of children, the sound rising and falling like the ocean itself. Joining me by the front of the car, Hannah gazed out onto the long crescent of golden sand, the clear blue water. 'You weren't exaggerating, were you?' she said. 'It really is beautiful.'

When we reached the sand, Hannah made her way ahead of me and began to dance by the water's edge, to the surprise of everyone else on the beach. With eyes closed and arms outstretched, she spun around again and again, her momentum taking her inch by inch into the sea. She was wet to the knees when a breaking wave clipped her ankle and she disappeared into the water. Another person in her position might conceivably have felt some sense of embarrassment, but not Hannah, who sprang back to her feet and smiled at her audience as if she might have expected them to throw off their clothes and join her. Taking a bow, she walked out of the water towards me. I was bent double on the sand, my stomach already hurting from laughter.

'What's wrong with you?' Hannah asked, when she reached my side.

'It was... You... The way you...' I went into another convulsion which lasted some time. 'My god, you're crazy!'

Hannah grinned. 'I'll take that as a compliment.'

I fought to catch my breath, wiped my eyes with the sleeve of my shirt. 'Oh dear, oh dear,' I murmured weakly. 'I'm so glad I was here to see it.'

When I could walk again, we made our way to a rocky outcrop on the east side of the beach, before turning onto a little path that led to a quieter stretch of sand. We took off our shoes and strolled along the water, watching as each small wave rushed our ankles in little eddies and then sucked our feet as it was pulled back into the sea. The sun had begun to set by the time either of us spoke again. It was Hannah who broke the silence. 'I bet you've walked these shores a hundred times before,' she said.

I smiled. 'Closer to a thousand, I think. Mum and Dad used to bring us down here all the time when we were kids. It didn't matter what time of year it was, there was always something to do; walks in the winter, paddling in summer, and in the autumn, we'd pick brambles over there in the dunes. We loved this place. Hardly a day passed by when we didn't ask to come.'

'You and Emma, you mean?'

'Mmm hmmm.'

Hannah nodded, bit her lip thoughtfully. 'James?' she said, after a moment. 'Your sister... I've heard people talking at work. She's really anorexic?'

I nodded.

'But she's okay?'

'Not so much. She's pretty sick, actually.'

'Oh. But I heard she was at university.'

'She was. But it didn't work out so well.'

'What do you mean?'

I looked up towards Hannah. 'Do you really want to know?'

Hannah nodded. 'Tell me,' she said.

So, I did. I told her everything, about Emma's childhood, about the night Dad had uncovered her secret, and about everything that had happened in the years that followed. This later period, I told her, had been marked by a steady decline in Emma's health. She became obsessed with her schoolwork and increasingly closed off from her friends. She ate less and less, and the excuses she used to avoid food became ever more elaborate. Mum had taken her to the doctor a number of times, but little had come of the visits and Emma was no closer to admitting to anyone that she had any kind of problem.

Then, in the spring of 2002, she accepted an unconditional offer to study geography in St Andrews. Suddenly, Mum and Dad were frantic. In the months that followed, they tried everything to talk Emma out of going to university, to stay at home and work on improving her health. Emma, though, was determined not to miss out on the opportunity to escape their prying eyes, so spent the summer working to convince everyone around her that St

Andrews was actually the best place for her shake off her issues with food. Mum and Dad didn't believe her, but what could they do? Short of locking her in her room, there was no way in the world to stop her from leaving. In the end, they just had to say goodbye and pray that she'd cope.

She didn't cope at all. As soon as term began, she settled into a routine of working from six in the morning until eleven at night. Literally every waking hour was spent working or preparing to work. I think the only time she ever really stopped was to make her way to and from classes.

I visited Emma every two or three weeks during that first semester, always hoping she might have staged some kind of sudden, miraculous recovery. But every time I arrived she looked worse than the last – sometimes quite a lot worse than the last – and often her eyes were red and swollen from the hours she'd spent crying over her books.

A few times, I managed to needle her into having lunch with me. After ordering the smallest thing on the menu, she'd fall silent, disgusted she'd actually just asked for something to eat. Disgust would turn to panic when the food arrived, her eyes darting around the room, searching for people who might be judging her for being so greedy. Then she'd start to cry, tell me she couldn't do it, couldn't eat in front of an audience, and I'd tell her it was fine, that she could take the meal home with her and eat it there. She'd nod and wipe away her tears; wrap it carefully in a napkin. A year later, she'd admit that every single one of those lunches ended up in the toilets of her halls of residence.

When Emma returned to university after the Christmas holidays, she became even more withdrawn. In the rare hours she wasn't working, she exercised. She took long walks around town, or otherwise went out to run a few laps of the local racetrack, desperate to burn off whatever fat she still imagined was clinging to her body. To look at her, it was impossible to believe she had the strength to do any of this, but starvation had brought a surge of wild, unstable energy, a rush of pure adrenaline that allowed her to push her body to its absolute limits.

When her body reached its limits, Emma began to collapse. More than once she left the bathroom after her morning shower with enormous bruises covering her face and shoulders. Terrified, the girls in her corridor met with the head of student support, who in turn arranged to meet with Emma the following week.

Just as she had with the doctors the previous summer, Emma tried to convince the counsellor that she was well enough to stay at university. But there was no fooling anyone by then. In the past few months, her breasts and hips had vanished almost entirely, and it was possible to make out every single one of her ribs through her clothes. When she spoke, she spoke slowly and awkwardly, as though her tongue had grown heavier. Her skin was a ghostly white, and her body permanently shivered. It would have been a crime not to send her home.

Three weeks later I arrived outside University Hall for the final time. There was a sickness in my stomach as I walked towards Emma's floor. She'd more or less convinced me since her meeting with the counsellor that her friends had turned against her for the pain she'd caused them, for ruining their first year in St Andrews. And yet, when the moment came for her to leave, every single one of them gathered outside her room to say goodbye.

'I hate to think of all the fun they'll have without me,' Emma had said as we reached the outskirts of town. But even as she spoke, I knew she'd never been more grateful for anything in her life. Throughout her months in St Andrews, she'd been torn between sticking things out and throwing in the towel. Now, finally, the decision to leave had been taken out of her hands. An enormous weight had been lifted from her shoulders.

When I'd finished talking, I glanced towards Hannah. She looked deep into my eyes, her own full of pity. 'What happened then?' she asked.

'The village doctors barely recognised Emma when she walked into the surgery for the first time after coming home. I've no idea what she weighed by then, but the starvation diet she'd been on had taken an enormous toll on her body. Within half an hour, the doctors had already begun searching for an available hospital bed. It usually took three months or more to find one, but time wasn't on Emma's side by that point. Five days later they rushed her into the Hope Park clinic in Glasgow.

'It was great there for a while. Emma put on weight and began to look healthy for the first time in years. She developed an understanding with her key worker and took part in group therapies and laughed and talked with the other girls in the ward and it truly seemed that she was on some kind of road to recovery. But after about five months something snapped in her. She began exercising in secret in her room. She began to vomit for the first time in a decade. She turned against the nurses and doctors who were trying to help her and suddenly all the good work of the past half year was undone.

'The doctors must have known she didn't stand a chance of succeeding on her own - too much of her was still clinging to her illness for that to happen. But she'd stopped complying, and her weight was at a 'safe' level, so they decided to discharge her. She was home for less than three weeks before an ambulance arrived at our door to drive her off to St Jude's. The less said about that place, the better.'

'She's back home now?' Hannah asked.

'Yeah,' I said. 'Though it won't be long before she's back in hospital again.'

'I'm so sorry,' Hannah said. 'I hope it will get better someday.'

'Yeah, well,' I said. 'That's the dream.'

We'd walked quite far along the beach, to a point where the sand began to give way to a crop of sea buckthorn. It was dark now, and near impossible to travel through the jungle of prickly bushes, so we lay down against a dune and stared into the glowing Milky Way.

'You see?' Hannah said. 'There's nothing more beautiful than a sky filled with stars.' She began to point out a few constellations, but I wasn't interested. After falling in the water Hannah had removed her cardigan, leaving her with only a thin tank top that clung tightly to her chest and stomach. I continued to watch her from the corner of my eye, noting the way her breasts rose and fell with each movement of her outstretched arm, swallowing back the yearning that this brought upon me.

We remained against that dune for three hours that night. I don't remember our conversation, only our proximity. We were lying so close that our arms brushed with every movement we made, and I was acutely conscious of every slightest contact. More than once, I was forced to remember the promise I'd made to Holly. Hannah and I were friends now. This was our new base. Forget the moments we'd shared. Ignore the chemistry. Stop chasing her around. End of story.

At around midnight I suggested we go home. 'Just a little

longer,' Hannah said, and reached over to hold my hand. Which was fine. After all, friends held hands sometimes.

By the time we arrived back to Hannah's apartment it was one in the morning. Having decided it was too late for me to drive home, Hannah set up the sofa bed in the living room. I lay down and she made herself comfortable next to me. Did friends normally lie next to one another in bed? Hannah's body was nice and warm. I decided they did.

'Thank you for tonight,' Hannah said. 'I had a wonderful time.'

'Me too,' I said, as Hannah moved closer towards me.

Oh god.

She shuffled up some more, placed her head on my chest.

Okay, I told myself. *Just ignore the chemistry.*

But her breasts were pressing against my side.

Ignore the chemistry, James...

I tucked down my chin. She looked up at me.

Uh, James?

Her eyes were so amazingly blue and twinkly...

I said, 'Can we share a kiss?'

Hannah seemed ready for the question; she moved so gently towards me that her lips had touched mine before I even knew her answer. It was a blissful, startling moment that stopped my heart for a second.

4

————

FOR A GIRL WITHOUT A JOB, OR HOBBIES, OR ANY KIND OF social life, Emma's schedule was remarkably crowded. Dieting, walking, worrying, writing, exercising, surviving – all of these things ate into a day that might have offered endless possibilities had Emma not felt obliged to fill her great unfenced acres of spare time with the kind of trivial concerns and ridiculous compulsions that her doctors had been trying for years to clear from her head. This habit shone most brightly every Tuesday, when she took her place by the living-room window to await the arrival of her care team from Edinburgh. No matter what was going on around her or within her head, she arrived by the window on the stroke of noon every single week. The team never arrived before half past one.

Whenever I could, I grabbed the chance to join Emma by the window. Her vigils offered little in the form of entertainment, but with Emma increasingly holed up in her room, they were among the few opportunities I still had to spend time with her. Each week, our schedule followed the same pattern. I'd begin with a few attempts at conversation, which Emma would ignore completely. Then I'd grab some snacks from the kitchen and throw myself down on the chair by the window. For the next hour, I'd divide my time between watching crap on TV and offering Emma the reassurances she needed to get through her latest stretch of guard duty.

On the first Tuesday of May, I was sitting in my usual place, but instead of pretending to give a shit about the programmes that were showing on telly, I was trying desperately not to go batshit crazy with Emma, who, for the past hour, had been drumming her fingers frantically against the back of my chair.

'Okay,' I said, when I could stand it no longer. 'You really need to calm down.'

Drum-drum-drum. 'That's not an option.'

'Maybe I could take over for a bit.'

'No.' Drum-drum-drum. 'You might miss them.'

'The Simpsons is coming on,' I said, resisting the impulse to stand up and force her onto the chair.

'I'm fine where I am,' Emma said. Drum-drum-drum.

Drum.

I breathed heavily through my nose, snatched up my sandwich. 'Whatever,' I said.

Emma ignored my tone, fixated on my food. 'Watch out for crumbs,' she said. 'And get rid of that plate before they arrive.'

'It's not like they're going to think you suddenly fancied an actual meal,' I said. But a car door had slammed in the street and Emma was already turning back to the window to peer out from between the curtains.

It wasn't them.

'For fuck's sake!' Emma yelled, banging a fist against the windowsill. 'They were supposed to be here at two.'

'It's not even five past yet.'

'I must have missed them,' she said. 'What if I missed them?'

'That didn't happen, Emma.'

Emma hardly seemed to hear me. 'Maybe I didn't hear the doorbell ring,' she said. 'Maybe the television... Oh god, Jamie, you've had the television turned up too loud!'

To watch Emma then, you'd have thought she was truly looking forward to the arrival of her guests. But the truth was that she dreaded these visits with every part of her being. For nearly three months, her health had continued to deteriorate, and the ever-decreasing numbers on the scales had brought the threat of hospitalisation and recovery closer and closer with each passing visit. Then there was the opposite, and possibly even more serious, worry that she'd piled on a stone or two in the previous seven days. Of course, anybody who'd watched Emma starving herself since her last weigh-in knew this was impossible, but in Emma-land the most implausible fears were often the ones that seemed most likely to become real.

Two more endless minutes passed before the dietician's red Volvo turned into our street. 'Oh!' Emma said. 'Here they come! Quick, Jamie, wipe up those crumbs. Get rid of that plate.'

I did as I was told but did it slowly; slowly enough to ensure that I exited the kitchen in the same moment Emma and her company appeared by its door. Today, this company comprised Rosa, Emma's dietician, and her therapist, Elaine. Both smiled when they saw me. Emma, standing by their side, glared furiously.

'Hello James,' Rosa said. 'How are you?' Handing dietary advice to anorexics must surely have been one of the world's most thankless tasks, but in all the times I'd met Rosa I'd never seen her lose an ounce of cheer.

I considered answering Rosa truthfully, but Emma was already shattered, and I wasn't sure that she would survive the betrayal. I said, 'I'm fine'.

Elaine, too, was smiling. Like Rosa, nothing ever seemed to penetrate her solid wall of cheerfulness. 'Looking forward to the summer?' she asked.

'Oh yes,' I said. 'I love the Scottish summer. It's probably my favourite day of the year.'

We all had a good chuckle at that, except for Emma, whose eyes were fixed on the bag Rosa was carrying. Inside the bag were the sacred weigh-day scales that would either make or break Emma's week. I decided it was time to put her out of her misery. 'Well, I better leave you guys to it.'

Emma breathed a sigh of relief so deep it seemed to come all the way from her feet, then ushered her guests into the living room and closed the door. It was a gentle close, not a slam, but I knew if I so much as sneezed again before the meeting was over, there'd be hell to pay.

And yet, I couldn't quite bring myself to walk away, to go to my room and stay there until I was given permission to come out again. For the past two months I'd been a good little boy, done exactly what I was asked to do precisely when I was asked to do it. Today, though, I found I'd had enough of uncertainty, of being kept in the dark. I understood that Emma was entitled to her secrecy, but I resented it too because, after all, I was living in the same house as her, watching her basically trying to self-destruct, and I felt I deserved at the very least to know whether she was likely to be rescued before her efforts proved successful.

Before I could think better of it, I turned back towards the living room and pressed an ear to the wall.

'So, how have things been this week?' I heard Elaine ask.

'Yep,' Emma said. 'Good. Much better.'

There was a pause. Then Elaine said, 'Well, that's great. Really great. So, you've been spending a bit more time with James and your parents?'

'Mmm hmmm,' Emma said. 'Yep.'

'Fantastic,' Elaine said. 'And the rest of the time? Have you been finding things any easier?'

'Yes,' Emma said. 'It's been much better.'

Okay, well that wasn't true. In the past week alone, I'd caught Emma counting calories on the internet three times, and on every occasion, she'd shouted at me to get the fuck out of the room, which seemed unfair, because it was my room she was in, my computer she was using. Her daily route marches around Myreton had also begun to stretch far beyond the one-mile distance that Emma and the team had agreed upon.

I was trying to picture how much more of this bullshit Rosa and Elaine were going to take when a floorboard behind me creaked and I almost screamed. When I threw my head around to face the offender, they took a respectful step backward, raising their open hands.

'Jesus, *fuck*, Mum!' I hissed, clutching a hand to my chest.

'Sorry,' Mum whispered. 'My leg was falling asleep.' She gave her foot a little wiggle, fending off the pins and needles.

'How long have you been here?'

'A couple of minutes,' Mum said, before adding, 'We really shouldn't be doing this.'

'I know,' I said.

'Emma would be furious.'

'I know,' I said.

We looked at one another, conversing with our eyes. It went on for some time – ten seconds, maybe. Then, finally, our decision made, we leaned guiltily back against the wall and resumed our eavesdropping.

'So, have you been following your meal plan this week?' Rosa was asking.

There was a long pause. Then Emma said, 'Some of it'. Strictly speaking, I suppose this was true; after all, the apple she ate each day probably *did* feature on the plan somewhere. However, as apples were the only thing she'd eaten for the past seven days, it would have been more accurate just to say 'no'.

Rosa was clearly aware of this. 'Emma, if you're not able to follow the plan, then –'

'I am following the plan!' Emma said.

'But not all of it,' Rosa said.

Emma was silent for a moment. Then she said, 'I'm not like you, I don't need to eat like other people.'

'Emma, you do.'

'No, I don't. I have a small frame and a fast metabolism.'

'Emma,' Rosa said, gently. 'If you're not coping, if your weight continues to drop...'

'Then, what?' Emma said. 'You'll throw me back into hospital?'

'It might be something we have to look at, yes.'

I sensed Emma's heart sink then. 'I'll do better,' she said. 'I promise.'

The awkwardness of the silence that followed was palpable even from the hallway. Hours seemed to pass before Rosa cleared her throat. 'Well,' she said. 'Let's get you weighed for now and see where we are with that.' When we heard Rosa rifling around in her bag for the scales, Mum and I looked at one another. There was a hint of panic in both of our eyes; to learn Emma's weight would have been the ultimate betrayal. After another, much briefer, unspoken conversation, I turned to leave. A second later, Mum did too.

Back in my room, I wondered whether it really had been the fear of betraying my little sister that had forced me from the dining room. It was easy enough to believe this was the case. After all, my parents and I had understood for years that proof of our loyalty to Emma lay in keeping our distance, in accepting what was told us, in turning and walking away when a door was shut in our face instead of swinging it open again. But there was another possibility; that I'd simply been too frightened to listen to the number that was read out from the scales. It was painful to consider this, but it often seemed that much of my relationship with Emma was not allowing myself to ask the questions I knew I ought to, because I was too afraid of the answers.

At the end of the day, I supposed it didn't really matter. The important, awful, terrifying fact was that Emma's situation was even worse than I'd imagined, that we were even further from being the happy, stable family I wanted so badly.

Mum had been right all those years ago when she warned me never to eavesdrop. I only wished she'd taken the trouble to remind me of that as we'd stood with our ears to the living room door.

Thank god for Hannah. Time and again in the weeks that followed our first kiss she saved me from misery. As often as I could, I picked her up from her apartment after I finished work and we drove off in search of adventure. We listened to live music and watched movies in the city. We sat in late-night cafes, drinking coffee and feeling terribly chic. We sang our hearts out to our favourite songs at karaoke bars. And on those evenings when we found nothing to interest us in Edinburgh, we simply walked – walked for miles and miles, over sand and fields, into the early hours of the morning, while we spoke about days gone by and our dreams for the future.

The final hours of May found Hannah and I lying together on the grass by the entrance of Hopetoun Castle, an ancient ruin that stands on a cliff edge high above the Firth of Forth. The castle's a major draw to tourists during the day, but that night, after parking the car by the gates and creeping through a quarter mile of darkness, we had the place entirely to ourselves. With no houses or traffic for miles, the moon and stars had made the sky their own. Not a sound could be heard apart from a delicate breeze and the gentle waves of the North Sea lapping against the rocky shore below.

Hannah lay with her eyes closed, her head nested in the crook of my arm. 'It's so beautiful here,' she said, her breathing soft, her lips parted. Silently, confidently, I leaned in to kiss her.

But she didn't kiss me back. Instead, she wrinkled her nose and made a strange, whimpery noise. Then she turned away from me.

'James, please don't take this the wrong way...' she said. 'It's just that, recently, I've started to get this strange feeling we're together.'

I tried to laugh. 'So, what?'

Hannah dared a look up at me. 'So, this is beginning to feel way too much like a relationship.'

This was clearly a night for strange, involuntary noises;

my throat let out a little gurgle. It could have been worse. I might have screamed.

'This feels like a relationship?' I said. 'Hannah, I've spent the whole of the last month assuming we were already in one.'

'What?' Hannah said, rolling up onto her knees. 'Have you told anyone this?' When I told her no, she pressed a hand against her stomach and exhaled deeply.

'You seem relieved by that,' I said.

Hannah sighed. 'I'd just... I'd like it better if you didn't say anything.'

'What do you mean?'

'About *us*. I'd just rather you kept things quiet.'

I narrowed my eyes. 'Are you seriously worrying about your reputation?'

'No, it's not that. I just don't want people talking.'

'Talking about you.'

'Yes.'

'Having an affair.'

Hannah grimaced. She didn't like that word. 'Talking about this... thing,' she said.

'And ruining your reputation,' I added.

Hannah's hand moved from her stomach to her forehead. 'James, this isn't about *me*. I just don't want anyone to get hurt.'

And then it struck me, her reason for asking. 'Oh dear,' I said, blowing out my cheeks. 'You mean Christian, don't you? You don't want Christian to get hurt.'

Hannah's head dropped. I sucked my teeth, closed my eyes tightly for a few seconds. It had been a pipe dream, hadn't it, all this Hannah stuff? I'd been kidding myself that we could ever have been anything more than friends. Whichever way I chose to look at it, I was the second man in her life, a pawn to Christian's king. Suddenly, I saw that the moments we'd shared had only filled me with false hopes. Suddenly, I almost regretted every one of them. I told Hannah this.

Now it was her turn to be hurt. 'Well, I don't regret anything,' she said.

'So, what? I mean, that hardly helps us, does it?'

Hannah didn't answer. I shut my eyes again, tried to swallow down the anger that was building in me. 'You know, this relationship, friendship, whatever the hell it is, is a complete sham. You make all this effort to spare Christian's feelings, but what about me? What about how I feel about all of this?'

Hannah stared hard at the ground for what seemed like an eternity. Finally, swallowing hard, she looked up. When she spoke, her voice was no more than a whisper. 'You always want more from me, James.'

'Yes, that's true,' I shouted. 'Of *course,* it's true. What else do you *expect*? I'm not a *saint*, you know. I'm not just in this thing to offer cuddles and snuggles whenever it suits your conscience.'

Hannah's eyes returned to her shoes. 'So, what are we going to do?' she asked.

'I don't know,' I said. 'I genuinely haven't a clue.'

With nothing else to say, we trudged miserably back towards the car and drove in deathly silence to Cranston. The journey was only a couple of miles, but it seemed to last a very long time. When, finally, I parked the car outside Hannah's apartment, she grabbed her bag from between her feet and clutched it close to her chest. 'So, this is where we leave things,' she said.

'For now, I guess,' I said. 'Unless there's something about the situation you want to change.'

'James, I –'

'Because,' I said, cutting her off mid-sentence, 'it's hard to see how we can continue like this. Something's got to give, Hannah. Do you understand what I'm saying?'

Hannah nodded sadly, touched a hand against my cheek. Then, turning quickly from the car, she dashed across the street to her door, fumbling for her keys. I drove home with a strong feeling that the evening might have gone a great deal better.

3 JUNE 2005

My birthday

I have to stop vomiting before it gets even more out of hand. I spent ages this morning shuddering by the sink, bringing up blood and feeling as though my insides were about to pour out. I feel so angry with myself. I'm stupid. I tell myself 'just one more time', but I'm lying to myself. It's never the last time.

I feel so frightened and confused. Nothing is making sense anymore. I can't stop thinking about the pills 'hidden' in Mum and Dad's room, and the stash I've collected since I got home. I used to think I had a purpose in life, but now I know that's not true. I'm not sure I can keep going through the motions any longer. I'm not sure that I can stand this pain.

5

The following week, Emma had her twenty-first birthday. I say 'had' rather than 'celebrated' because, instead of spending the occasion partying with friends by a bar, she settled for another day of skipping food and exercising secretly in her room. Mum tried her best to instil some normality to the day, even taking the time to bake Emma a birthday cake. In the afternoon, she brought it through to the living room, candles all lit, and began to sing *Happy Birthday to You*, as if everything was normal, as if everything was what she liked to call 'Hunky Dory'. Emma didn't eat any herself, just sat and watched, enthralled, as Mum passed around thick wedges to the rest of us. It seemed strange to me; unnatural, almost. I had one bite, and then I couldn't swallow any more.

By the time I readied myself to leave work that evening, I felt completely drained. I also felt stupid, because I'd agreed to visit Hannah when my shift ended, despite knowing she was due to meet Christian in Vienna the following day. Like an idiot, I'd even promised to drive her to the airport the following morning. I felt shitty about *that* as well.

It wasn't my fault. For the past four days, I'd actually worked really hard to stay away from Hannah, and until that morning I'd been perfectly prepared to continue doing so for another week at least. But then Hannah had sent me a message over breakfast to say how much she missed me and I'd caved immediately – my reply was with her before she'd even gone back to eating her Cheerios. I wasn't proud of the fact, but I wasn't ashamed either. I supposed that the whole separation had just happened too quickly. Perhaps I'd just been asking too much of myself to go cold turkey. Probably I just needed another chance or two to get over her. I really hoped so, because the constant fucking thought of her was driving me crazy.

I was getting ready to set off for Hannah's when Gary Collins walked into the County. Gary was an old classmate of mine, though back in school we'd moved in very different circles. While I'd been one of the quietest pupils in our year, Gary had made himself the clown of every classroom he ever entered. In the years since finishing school, he'd worked hard to cement this reputation. In the Grange a few summers back, I'd watched him run a finger down his arse crack and lift it to a girlfriend's nose, claiming he'd just fingered the barman for a packet of beef jerky. On another occasion, a couple of his friends had distracted another of our contemporaries, Janey Pettigrew, while he dipped his cock in her gin and tonic. Janey had always denied this was true, but the way she'd smacked her lips after every sip had suggested that the drink was somewhat more flavoursome than she'd anticipated. She hadn't spoken to Gary in four years.

Though his chubby face and expanding waistline were testament to his complete lack of physical prowess, his personality was far more suited to the local rugby club than a quiet provincial bar. Yet I enjoyed his frequent visits to the County and had even started to consider him a friend. He typically arrived late, after finishing his shift as head waiter at a neighbouring hotel, and was always surrounded by a band of minions who worked frantically to find a way into their manager's good graces.

Gary was also regularly joined by Katie, the hotel's young assistant manager. Katie had soft features and a wide, honest smile that gave her a certain kind of understated grace. She'd worn her dark chocolate hair in a cute pixie cut when I'd met her, but she'd recently started to grow it out, and now fought endlessly with several unruly strands of hair that fell down over her eyes whenever she made the slightest move. She was charming and teasing and sweet and funny, and in the three months since her first visit even the most cynical of the hotel's regular customers had fallen a little bit in love with her.

I'd assumed at first that Katie and Gary were seeing one another, that Gary had called on some hidden reserve of charm to win Katie's affections. But more and more over the next few weeks Katie had begun to spend her time chatting to me as I cleaned glasses she'd collected from the tables, and I'd realised it was me, rather than Gary, that she was coming to see.

'I hope you weren't expecting any drinks,' I said to Gary as he reached the bar. His face was flushed, as were those of his colleagues. They often toasted the end of their shift with a few beers in the staffroom of their hotel, and the celebrations tonight had clearly been more enthusiastic than usual. Even Katie seemed a little merry.

'What?' Gary moaned. 'You can't even sell us some shots of tequila?'

'Nope,' I said. 'Not even that.'

'Aaw, please James,' Katie pleaded. She propped her chin against the edge of the bar and looked at me through her scattered hair.

'Sorry,' I said, pointing to the clock behind me.

Katie shrugged. 'No matter,' she said. 'We have plenty to drink at the James. No, wait, plenty to drink at the *flat*. Whoops! Sorry, I'm a wee bit tipsy.'

Gary grinned. 'I think what Katie's trying to say is that we're having a party at my place. And she wanted me to ask you if you'll come.'

Katie's mouth fell open. 'Gary! Jesus!'

'Well, you did, just outside. You asked whether I'd invite him along tonight. Remember?'

Katie shook her head. '*Ass*hole.'

Gary turned to me. 'She did ask, you know. And she's right. You should come. It'll be fun.'

I had no doubt it would be; after all, a glass of wine and some good company were precisely what I needed after such a crap day. As quickly as I could, I ushered everyone out of the bar, left Hannah a message to say I was running late, and set about locking the hotel.

By the time I arrived at Gary's apartment the party was in full swing. I grabbed a bottle of wine from the kitchen, then made myself comfortable on Gary's living room sofa. A handful of Gary's minions were sitting cross-legged around a small television screen playing war games on a PlayStation and drinking shots of crème de menthe, which was presumably the strongest alcohol they'd been able to find in Gary's cupboards. A girlfriend of one of the gamers, who looked about twelve, was dancing alone in front of a large mirror to Eminem, watching every move she made in drunken fascination. I was watching her myself when, ten minutes after I arrived, Katie approached me. 'Oh, to be young again, huh?' she said.

I smiled. 'It does make you feel old, doesn't it?'

'A little bit. Not that we're anywhere near death's door quite yet.'

'No, that's true. Uh, do you want some of this?' I asked, waving my bottle of wine at her. She nodded and sat down next to me.

Two hours later, the last of the revellers had stumbled off towards home, but Katie and I remained on Gary's sofa, deep in conversation and sipping the last drops of a third bottle of wine. I was considering grabbing a fourth from the kitchen when Gary swaggered into the room, dressed in only a pair of boxer shorts. From the size of his grin, I could tell he'd already awarded himself full credit for the events that had been unfolding on his sofa. 'Well, lovebirds,' he said, 'don't let the fact the party's over stop you from getting on with whatever you were doing. I'm off to bed, so the room's all yours.'

I looked towards Katie. 'Don't you need to get home?'

Katie smiled. 'After all the wine I've drunk, there's no way I could drive back to Cranston.'

'And you're okay if I stay?' I asked.

Gary threw out his chest. 'If you even try to leave, then I swear to God I will *kill* your dick.'

I looked at Katie and smiled. 'I guess it's settled then.'

'Excellent,' Gary said, grinning at us both. 'Just be sure not to do anything I wouldn't. Which, in this case, would be to pass up the chance of a fucking good shag.'

With this, Gary turned and exited the room. Katie and I rolled our eyes at one another, a desperate attempt to diffuse some of the awkwardness Gary's last comment had created.

Then we turned and looked at the sofa. 'You think this thing's even big enough for two?' I said.

Katie shrugged, offered an embarrassed smile. 'Shall we find out?'

We crept self-consciously onto the sofa, cuddling close to prevent ourselves from rolling onto Gary's deeply stained carpet. By the time we'd settled our arms and legs were overlapping. I waited for Katie to say something but no words came. Instead, she found my hand, laced her fingers in mine and squeezed.

Then we were together, first fumbling, then holding on tight. Katie kissed me hungrily, pressing her mouth so hard against mine that I thought my lips might bruise. My arm went around her waist, pulling her closer into me, so that she was almost sitting on my lap, and my other hand drifted up the back of her neck, getting entangled in her hair. Breathing hard, Katie took her lips away from my mouth and placed a row of kisses against my neck, sending shock waves through my body. I let my hand drift down her back and beneath her shirt, relishing the touch of her skin, the soft lace of her bra. When my hand found her breast, she gasped in pleasure and her head fell forward against my shoulder. 'My god,' she said, breathlessly. 'I can't believe this is happening.'

'I know,' I said, and smiled at her. Through the darkness, I could make out the silhouette of her face and her large, bright eyes gazing tenderly towards me.

It was a beautiful moment, but with Gary in the next room, and quite possibly with an ear to his wall, we both knew that our petting would progress no further that night. We kissed quietly and laughed softly for some time more before laying down on the sofa, huddling close to stay warm. I was cramped and cold and my neck was close to spasm, but as I lay there, listening to Katie breathing softly beside me, I felt as comfortable as I'd been for quite some time.

When my alarm buzzed in my pocket five hours later, I was greeted by a hellish ache in my head and the nauseating taste of stale wine in my mouth. My stomach was churning so badly that I considered turning over and falling back asleep, but I was too full of pride to break the promise I'd made to Hannah. As discreetly as I could, I rolled off the sofa and grabbed my trousers from the floor. I was halfway to the door when Katie groggily lifted her head and asked where I was going.

'I need to go,' I said, pointlessly, before adding, 'to see my, uh, mum.'

Katie tried to consider this, but thinking clearly hurt, so she nodded twice before allowing her head to fall back onto her cushion. I moved back to the sofa and kissed her quickly, remaining careful not to add to her woes by exhaling near to her face. She'd already fallen back asleep by the time I was out of the room.

Outside Hannah's apartment, I took a moment to prepare myself for the frosty reception I was about to receive. Then I threw on my most charming smile and rang her doorbell.

After a moment, the door opened. Hannah stood by it and stared at me. It was some time before she spoke. 'Where the fuck were you last night?' she said.

Still smiling, I mumbled something false about an aching throat.

Hannah's eyes were blazing. 'I waited for you outside the apartment until three in the morning.'

'Really?' Come to think of it, she did look a bit pasty today. 'Damn. I really am sorry.'

Hannah continued to glower at me for so long that I started to wonder if she was going to let me in. But then, at last, she pushed the door open and, without looking back, made her way ahead of me to the hallway.

Hannah remained silent throughout the journey to the airport, pointedly avoiding conversation and listening sulkily to an old Bob Dylan cassette she'd brought from home. I knew she was waiting for me beg her forgiveness for letting her down, but with her only hours away from being shagged by Christian I really wasn't in the mood to apologise for anything I'd done.

I'd been driving for a half hour when *It Ain't Me, Babe* started to play. Hannah immediately reached for the dial and turned up the volume. I rolled my eyes; why did she insist on finding these deeper meanings everywhere? Why did everything we did have to be filled with such drama? Hannah waited for me to make a comment, but I didn't have the energy to argue.

The situation was still tense when we reached the departures lounge. We said a stifled farewell to one another before Hannah turned and walked the few yards to have her ticket inspected. I could tell she was disappointed. She'd expected me to kiss her goodbye. I thought she might stubbornly continue her journey towards departures, but at the last moment she turned and walked back towards me.

'Do you want me to stop?' she asked, when she was by my side. 'Shall I be the smart one and put a stop to things?'

I sighed. 'Probably not. I guess I'd kind of miss you.'

Hannah looked up at me, relieved. 'Okay. So, I suppose we just see how things go.'

When I nodded my head, Hannah smiled and kissed me quickly on the mouth, before walking again towards the ticket inspector. 'I'll see you in a week,' she shouted back to me.

'I'll call you,' I said.

'Promise?'

'Yeah.'

At the time, I think I actually believed that I'd keep this promise, but as the hours passed I became less and less sure of it. It would be hard to break my word to her, but if I was going to save myself from hurt then it had to be done. After all, what was the point in loving her if it only brought pain? What was the point in filling my mind with hopes if they were only going to crush my heart? No, it had to be done. It was time to tidy up my life. It was time to start again. And so, reluctantly, I surrendered my impossible dreams of a life with Hannah. I didn't call her once in the entire week she was away.

7 JUNE 2005

I'm back in Hope Park. I thought when I got here that I'd fight them all, but I can't fight any more. There are no more choices I can make. This is all too painful, too frightening. I'm cold, exhausted, weak, and dizzy. I had a hard time breathing this morning and have felt so sore all day long. Every inch of me is sore. Every inch of me aches.

It will be over soon. All this pain and torture will soon be forgotten. I've so many regrets about the way things have gone, so many wishes that will never be fulfilled, but I shouldn't focus on these things. I just need all of this to be over. I've had as much as I can take. I can't even cry any more.

Leave me alone now. You've had your fun. I give up. You win.

6

I'd expected Emma to hit the roof the morning she was finally readmitted to Hope Park, to have to drag her kicking and screaming out of the house, or something. After all, it wasn't as if she'd chosen to go there. In the past few weeks, with her health fading fast, her doctors had made the necessary arrangements to place her under section. Emma had been sectioned once before, so she could be sent to London, and back then we'd practically had to prise her out of her bedroom. But when the time came to leave for Hope Park she just slumped into her coat, picked up a bag of her stuff, and made her way, silently and without emotion, to the car. It was horrible to see that. It was as if she'd waved a white flag, surrendered her campaign against the tyrannical doctors. Suddenly, her fighting spirit had gone.

For the past three months, I'd waited anxiously for Emma to be sent back to Hope Park. Her first spell there had obviously failed to bring any miracle cure, but I felt certain it was her best chance of recovery. Looking around the ward, it was impossible not to be filled with hope. It was every bit as posh as it was made out to be in the celebrity magazines, with en suite bedrooms, Sky TV, gourmet meals, and nurses who displayed a kindness and patience I'd thought were reserved for saints. On the whole, the patients were pretty positive, too. Most of the girls on the ward were looking to get better, and many seemed to be well on the road to recovery.

Emma would hate it, of course; she'd be miserable and depressed and angry and defiant. Any increase in her weight, even the merest fraction of an ounce, would be treated as a disaster and used as an excuse for a new wave of rebellion against the hospital staff. But she'd also be safe, and right now I needed more than anything to know she wasn't going to die. Since the early spring, I'd felt like I was a passenger in a car that was going out of control. For three months, I'd been swerving across the road, narrowly missing fences and oncoming vehicles. Now, finally, the car was under control again and unimaginable disaster had been averted.

But I didn't breathe easy for long. The morning after Emma was readmitted to Hope Park, Mum barged into my room. 'James,' she said. 'The doctors just called. I need to go to Glasgow.'

The sound of her voice, loud as it was, took a moment to reach me. When it did, I looked up from my pillow. 'What time is it?' I asked, stupidly.

'James, did you hear me? There's been an accident. I'm going to see your sister.'

Finally, I woke. 'What sort of accident?'

'Emma had a fall. At breakfast, she… She collapsed.'

'She… Oh fuck.' I jumped out of bed. 'I'm coming with you.'

'You have to work,' Mum said, but she said it half-heartedly. Even she knew that she was in no fit state to drive.

Mum scribbled a note for Dad, who'd already left for work, then paced around the house as I hurriedly got washed and dressed. By the time I came out of the bathroom she was gazing distantly at the dining room sideboard, her clenched fists pressed against its polished surface. After a moment, she looked up at me, her eyes so sad that I felt my heart break inside of me. 'It'll be alright,' I said gently, placing a hand on her forearm. 'Sometime soon the doctors will sort her out, and she'll come home and be safe and well and we'll be a family again.'

Mum smiled a tight little smile, gave my hand a little squeeze. I wanted badly for her to agree with me, to tell me that, yes, I was absolutely right. But she said nothing, just handed me the keys and made her way ahead of me to the car.

Emma's eyes were closed as we walked towards her bedside. The nurses had placed a blanket over her to keep her warm, but she was so painfully thin that it was practically impossible to make out her body beneath it. She looked as small as a child.

Margaret, one of the Hope Park nurses was sitting next to Emma's bed. When she saw us, she raised herself out of her chair and tiptoed towards us, an action that was completely at odds with her short, round frame. 'Now, you've not to worry,' she whispered, gently. 'The doctor says she's going to be fine. Absolutely fine. She just gave us a bit of a fright this morning, that's all.'

'What happened?' Mum asked.

'Well, we think she had some kind of seizure. She was making her way out of the dining room after breakfast when she just collapsed. It was quite a shock, but we managed to get the other girls upstairs while the head nurse got her breathing again. It took her a minute or two to come around, but the doctors don't think there'll be any long-term damage.'

I stood, looking dumbly at Margaret. Emma had stopped breathing? The nurses had been forced to revive her? Oh god, it was worse than I'd thought, worse than I could ever have believed. I looked towards Mum, and it was clear from her expression that she was thinking the same thing as me. We'd nearly lost her. If she'd stayed an extra day in Myreton, she'd probably have died.

I wanted to curl up into a ball on the floor, but when I looked over Margaret's shoulder again I saw that Emma had opened her eyes. I nailed a smile to my face and trotted up to Emma's bed, an artificial swagger. 'Hey, there she is,' I said. When I stooped down to kiss her, the skin of her cheek was unnervingly cold.

Emma looked back up at me through half-closed eyes. 'They put a drip in my arm, Jamie.'

'Hey, that's great,' I said, sitting down on the chair by the side of her bed. 'They'll have you feeling better in no time at all.'

'They're trying to make me fat.'

'What?' I glanced towards Mum, who'd seen Margaret out of the ward, and was now settling herself on the edge of Emma's mattress. 'No,' I said. 'No, they're just trying to get you back on your feet.'

Emma looked at the IV bag that hung over her pillow. 'Oh god,' she sobbed. 'Look at the size of it.'

'Emma, it's what you need. They –'

'I'm going to be huge, Jamie.'

'Emma –' Mum said.

'I bet they're all having a good fucking laugh about how enormous they're making me.'

'Emma!' Mum said, more firmly this time. 'You're *not* fat. You're not going to *get* fat.'

Emma looked again at the drip, shook her head. 'I need to get this out of me,' she said, grabbing weakly at the tube.

I took hold of her hand. 'Emma, what the hell are you doing? Are you seriously planning to burst your arm open in front of everyone here?'

Emma considered this for a moment, then fell back against her pillow. I couldn't believe what was happening. I couldn't believe Emma's collapse had done nothing to frighten her out of the illness, nothing to put her off the idea of losing weight. Holding back tears, I stood up and walked out of the room – got the fuck out of there before my fucking head exploded.

Sitting in the car in the hospital car park a few minutes later, a sick feeling washed over me. I rested my face against the steering wheel, trying to quell the sense of panic that filled my thoughts. *It's okay,* I told myself. *Just breathe. Just keep breathing. Gaagh!* My eyes began to water over, and I slammed the dashboard with my fist. *Fuck! Why is this happening? Please, don't let this happen. Don't do this to me. I love you so much. I'll do anything, I promise. Please, just come back.*

I arrived back at the ward half an hour later. When she saw me walking towards her, all puffy eyed and sniffly, Emma smiled sadly. 'Don't worry, Jamie,' she said. 'I'm better now.'

Her skin was pale and tight against her cheekbones. She was so exhausted that she could hardly think how to speak. But I nodded and told her I knew she was okay.

Dad swung the garage door open the moment he heard the car turning into our street. As he walked towards us, his whole body was tensed, his face pale and sweating. 'Where the hell have you been, Mary?' he said, his voice trembling. 'I've been calling you for hours.'

'I know, John, I know. I'm sorry. We forgot the phone.'

Dad's eyes were shifting restlessly between Mum and me. 'I've been... I was...'

'She's alright, darling. It's going to be alright.'

'You should have bloody called.'

Mum found Dad's eyes, held them carefully. 'John,' she said, gently. 'She's going to be fine.'

This time the news seemed to penetrate. Dad took a few short breaths before lowering his gaze to a crack on the driveway. 'What happened?' he asked.

'They don't know. It was some kind of a seizure.'

Dad winced. I could see how terrifying he was finding this; how hard he was having to work to force the questions from his mouth. The answers were hitting him like bullets to the chest, but they had to be found, however painful they were. 'Are they expecting any more of them?' he said.

'No,' Mum said. 'Not necessarily.'

Dad nodded, kept his eyes on the ground. 'Aye,' he said. 'It's a shame.' Then, without another word, he turned and made his way slowly back to the garage.

The County was almost deserted when I walked through its doors a few hours later. That was fine; I wasn't looking for conversation anyway, just some background noise to distract me from my thoughts and a few drinks to steady my nerves. I gave my order to Fiona, then took a seat in a quiet corner of the bar, where I'd remain for the next two hours, drinking back one deep, hot throatful of vodka after another.

I saw Emma. I saw her when she was eight years old, dancing and singing along to *The Sound of Music* in our living room. I saw us wrestling together in the garden during the endless days of our summer holidays. I saw her skimming stones on Loch Lomond, watching fascinated as her pebble bounced along the surface of the water. And I saw her now, frail and gaunt and carrying the weight of the world on her shoulders. What had happened to her life? What had happened to the happy little girl I'd spent my childhood with? Where the fuck had it all gone so wrong?

I let my head sink back and closed my eyes. Little pricks of water began to form behind my eyelids. I decided it was time to go home. I rubbed my eyes, grabbed my coat and stumbled towards the exit. In the same moment I reached the door, Katie arrived through it. 'Hey,' she said, smiling brightly. 'I hoped I might see you here.'

I tried to smile back, but it didn't work very well. Katie looked at me, and her eyes narrowed. 'Are you alright?' she said.

'Yes,' I said. 'No. I don't know.'

'Well, that covers your options,' Katie said, gently. 'Okay, you sit down there. I'm going to buy us both a drink.'

I watched Katie as she stood by the bar, a look of quiet concern covering her face. She returned to the table a couple of minutes later, still wearing the same expression, and laid our drinks on the table. 'Now,' she said. 'Tell me. Tell me what's happened.'

I started to tell the story, but everything had happened so quickly that it was hard to remember – it was like a terrible dream, the kind you can only remember parts of. By the time I'd finally managed to put all the facts together, my glass was empty and my head was sore. 'The thing is,' I told her, 'I spend each day waiting, hoping for it to get better, but it just... it never does. And it's hard, you know? I wish I knew what to do.'

Katie laid a hand on mine. 'Well, for one thing, I think you need to look after yourself.'

'*Me*?' I said. 'No, no, I'm okay. Really I am.'

'You're not. Look at yourself. Look at the weight you're carrying. You're exhausted.'

'Well...' I looked down at my glass, breathing deeply to stop the tears from falling. 'It's hard to know what to do about that.'

Neither of us said anything for a while, though I could tell from Katie's subtle fidgeting that she was working up the courage to say something. Sure enough, as soon as her drink was finished, she stood up and reached for her coat. 'Come on then,' she said.

I looked up and saw that she was blushing. 'Where are we going?' I asked.

Katie tried to hold my gaze but failed. 'Well, if you like, to mine. I think it would be good for us both if you stayed with me tonight.'

'I'd like that,' I said. I took her hand and together we turned from the bar and walked out into the night.

'Another one?' Holly said, when I told her about Katie the following evening. We'd tucked ourselves away in a quiet corner of the Grange, as far as possible from the bar, where Will was providing guests with a real-time analysis of his performance in the previous weekend's rugby match. 'But what about you and Hannah? I thought you two were getting close.'

'Yeah, well, she has a boyfriend.'

'And that's suddenly an issue?'

'It always was,' I said, impatiently. 'I don't want to be a pawn. I don't want to be some stupid little plaything for her to make do with until she goes back home to Christian.'

'Okay. So that just leaves Katie. Do you think she can make you happy?'

'I suppose so,' I said. 'She seems nice.'

Holly snickered. 'Nice?'

'Yeah, she's nice. She's...'

'Okay, I get it. Maybe not pretty or funny or interesting, but nice. She sounds like a dream.'

'I know what you're getting at,' I mumbled. 'And, actually, she *is* quite pretty.'

Holly leaned back with folded arms and regarded me suspiciously. 'If you say so. And yet, I do wonder. Is this really the best way to be dealing with your problems?'

'Works for me,' I said.

'And Katie?'

'Katie will be fine.'

'So, you've told her about Hannah.'

'What's to tell?' I said. 'We were friends. Now we're not. It's done with. Finito.'

Holly put her head on one side, half signalling her doubt, but let it pass. 'Well, do what you have to do,' she said. 'But don't forget to consider her feelings as well. Especially if the poor girl really has decided she fancies you.'

I paused to consider this, my eyes narrowed attentively at Holly's face.

'Because,' Holly said, 'I doubt she'd want to be just some

stupid little plaything for you to make do with until something better came along.'

I wasn't expecting that, and it hurt. I tried to think of some equally biting comeback, something to show Holly she was wrong somehow, but my mind drew a blank. Defeated, I pushed my chair back and retreated towards the bar. I'd taken a few steps when I turned back to Holly. 'You're not as bloody clever as you think, you know,' I said.

Holly smiled. 'Be nice,' she said.

7

———

DESPITE HOLLY'S INSISTENCE THAT I WAS USING KATIE AS A glorified sex toy, I was not, in fact, against the possibility of a relationship with her. It's just that I wasn't completely certain I wanted to be with her, either. It seemed silly, in a way, to be so unsure, but the past seven days had been filled with such drama that I'd completely lost track of what was really going on. I'd been swept along by the excitement, one drama bleeding into the next, with no time to stop and consider the relationship between events, no chance to gauge the consequences of the decisions I'd made.

The opportunity to reflect on the past week finally arrived two days after my conversation with Holly, when Katie left Cranston to spend a week with her girlfriends in Spain. I welcomed the prospect at first, but only until the fog started to clear from my head and I began to wonder whether I might, in fact, have fucked things up somewhere down the line. It wasn't that I regretted anything that had happened with Katie. I didn't. It's just that everything had happened too quickly, before I'd really considered it possible, before I'd been able to decide whether or not my intentions towards her were genuinely honest. Katie was an unconditionally good person, far too good to have her heart broken by some two-a-penny arsehole. The thought that I might be that creature, after all the kindness she'd shown me, was frightening.

Wracked with guilt and anxiety, I fell into a black pit of depression. Less than twenty-four hours after Katie left Cranston, I lay down on my bed and simply refused to get up. For three days I slept badly and drank coffee and listened to music, trying for all the world to forget about all the shit I'd been dealing with. I received a bunch of texts from Katie, to say hello from Spain, and from Hannah, to say she was back in Scotland, but they did nothing to cheer me. I thought more than once about returning the messages, but in the end, it proved far easier to let them pile up on my phone.

I might have stayed in bed indefinitely, but on Saturday evening the doors of the village hall opened on Mum's fiftieth birthday party. Ninety-five of Mum's nearest and dearest were invited to the celebration, and although Hannah hadn't confirmed it, I was pretty sure she'd be making an appearance alongside her Rose Glen colleagues.

I was right. The party had barely started when Mum came over to me. 'I need you to pick up Hannah and Elisabeth in Brookfield,' she said.

'In *Brookfield*?' I asked. 'Why didn't they catch the bus here from Cranston?'

'I need you to go and get them. They're on the village green. I told them you'd be there in ten minutes.'

I was confused, but who was I to argue with the birthday girl? Mum had been excited about this day for months, discussing potential outfits and hairstyles with her sisters whenever they called. This evening it had taken her two hours to get these two things – a red Marks and Spencer's dress and a near-identical version of her usual short bob – just right. She'd almost cried when Dad told her how nice she looked.

I spotted Elisabeth as soon as I arrived in Brookfield, standing on the village green with two of her colleagues. All three women were staring intently at a red coat on the grass, which seemed odd to me until I pulled up alongside them and realised Hannah was inside it. I brought the car to a stop and stepped nervously outside.

"What happened?" I asked.

Elisabeth walked up to me. "Hannah wasn't feeling too well on the bus, so we had to get off and grab some air."

'She's unwell? In what way?' I looked over Elisabeth's shoulder towards Hannah. The other two girls were picking her up off the ground. Her eyes were only half-opened and she was smiling stupidly. I looked back to Elisabeth, suddenly pale. 'How much has she had to drink?'

Elisabeth glanced towards Hannah. 'A little too much. Quite a lot too much, actually.'

'Oh my god,' I said. 'She's gonna puke in my car.'

'No, she won't,' said Helen, another of Mum's work-mates. She was holding Hannah up by her armpit. 'We'll just pop her head out of the window and she can enjoy the fresh air. Can't you, sweetie?'

Hannah looked dreamily at Helen and smiled. Sensing that Helen wanted her to nod her head, she nodded her head. As the others tried to manoeuvre her into the car, I turned back to Elisabeth. 'So, the bus?'

Elisabeth nodded. 'We got thrown off. She was sick on the floor.'

'She...?' I looked around again at Hannah. She was

sitting in the car with her face against the back window. 'I'm going to kill Mum when I get back.'

The drive back to Myreton was gruesome. Hannah refrained from vomiting *in* my car, but a misdirected retch out of the back window left a streak of puke all down the paintwork. When we got back to the village hall, I made a hasty exit from the car, having decided, for the sake of my stomach, to avoid Hannah until visions of her throwing up had cleared from my mind. Half an hour later, though, she still hadn't appeared in the hall, so I went outside to check on her. I found her by the corner of the car park, on her knees and puking into some flowers. 'You okay?' I called to her.

She looked around, startled. 'Would you *please* just go *away*!'

Her tone took me by surprise. 'Hannah, I hope I haven't upset you. I...'

'James,' Hannah shouted. 'I don't want you to see me like this. Please, just go away.'

'How is she?' asked Mum when I got back inside.

'A bit better. She's being sick over the marigolds.'

'Well, I wouldn't worry. They'll survive.'

I laughed, then realised she wasn't joking. This night was becoming very strange.

An hour later the party was in full swing. Mum and her sisters, as usual, were shuffling arthritically around the dance floor, while Dad had joined my uncles by the bar to drink beer and reminisce about the Good Old Days. I stayed away from the action, wondering whether Hannah was okay. Then, just as ABBA gave way to Phil Collins, I saw her stumble through the back door of the hotel and towards the centre of the room. Without a word to anybody, she began to dance.

She danced the way she always did, holding her body and arms still while her legs and feet sprang across the floor. When she was sober, her head remained stationary; when she was drunk, it nodded in time to the music. She always closed her eyes. She always wore the same, ecstatic smile. And I, always, watched in wonder.

She'd been dancing for ten minutes when Dad walked over to me. He was dressed in a suit that was older than I was, and which he'd worn only twice, to the funerals of his parents. The jacket hung awkwardly on his shoulders, making his bony chest appear concave and emphasizing his small paunch. His skinny legs appeared lost in his trousers. 'So that's her, huh?' he said.

'What?'

Dad nodded towards Hannah. 'Riverdance. That's the thing you've fallen in love with?'

Fell in love with, I wanted to say. *It's over now.* But this was hardly the time to talk about my problems. 'She's not usually so strange,' I said.

'Well that's a relief,' Dad said, laughing.

'Dad, don't. She's a good person.'

Dad held up his hands in a gesture of surrender. 'Do whatever you like,' he said. 'As long as you're happy.' He was still laughing, to show that this was just some silly little thing, to show that the moment meant nothing. But I knew what he was really saying. *Keep smiling, son. Just keep smiling. I need you to be happy. I need one of you at least to be happy.*

I nodded self-consciously and was about to turn away when Dad reached out and held a hand against my shoulder. When I looked up at him, I saw his expression had become serious. 'You're doing grand, son,' he said, his grip tightening on my collarbone. 'You're doing just grand.'

I stared in disbelief, trying to remember the last time Dad had spoken so gently to me. I had no idea. With this realisation, my throat began to tighten and my chest began to hurt. I wanted to say something, but I could think of nothing. I wanted desperately to weep, but I had no way of releasing it. I was locked up as hard as stone.

Perhaps we weren't so different after all, my father and I.

I stared at Dad, and he stared at me. For a long moment, we stayed that way. Then, without a word, Dad turned from me walked away. I watched his back receding as he took a cigarette from his pocket and made his way out into the night.

It wasn't until around midnight, with the party in its final throes, that Hannah finally made her way to my side. There, she stood in silence, sheepishly inspecting the carpet beneath her feet. 'How are you feeling?' I asked her.

Hannah sighed. 'Embarrassed, mostly. And you?'

'Emotional,' I said. 'I'm sorry she couldn't be here.'

Hannah nodded solemnly. 'I'm sorry,' she said.

I shrugged. 'It's not your fault.'

'No,' Hannah admitted. 'But I've hardly helped matters. I mean, I'm the one to blame for messing everything up so badly between us...'

'Hannah –'

'And before you say anything, I know I did. Just like I know how deeply you're holding it against me.'

I laughed then. 'What makes you think I'm holding it against you?'

Hannah tilted her head to the side, raised her eyebrows. 'James, you did *not* have a sore throat the night before I left for home. But you *did* have a hangover when you arrived in Cranston the next morning.'

I considered that. 'Okay. Good point.'

'Then there were the missed calls,' Hannah continued. '*So* many missed calls.' She gave a little half-laugh, which really wasn't a laugh at all. 'You should be flattered, you know. I don't usually do that.'

I gave an ironic snort. 'Sweetheart, my chest's just bursting with pride.'

Hannah's lips thinned. 'Fine,' she said. 'But will you at least tell me why you've been ignoring me this past week? Or am I just to keep guessing that you don't care about me at all anymore?'

I let out a little half-laugh of my own. 'Hannah, do you really think I'd be this hurt if I didn't care? Of course, I do. But where's the sense in going around thinking about it? Why drive myself crazy wishing for things that are never going to happen? It's pointless – a waste of fucking headspace.'

Hannah's dark eyes lifted to mine. 'When did you decide this?'

I held Hannah's gaze for a split second, then looked away from her. 'This thing with Christian.' I swallowed, then said. 'It's like I told you. I just can't look past it. I'm sorry, Hannah.'

Hannah opened her mouth to speak, but before she could get her words out Elisabeth stumbled over to our side.

Elisabeth had apparently taken up drinking where Hannah had left off – five hours into the party, she seemed wobbly on her feet and her eyelids were only half open. 'They closed the bar,' she complained, her speech a slurred mumble.

I was still staring at Hannah, searching her eyes for some clue about what she'd been going to say, but the moment had passed. Shaking my head, I turned to Elisabeth. 'The County's still open if you fancy one last drink,' I said.

During the short walk to the hotel, Hannah took hold of my hand, and because I'd missed her and it felt really nice, I didn't stop it from happening. But I should have, because when we arrived at the County, we came face to face with Gary and a bunch of his colleagues, who were getting boisterously drunk by the jukebox. Panicking, I threw down Hannah's hand and gave her and Elisabeth some money to buy a round of drinks. They hadn't even reached the bar before Gary began to stagger towards me. 'YOU!' he yelled dramatically, pointing an accusing finger in my direction.

'Who?'

'*You*. And *her*. I *saw* you. Holding hands.'

'We're just friends,' I said. I sounded like somebody who was lying.

'Fuck off.'

'We *are*!'

'Fuck off. But okay. Let's pretend you're friends. Who is she?'

'A friend,' I stammered. 'A friend from, uh...'

'You're a fucking *liar*!' Gary shouted. 'Come on, tell me. Who is she? What's her name? Have you shagged her yet? Was she any good?'

'Shit, Gary,' I said, throwing up my hands in a desperate attempt to shush him.

Gary smiled. 'No comment, huh? I guess I'll just have to wait and ask *her*...'

'No, don't say anything!' I shouted. 'Nobody's supposed to know about us.'

'Us?' Gary said, grinning. I shot him a warning look. 'Okay, okay,' he said. 'Consider me shushed. But at least bring her along to mine tonight. We're having another little get-together.'

The party was a carbon copy of the one I'd dropped into three weeks earlier. A bunch of girls threw on a Franz Ferdinand CD and began to bop self-consciously by the living room window. Five or six smokers crowded together in the hallway, working hard to preserve their fake smiles of indifference as the smoke began to sting their eyes. The crème de menthe boys cheered when they found a crate of discount beer on the living room floor, and immediately began setting out the rules of some obscure drinking game. Smiling contentedly, Hannah slipped off her jacket and sat down by their side.

I was still hovering by the door to the living room when Gary strolled up to me, his eyes fixed on the crème de menthe crew. 'Look at them,' he said. 'Gulping down that horse piss like it's manna from heaven.'

'It's not?'

'Fuck, no. That stuff is bad. I mean, I'm talking dinner-date-with-Hitler bad. Truly, dude, it tastes like ass.'

'So, I should pass on the drink you promised me?'

Gary brightened suddenly. 'Not at all, my adulterous little friend. I have vodka, too, a whole bottle of it nestled safely away in the fridge. Help yourself to as much as you want. Only don't let the dumb-fucks over there find it. The ass-juice is good enough for them.'

Five minutes later, I was in Gary's kitchen pouring myself a drink when Elisabeth appeared in the doorway. She walked across the room and lifted herself onto the counter, and something about her expression told me she had something on her mind. I handed her the drink I'd made and poured myself another, then leaned back against the sink and waited for her to begin talking. It didn't take long. 'James,' she said, 'I promised Hannah I'd keep my mouth shut, but this thing between you two is driving me crazy. Please, you have to tell me what's going on. Why are you acting so strangely to one another?'

I raised an eyebrow towards Elisabeth. 'I'm sure Hannah's already told you everything there is to know.'

Elisabeth put her glass down and stared straight at me. 'James,' she said. 'Just... tell me. Please.'

So, I did. I told her about the adventures Hannah and I had shared, about how happy we'd been together until our night at Hopetoun Castle. I told her how things had changed the moment she turned from my kiss, about the things that moment had stood for and the tensions it had caused between us in the hours, days and weeks after it passed. I told her absolutely everything about Hannah and I. But I told her nothing about Katie.

'It doesn't sound so bad,' Elisabeth said, when I was finished talking. 'For one thing, you know what you want.'

I looked hard at her. 'Do I?'

'Sure, you do,' Elisabeth said, cheerily. Then she noticed the way I was staring, and an air of uncertainty crept into her face. 'Don't you?'

'No,' I said. 'Not when she doesn't want me back.'

'You don't know that,' Elisabeth said.

I laughed bitterly. 'Elisabeth, she just spent an entire week in Vienna with her boyfriend.'

'Are you sure about that?' Elisabeth asked.

'Yes, of course I am!' I said. Then I saw the teasing look in her eyes. 'Aren't I?'

Elisabeth glanced quickly at the door, careful to check for any eavesdroppers. 'James,' she said, 'Hannah and Christian argued during her first evening back in Vienna. They hardly saw one another while she was home.'

I had no response for a moment. The idea was absurd. 'What happened?' I asked.

'She told him she had a crush in Scotland. He didn't take it well.' Elisabeth was silent for a moment, contemplating her next words carefully. 'James, it wasn't a coincidence that Hannah chose tonight to get as drunk as she did. She's been nervous all week about seeing you again. She's been convinced that this was the night you'd break things off with her.'

'She didn't sleep with Christian?' I asked.

Elisabeth shook her head.

I remembered my night with Katie and blushed. 'I didn't know,' I said, the words catching in my throat.

Elisabeth shrugged. 'How could you have? You've ignored her all week.'

'I thought... I thought she was ...'

'But she wasn't,' Elisabeth said. 'She didn't.'

'Oh, man,' I said thickly. 'I should probably go and talk to her.'

The ghost of a smile flickered on Elisabeth's face. 'Yes,' she said, 'you probably should.'

Back in the living room, Hannah remained enthralled by the boys' drinking game. The game had already claimed its first victim, a skinny high-schooler who'd vomited from a bedroom window after only his third shot, while a second participant had quit the game in protest over a debated rule. Now, the game had descended into a crazy, hedonistic free-for-all, the competitors throwing out new rules and pouring ever-larger drinks in a bid to increase consumption and the possibility of new drama.

When I sat down on Gary's sofa, Hannah climbed up from the carpet and cuddled in close to me. It felt like forever since I'd held her like that. I'd forgotten how comforting it was, how she always made me feel as if all the parts of me were finally in one place. Hannah rested one hand on my knee and the other on the back of my neck, her fingers playing idly with the ends of my hair. We passed several minutes in silence, before I turned to face her. 'By the way,' I said. 'I think I might be in love with you.'

Hannah stared at me. 'You think?'

I placed my face so close to hers that her features became indistinct, and I began to lose myself in them. 'Actually,' I whispered. 'I'm pretty sure of it. I just didn't want to freak you out.'

'Oh, Mister. You should know me better than that by now.' Hannah said.

'I probably should, huh?'

Hannah nodded, stared at me a moment longer. Then, smiling gently, she pressed her head into my chest and kissed my neck, my cheek, my lips. And told me she loved me, too.

8

IN THE WEEKS AFTER OUR FIRST KISS, HANNAH HAD TAKEN care to distance herself from me whenever we were in the company of friends. Even on our best days – days when she wasn't freaking out beneath castle walls or I wasn't feeling sorry for myself about Christian – she rarely agreed to hold hands or cuddle outside the confines of her apartment. After Mum's party, though, she threw caution to the wind. The very next morning, she took hold of my hand as we walked along Cranston beach. Later that day, she kissed me on the mouth in front of Elisabeth. And two days after that, she draped her arm around me as we walked into the Grange. I'd expected Dan and his boys to go batshit crazy when they saw that, but when I looked towards their table there was no noise, just nine mouths and eighteen startled eyes gawping at us in amazement.

'Well, well,' said Dan, as Hannah and I took our seats at the table. 'For once, the rumours were true.' He turned to Holly. 'You didn't tell us Jamie was off the market.'

Holly glared at me, disapproval radiating from her like heat waves. 'I didn't know,' she said.

I grinned sheepishly at Holly as Hannah laid a hand against my lap.

'So, are you going to tell us what old Jimbo's like in the sack?' Will said, leaning towards Hannah.

'Just ask your mum if you want to know,' said Dan.

Will slapped a hand over his heart in mock surprise. 'Daniel, my mother would *never* kiss and tell.'

'Really?' said Dan, grinning. 'She told me plenty when I was banging her last night.'

'Ha! There's no way in hell my mum would ever bang you.'

'Dude, your mum would bang a horse if it winked and got its cock out,' Dan said.

Will laughed. 'Honestly? I don't think she'd care if it winked or not.'

As the boys continued to poke fun at one another, I sank back into my chair, as happy as a pig in shit. Hannah scooted her chair even closer to mine and snuggled against me, warm as a blanket. She moved her hand further up my thigh and smiled at me. Smiling back, I touched her cheek, drew her mouth to mine and kissed her softly...

Then looked up to find Katie staring at me in disbelief from the other side of the bar.

Having noticed the way my mouth was hanging open, Holly and the boys followed my stunned gaze to Katie, and Katie's stunned gaze back to me, then began to search each other for some explanation of what was happening. For all I knew, Hannah was doing the same, but I couldn't bring myself to look at her. My legs felt like jelly as I stood up and made my way towards Katie.

We walked outside of the hotel, the air around us thick, dragging with awkwardness. We stopped when we reached the edge of the car park, standing self-consciously with our eyes to the tarmac. We still hadn't spoken a word to one another and for a time I thought we might never break the silence. Eventually, though, Katie lifted her head and asked, 'Who was that girl in there with you?'

'The girl I was... oh, you mean –'

'The one with her hand on your crotch,' Katie said. 'Yes.'

'Right.' I said. 'That was Hannah.'

Katie's brow furrowed as she forced her eyes to meet mine. 'Hannah? The Austrian girl?'

I nodded.

'I don't understand,' Katie said, slowly. 'You told me you didn't like her. You told me she was mean.'

'Well, yes, she is,' I said. Beads of sweat were forming on my forehead. 'Or, at least, she was. A little. To be honest, I think I was a little bit harsh on her.'

'So, let me guess,' Katie said. 'Having realised your mistake, you took the chance to get together with her while I was away on holiday.'

I dropped my eyes to the ground. Katie closed her own tightly.

'Well, this leaves me looking a bit foolish,' she said.

'No, no,' I said, stupidly. 'Everything's fine.'

'James, I've told all my friends about you. I even told my parents. They wanted to know when they can meet you.'

'Oh.' I said. 'I, uh –'

'No,' Katie said, waving a hand to cut me off. 'Like you say, everything's fine. Don't worry yourself about it.'

'Katie –'

'*I said it's fine!*' she said, as she began marching towards her car. I marched alongside her.

'Katie, I'm sorry, I really am.'

'Doesn't help,' she said sharply, quickening her pace. I was struggling to keep up with her.

She turned to me again as she reached her car. 'So, I suppose this was why you never bothered to reply to my texts while I was gone.'

I nodded guiltily.

'You know,' Katie said, 'I spent my entire holiday thinking about you. To think that all the while you were back here in Scotland shagging some other girl.'

'If it helps,' I said, 'we didn't actually sleep together... We, uh...'

It didn't help. Katie's eyes began to fill with tears. 'Katie –' I said.

'Don't,' Katie said, wiping a sleeve across her eyes. 'Please don't. This is humiliating enough already.' She swung the car door open.

'Katie, listen.' I took a step towards her, but she threw out a hand.

'Just leave me alone,' she snapped. 'And don't ever speak to me again, you... you *fucking* arsehole.' I watched, unable to speak, as she climbed into the car and sped off for home. Then, miserably, I turned back towards the hotel, my guilt following me like an ugly shadow.

There was no question of coming clean to Hannah in the confines of the Grange, so I took her hand and led her the short distance to Cranston beach. I'd always considered it one of the prettiest spots for miles around, but that night I didn't give a damn about the scenery. I was thinking about the kind, trusting girl whose heart I'd just broken. I was thinking about the crazy, beautiful girl walking next to me. I was thinking about the two of us together, whether there'd ever be a time the two of us could *be* together.

Would Hannah even still want me after what I was about to say?

There was only one way to find out, of course. We sat down on the sand, which was still warm from the evening sun, and I told her everything that had happened in the past two weeks.

When I was finished talking, Hannah took a deep, stuttering breath and said, 'It's only fair. If that's what you want, if that's what you need.'

'I didn't need it,' I told her. 'I'm not even sure I wanted it... oh, that sounds so cruel! I didn't mean it to sound like that. She was so kind to me. She's such a good person.'

Hannah raised her hands to her side. 'Well, there you are.'

'No,' I said, 'it wasn't that. I mean, I liked her and all but... it all just sort of happened.'

'Things happen for a reason,' Hannah said.

I raised my brow. 'In that case, maybe if you hadn't vanished off to visit Christian...'

'Ah, so the whole thing was *my* fault,' Hannah said.

'Well,' I said, attempting a smile. 'I wouldn't be *too* hard on yourself.'

Hannah punched my arm, hard. 'You're an asshole. Do you know that?'

I nodded but said nothing. Sighing, Hannah took a stick and drew a heart in the sand. I didn't notice. 'The thing is,' she said, after a few moments, 'I wish I could be so romantic that I could throw away everything I have with Christian and live for the moment. But I can't. James, you *have* to understand that it's not a choice between him and you. It's a choice between living for the future and living for the present.'

'Ah,' I said, my heart sinking. 'So, you still think your future lies with Christian.'

'I don't know,' Hannah said.

'Because if it's true, then please tell me and I'll leave this whole thing alone. I've got no right to be here like this if you really do love the guy.'

Hannah swallowed hard and nodded. I took hold of her hand, looked hard into her eyes. 'Listen,' I said. 'If you choose him, then I get it, okay? But I want you to know that if you choose me, I'll be ready. I'll be patient and I'll go through everything we have to go through until it's just us, just the two of us, together. The thing we can't do is spend forever like we are now. We've both proved that in the past couple of weeks. Like it or not, you have to make a choice. And you need to make it soon.'

Hannah sighed heavily, then stood up and brushed the sand from her skirt. Turning towards her, I noticed the heart she'd drawn by our feet and blew out my breath. 'We really don't make things easy for ourselves, do we?' I said.

Hannah looked at me and smiled gently. 'If life was easy, then where would all the adventures be?'

9

HANNAH AND I COULDN'T HAVE BEEN MORE EXCITED WHEN WE arrived at the *Make Poverty History* rally in Edinburgh. The protest had been organised to highlight the concerns of the nation to those world leaders who were about to meet in Scotland for the G8 summit. Unsure of the exact concerns of the nation, Hannah and I had joined through curiosity more than anything else; the organisers had talked of creating a human band around the centre of Edinburgh, and we wanted to see whether or not they managed.

They did. For five hours a great circle of people continued to snake around the city, making it the largest protest Scotland had ever seen. Hannah and I joined the march mid-way through, blowing heartily on the whistles we'd bought and taking blurry photographs of the crowds that surrounded us. Further along the route, on Princes Street, we chanted songs and waved banners to the sound of beat drums. Policemen and shoppers stopped to cheer us on our way and Hannah and I cheered back, smiling gleefully, drunk with happiness.

By late afternoon, the sun was shining more brightly

than it had all summer. Hannah was clutching a white rose that she'd picked from a Marchmont garden as a souvenir of the day. We climbed into my car, threw on the radio and sang along joyfully to each of the crappy pop songs that played. An hour later, we arrived back at Hannah's apartment. In the quiet of the hallway, Hannah placed an open hand on my chest and drew herself in towards me. I draped an arm around her waist, combed my fingers through her hair, and as I stood, gazing into her eyes, I realised how much I loved this girl, how perfect we were together, how completely...

'Hello, Hannah.'

I jumped so violently that I cracked my nose against Hannah's forehead. Hannah and I spun around to find a tall youth watching us from against the frame of the living room door.

'Christian!' Hannah shouted. 'Oh my god, what are you doing here?'

'A little surprise,' Christian said, nudging himself gently from his resting place. 'I hope you don't mind.' Hands in pockets, he crossed the room and planted a kiss on Hannah's cheek. He was standing only a foot from me, but kept his eyes firmly on Hannah, desperate to delay the moment he'd be forced to acknowledge my presence. To his credit, he gathered his wits about him pretty quickly; by the time he turned to face me, he'd even managed to nail a smile to his face.

'And you are...?' he asked.

'James,' I said, taking the hand he'd offered me. Even through his false cheer, I noticed him wince at the name. He gave my hand another couple of sharp pumps with his fist, then let it go and turned back to Hannah. He said something to her in German and she nodded guiltily, before mumbling something back. I couldn't be certain, but it sounded like 'fortified horse goblets'. It seemed like as good a time as any to join the conversation.

'So, uh, Christian, did you have a good journey?' I asked.

But Christian didn't answer, just squared his shoulders as he threw his head round to face me. Though we were the same height, I was relieved to note he was slightly scrawnier than me. 'So, you're the friend I've heard so much about,' he said.

This, I knew, was the point where I was supposed to press my forehead against his and offer some masculine reply, but I didn't feel angry or bitter, only sorry for the whole situation. Sorry, especially, for Christian. I stared into the space above his left shoulder and nodded.

'You've been a good friend to Hannah,' Christian said. 'And I thank you for taking such good care of her. But she won't be seeing you again for some time. I'm here for her now, and I don't plan on leaving anytime soon.'

'Stop it, Christian,' Hannah said, reaching for his arm. Christian took a step backwards and laughed.

'Calm down, Hannah,' he said. 'I'm just trying to get to know your friend here.'

'You're sounding ridiculous,' Hannah said, with a frown.

'Well, FUCK!' Christian shouted. 'I'm sorry if I'm making this awkward for you.'

Hannah closed her eyes, took a deep breath. 'Okay,' she said. 'I'm sorry.'

Christian glared at Hannah a moment longer, then turned to me with such violence that I felt sure he was going to punch me. 'And *you*,' he said, jabbing a finger in my face. 'You knew about me and still you tried to take her away. What kind of man are you?'

I forced myself to hold Christian's gaze, though tears

were welling in his eyes. 'I'm sorry,' I said.

'You won't fuck this up for us,' he said. 'Do you hear me? I won't let you fuck this up for us.'

Hannah moved slowly forward to Christian, like she was afraid he might run away. Then she wrapped her arms around him, pulled him towards her, and began to stroke his hair. The two of them stood there for a long moment, and when Christian finally spoke, it was through heavy sobs. 'He won't fuck it up for us,' he said. 'I need you so much.'

There was nothing more for me to say, and so I turned and left the apartment in silence. The pain I felt as I stepped outside was like a knife to the heart.

For the next twenty-four hours I traipsed aimlessly around the house, waiting for Hannah to call. But the longer I waited, the more the phone didn't ring, and the more the phone didn't ring the more convinced I became that Hannah had chosen Christian over me. I suppose it was living around Emma all those years, but in difficult times I always readied myself for the worst possible outcome. That way I could feel happy with anything that fell short of Armageddon.

It was late on Sunday evening when Hannah finally asked me over to her apartment. When the call came, I practically leapt into my car as I raced towards Cranston. Hannah arrived at the door in some sweatpants and an old Sex Pistols T-shirt that had seen better days even before she'd stolen it from her brother a few years earlier. Her unwashed hair was swept back in a pony-tail, and she looked pale and tired, her eyes swollen from crying. It seemed for all the world like she needed a hug, but when I moved towards her she simply leaned against her door, making room for me to pass. I glanced tentatively over her shoulder.

'It's okay,' Hannah said. 'He's not here.'

I made my way to the living room and sat down on the sofa. Hannah followed a moment later and sat down opposite me. She looked exhausted.

'You look exhausted,' I told her.

'Thank you.'

'No, no, it's not that you look bad,' I said, backtracking. 'You just look more tired than usual.'

'Mmm hmmm,' said Hannah.

'Not that you usually look tired.'

Hannah rolled her eyes. I decided I was talking too much and turned my attention to the pitiful collection of '80s music cassettes that she'd inherited when she moved into the apartment. Then I started talking again. 'You know, you're only one album away from owning *Bananarama's* full back catalogue.'

I looked over to Hannah. She wasn't laughing. That felt strange. She always laughed at my crappy music cassette jokes.

I tried another.

'Have you managed to fill that hole in your *Wham* collection yet?' I asked.

Hannah looked to her knees. 'We broke up,' she said.

Perhaps I should have expected that. Or half expected it, at least. But after spending the past twenty-four hours preparing for the worst, it seemed almost impossible to consider such a happy outcome. I told myself to stay calm, that I might even have misheard Hannah's words, but as soon as I spun my head around to face her I knew I hadn't. Her chin was already starting to wobble.

'When?' I asked.

'This morning. After you left, we spoke for... God, I don't even know how long. The sun was rising by the time we were done talking.'

'So, when you said Christian's not here...'

Hannah dropped her eyes to the ground. 'He left. Around lunchtime – just grabbed his bags and left. I asked him to stay, but he wouldn't. He wouldn't even look at me.'

I felt a guilty flutter in my stomach. True, I'd spent the past three months competing with Christian for Hannah's affections. But it had been a fair fight, and I'd never once held a thing against him, never once wished to see him hurt. Now, at the end of it all, he'd been hurt terribly, and as I pictured him, heartbroken and alone in some airport or hostel, I felt sorry beyond words.

'Are you okay?' I asked.

Hannah swallowed. 'I'm better than I was.'

'I'm sorry, Hannah. Truly. It's a horrible thing.'

Hannah nodded sadly. 'But it had to happen, didn't it?'

'Something had to,' I admitted.

Hannah considered that and sighed. 'I just wish I hadn't hurt him so badly. He didn't deserve that.'

'I know,' I said, gently. 'But his wounds will heal. He'll move on. Yes, there'll be a scar where his heart was broken, but time will make him whole again.'

Hannah stood up and crossed the short space that separated us. She sat next to me, took hold of my hand and placed a head against my chest. It was then, in the moment my body flooded with Hannah's warmth, that I felt the absolute happiness of being *with* Hannah, of knowing – truly knowing, for the first time – that she was mine. Even with a conscience as dirty as mine, that felt pretty incredible.

6 JULY 2005

It's taken me an hour to finally decide on what to wear this morning as I'm so anxious about meeting Jamie's new girlfriend. I don't want to look fat or any more disgusting than I have to. I wanted to hide under baggier clothes but the fucking sun has come out following a storm and has brought with it a sticky heat wave that's forced me into summer clothes that were clearly designed to kill me through shame. I've never felt more uncomfortable in my own skin.

10

WHENEVER I CHECKED IN TO HOPE PARK, I LIKED TO CREEP along the ward and sneak a peek at Emma before officially announcing my arrival to her. Those little glimpses, I found, offered the strongest clue about how the visit was likely to pan out. If I found Emma curled up on her bed, I knew I'd be lucky to draw a single word from her before leaving for home. If I found her pacing around her room, I'd likely spend the entire visit answering a bombardment of anxious questions. And, on those rare occasions that I found her laughing and joking with another patient, there was a chance the visit might prove enjoyable, that we might even share a little small talk before the time came for me to make my way back home.

I was faced with none of those things when I glanced into the room on the sixth afternoon of July, 2005. Instead, I saw Emma standing near her window, examining her reflection in the glass with the care and precision of a surgeon. From the way her shoulders were slumped, it was obvious that what she saw was not remotely close to what she wanted to see.

It had nothing to do with vanity, and a great deal to do with Hannah. Even on her best days, Emma was incredibly shy of new people; on her worst days – days when she was in hospital, growing more enormous with every meal – her shyness turned to pure terror. When, two days earlier, I'd told Emma that Hannah wanted to meet her, Emma had fallen silent for so long that I began to think she'd hung up on me. It had taken ten minutes of pleading to make her agree that Hannah could join me on my next visit.

When Hannah and I entered Emma's room, Emma jumped away from her window and threw a smile onto her face. I moved to hug her, but as usual she ducked away before I made contact, fearful that I might grab hold of the imaginary fat that covered her body. When I stood aside, Hannah edged forward and shook Emma's hand before stepping back and moving in even closer to me than before.

'How are you?' I asked.

Emma forced another smile. 'I need your opinion on something,' she said.

Right, I thought, *so it's going to be another of our question and answer visits after all*. I sat Hannah down on the chair by Emma's desk, then sat down myself next to Emma on her bed. Then, with some dread, I invited Emma to ask her question.

'I'm getting my hair cut tomorrow,' she said. 'Do you think my weight will go down if I get it cut short?'

I told her I didn't.

'Would getting it coloured and styled make it shoot up?'

I told her it wouldn't.

'Maybe the two would balance each other out. What do you think?'

I nodded heartily. Maybe she'd stop talking if I kept saying the things she wanted to hear.

'If I get my hair cut short then maybe people will focus on that instead of the weight I'm putting on,' Emma reasoned. 'Then again, a longer style would obviously disguise, well, this...' She pointed a finger to each side of her face and puffed up her cheeks. I laughed obediently, but really, I hated that kind of thing, that awful gallows humour.

Emma threw her hands in the air, a comedy gesture for Hannah's benefit. 'I don't know,' she said. 'I really don't know. Maybe I should just leave it as it is and save the torment. What do you think?'

'You could shave your head,' I joked.

Emma laughed. 'Well, they say I already *look* like a cancer patient. I suppose that would complete the effect.'

Even from across the room, I heard Hannah gasp. I looked towards her, smiling desperately to show her that everything was still okay, but she was already staring out of the window, her face and neck glowing like pink charcoals.

That pretty much set the tone for the rest of the visit. When Emma spoke, it was only to ask about her impending haircut, while nothing I said in reply came close to penetrating Emma's great wall of delusion. Hannah, for her part, said nothing at all, just continued to stare blankly out of Emma's window. By the time I made our excuses to leave an hour later, she looked ready to scream.

'I'm sorry,' I said, after a silence that had lasted all the way to the car. 'I should have given you more warning before we went in, made sure you were better prepared.'

Hannah was shaking her head before I'd even finished talking. 'James,' she said. 'It's not your fault.'

'It's just that sometimes I forget how bad it is.'

'James,' Hannah said, more firmly this time. 'Truly. It's not your fault.'

Tears started to rise up. I shut my eyes to hold them in.

Hannah let out an uneven breath. 'Anyway,' she said. 'It wasn't so bad. I just... I didn't expect her to be so thin.'

I looked at her sceptically. 'That's all?'

There was a very long pause. 'Well, some of her jokes were a little strange. Does she always talk like that?'

'Sometimes,' I said. 'Other times she doesn't talk at all.'

Hannah shook her head, running her hands up over her arms like she was cold. 'I can't even imagine...' she said. 'You poor thing.' She opened the car door and collapsed down onto the seat. When I climbed in a moment later, she'd already turned her body to face me. 'Let's *do* something,' she said.

The change of topic was so complete that I couldn't help but laugh. 'Like what?' I asked.

'I don't know,' Hannah said. 'Let's... let's go into Edinburgh, to the film festival. We can go and watch a movie at the Filmhouse, have a coffee afterwards. Just... *be* for a little while.'

We chose a dumb British thriller. It was by no means a classic, but it offered an escape from our thoughts of Hope Park, and we gladly took refuge in it. In the bar afterwards, we got talking to the film's lead actor, who was every bit as beautiful and charming as we'd expected him to be. But he took himself far too seriously, and so Hannah and I set about convincing him that we'd worked on the film, too, just to lighten our moods. He believed us, and even handed us his card before he left, insisting that we call him if any opportunities came up. We never did call, but I doubt he cared. A few years later, he ended up with a lead role in *Downton Abbey*.

Hannah and I drove home with the radio playing at full volume, singing along to all the songs we knew and making up lyrics to the ones we didn't. At around dusk, we arrived back to Hannah's apartment, hoarse but happy. I threw off my shoes and headed towards the lounge, but Hannah caught me by the sleeve of my shirt and, smiling sheepishly, shook her head before leading me down the hallway to her room.

Hannah sat me down at her desk while she tiptoed around, fluffing her pillows and lighting some scented candles on her bedside table. 'They smell nice,' I told her. Hannah smiled her acknowledgement. She was already over at her music player, pressing play on the latest Arcade Fire CD. 'Ooh, music, too,' I said. 'Whatever next? Coffee and biscuits?'

Nope. Next, Hannah walked over to face me in the dimmed light of her room and grabbed me by the crotch, pulling me hungrily towards her bed.

Hannah pushed me onto her mattress and threw off her t-shirt to reveal a flat stomach and a white lace bra. I gawped at her, trying to understand what was happening. It was dumb, I know, but I'd been so busy during the past ten weeks *not* having sex with Hannah that the thought of finding myself in such a position had come to seem almost absurd. There'd been the occasional spark of hope that it might somehow happen, but even in my wildest dreams I'd been made to move mountains before it came to pass. The thought that I might eventually be handed the entire thing on a plate had never remotely occurred to me. Yet here I was, in Hannah's bed, with her tongue in my mouth and her hand down my trousers. It was lovely and all, but it was terrifying, too. I cursed myself for being so fully under-prepared.

Hannah pushed me backwards and clambered on top of me. Her hands tugged at my shirt, pulling it over my head, tossing it to the floor. She moved her hands down my chest, my stomach; her hands grazed the inside of my thigh, awakening every nerve ending in my body. my heart was pounding as Hannah threw one leg over me and rolled onto her back where first she unhooked her bra, then wriggled out of her skirt and pants. Grinning a little self-consciously, she pulled me on top of her and pushed my trousers down over my hips and thighs, before kicking them the rest of the way past my ankles and onto the floor.

Hannah caught my earlobe between her teeth and gave it a little nip before flicking her tongue in my ear. 'I wanted this for so long,' she whispered. Moaning softly, she moved her hands to the back of my head, pulling me to her, raising her hips to reach mine and grinding herself against me. This went on for a minute or so, until it became impossible to ignore the fact that an integral part of our little adventure was missing. Suddenly, Hannah stopped gyrating and looked up at me with obvious confusion. 'Is everything okay?' she asked.

'Yup,' I said, trying to keep the panic from my voice. 'Just gimme a minute or two.'

'Is there something I can do to help?'

I shook my head. 'He's just a bit late to the party,' I said, my voice cracking. 'He'll be along in a sec.'

I continued to hold myself above Hannah for what seemed like forever, embarrassed to death but hoping against hope that my body would come to its senses and let me get on with what I was supposed to be doing. It did, eventually, but what followed was over so quickly that I didn't even find time to ask Hannah whether or not she was enjoying herself.

As I lay next to Hannah afterwards, I quickly began to worry that the whole event had fallen some way short of the high standards she'd come to expect during her time with

Christian. I considered asking, just to be sure, but deep down I knew it wasn't the time to talk about it. Maybe in a week or two, if the chance came up, but right now the important thing was to keep my lips zipped. That was obvious to anyone but a complete lunatic.

'Uh, Hannah?' I said.

Uh-oh.

'Can I ask a question?'

'Yes.'

'I'm not sure you'll like it.'

'James, just... Just ask it.'

'Well, it's just... was Christian better?'

Hannah turned her eyes slowly towards mine. 'Are you seriously asking about my sex with Christian? Do you really want me to describe it to you?'

'I don't know,' I said. And I didn't.

Fighting back a smile, Hannah propped herself up on an elbow and kissed me on the neck. 'Listen, it was different with him, okay? Which isn't to say it was better. What just happened between us was beautiful, even if it didn't go exactly as planned.'

'Really?'

'Yes. Really.'

'Because I'll get better, you know. If you let me practice a little more...'

Hannah couldn't help but giggle. 'James, are you even listening to what I'm saying? What happened just now was wonderful. It meant a lot to me. And I'm thankful it happened. Okay?' She looked at the clock on her bedside table. 'Look, it's getting late. Can we just stop worrying about silly things and get some sleep?'

I agreed we could.

So, we did. We went to sleep.

11

WHENEVER I MADE MY WAY TO THE GRANGE, IT WAS ALWAYS with a strong sense of apprehension at what I'd find when I stepped inside its doors. In the past year, I'd witnessed all manner of things, including – but not limited to – screaming, brawling, chanting, bawling, retching, groping, wild flirtation and countless public displays of nudity. The place had become so unpredictable that none of its goings-on should have been able to surprise me anymore. But when I arrived at the hotel a few days after my sexy time with Hannah, I was completely shocked to find Dan, Holly and Steve sitting quietly round a table and drinking pints of lager in what could only be described as a regular fashion. They were not singing. None of the bar staff were crying. I saw no trails of destruction. The room, for once, seemed entirely at peace.

'Where are the others?' I asked. I put the question to my friends at a normal volume, yet they still heard me. *How strange*, I thought. With Dan's boys around, you had to yell like a lifeboat captain in a gale to be understood.

'The others,' Dan said, 'are in Stirling, getting royally

drunk in preparation for their big cup match tomorrow. The question is, where have *you* been? Having watched you slink out of here with Hannah last week, we were starting to think you'd ended up fertilising her garden. You must be even more of a sweet-talker than I thought if she decided to forgive you.'

'How do you know she forgave me?' I asked.

'Where else would you have been for the past few days?'

I conceded the point.

'So, come on then,' Dan said. 'Tell us. Have you shagged her yet or not?'

I said nothing.

'Oh, come on, James. Just say it. Say you've shagged her.'

Silence.

Dan's eyes widened. 'Oh shit, you *have*, haven't you?'

I looked away, trying to hide the smile that had crept across my face.

'I don't believe it,' Dan shouted gleefully. 'You've been shagging the Vienna vixen!'

'Keep it down, will you?' I said, looking around the bar.

But Dan was enjoying himself too much. 'James, you dog!' He clapped his hands together and faced the others. 'My friends, it seems our little James is finally back in the game.'

'It's not so little,' I said quietly. The joke wasn't really all that funny, but Dan exploded into laughter. I suppose he was missing the risqué humour of his boys.

Wiping a tear from his eye, Dan leaned forward in his chair. 'So, come on then,' he said, conspiratorially. 'How was she?'

I shook my head. 'No comment.'

'Oh, come on,' Dan said. 'Just give us a little something

to go on.' And right then he grinned, struck by some sudden inspiration. 'Tell us –'

'Daniel,' Holly said, warningly. 'If the question you're about to ask includes the words 'shaved' or 'anal', then I swear to god I will punch you in the throat.'

Dan took one look at Holly and his courage collapsed. 'I was only asking,' he mumbled, before returning his attention to his drink.

Holly turned back towards me. 'So, I guess this means you're well and truly together?' she asked. When I nodded, she gave an irritating little roll of the eyes, which Steve immediately intercepted.

'Well, if you ask me,' he said, 'you could do a lot worse than Hannah.'

'*Has* done a lot worse,' Dan corrected.

'Did I say he hadn't?' Holly asked, at which point we all turned our heads to face her. This was unexpected. 'What?' Holly said. 'Jesus, guys. I'm not saying I'll ever be friends with the girl, but you have to hand it to her – James is finally smiling again for the first time in forever. I suppose she deserves at least *some* credit for that.'

'Wow,' I said. 'Thanks Holly.'

'Oh, don't get all soppy, James,' Holly grumbled. 'I still think she's a twat.'

I wished she hadn't said that. It kind of ruined the moment. And yet, I wasn't remotely offended. I refused to be. As Dan had pointed out, little James was back in the game now. And, for tonight at least, I was going to enjoy the fanfare.

12

As children, Emma and I very rarely heard our parents scream or shout at one another. We'd always known they argued, of course, but over the years they'd got very good at holding their 'discussions' – they always called them discussions – in hushed tones so as not to upset us.

This all changed after Emma got sick. Then, increasingly, they threw caution to the wind, their arguments growing fiercer and more recurrent as Emma's illness seized control of all our lives. Even from the safety of my room, the words of my parents frequently arrived through the walls as loud as any TV show.

Their discussions had grown even more than usually heated in the past few weeks, after Emma had snapped at Dad for leaving a coffee ring on the top of her desk during a family visit to Hope Park. Emma's sudden loss of temper had been nothing out of the ordinary, but Dad had taken it to heart, and since then he'd flatly refused either to visit Emma in Glasgow or speak to her during her daily phone calls to Myreton. The idea that he could somehow manipulate Emma into recovery seemed ridiculous to Mum and I, but Dad clearly hoped his persistence would eventually pay off. Unfortunately, the results so far had been a long way from positive, and the stress was telling on all of us.

I was forced to listen to this argument yet again a few nights after my trip to the Grange. Emma had called, like always, an hour after dinner and, like always, had spent a few minutes chatting first with me and then with Mum. Until recently, Dad would have taken his turn to speak when Mum was done talking, but tonight, to no one's surprise, he chose once more to refused conversation. I was in my room by then, so was spared having to watch Mum's heart break as Dad ignored her entreating looks from across the room. I could feel the tension, though, and knew that we were headed for fireworks. These began the moment Mum hung up the phone.

'You have to stop this,' she said. I could sense the anger and frustration surging through her. 'You have to talk to her, even if it's just to say a quick hello. She's missing you, John. She feels terrible about what's happening.'

'Good,' Dad said, gruffly. 'She's supposed to.'

'You can't guilt-trip her into recovery. That's not how it works.'

'It'll work,' Dad said. 'She just needs time.'

'Time?' Mum said, her voice rising several octaves. 'John, it's been nearly a *month*. It's driving Emma to distraction. You know she blames herself when things go wrong.'

Dad snickered, started to say something.

'Don't you dare,' Mum said, cutting him off sharply. 'Don't you dare say it. None of this is her fault. She's done nothing wrong.'

Dad, wisely, kept his mouth shut then, leaving Mum to fire her point home. 'Emma's mood's dropping further and

further each day,' she said. 'It's getting more and more difficult for me to put her mind at rest.'

'So, what are you saying?' Dad said, his anger returning.
'That I'm making things worse?'

'I'm saying you should leave Emma's treatment to the
professionals.'

'Oh, screw the professionals, Mary. I'm sick to the teeth
of those bloody people.'

'John –'

'I'm serious!' Dad shouted. 'I've had enough. I've had
ENOUGH!'

I listened as Mum made her way from the living room
through to her bedroom, where I knew she'd cry following
her latest argument with Dad. I sat up on my bed, took a few
minutes to gather my strength. Then I went through to the
living room, where Dad was sitting watching football on the
telly.

I hovered beside the sofa for a second, feigning an
interest in the football, hoping that Dad would acknowledge
my presence. I even said, 'Dad, how's the game going?'

But he didn't answer me. He was angry at Mum for ques-
tioning his new hands-off parenting style, so now he was
sulking. I knew from experience that he wouldn't say
anything for the rest of the night, so I skulked off back to my
room, threw some headphones over my ears, and tried to
forget everything that had just happened.

It was late and I was hungry when the batteries in my
Walkman finally died, so I crawled out from underneath my
duvet and set off towards the kitchen. On the way, I dared to
stop by the living room, where I found Mum working on a
cross-stitch by the hearth. Dad, unsurprisingly, was
nowhere to be seen.

'He's been in the garage for the past two hours,' Mum

said, when she looked up to find me hovering by the door. 'Just before you ask.'

I shook my head. 'Probably ashamed for acting like such a prick.'

Mum narrowed her eyes, laid down her sewing. 'You know, you really can be a little hard on your father sometimes.'

'He makes it difficult to go easy on him,' I said.

'He loves you very much, darling.'

I stared at her, expressionless. 'He has a funny way of showing it.'

Mum looked to the carpet and sighed impatiently, the way she always did when she was exasperated with me. When she looked at me again, there were tears in her eyes. 'James, when you had that nasty chest infection the winter after Emma was born, your dad rocked you in his arms for more than thirty hours. I told him again and again to put you down and get some rest, but he wouldn't hear of it. He went without sleep for two days just to see you safe from harm. You wouldn't remember that, of course.'

I dropped my eyes to the ground. I didn't want to let go of my anger, but Mum's words had hit me hard, left me too dazed to feel anything much. I found myself fighting back tears.

'We all have our different ways of coping,' Mum continued. 'Your father's methods are far from perfect, but he's trying hard to be strong, I can promise you that. You could try to be a little more sympathetic.'

'It's just... It's so hard,' I said, feebly. There was a lump in my throat. It was difficult to speak.

Mum nodded and patted my arm. I could see the liver spots and wrinkles on her hand. *Oh, god*, I thought. *Every-*

body around me is falling apart. Piece by piece, they're all falling apart, and there's nothing I can do to stop it.

'Try not to let it get you down, honey,' Mum said. 'Look, here comes your dad. Maybe you could watch a bit of telly together.'

But I couldn't. It was too much. It was all too much. Without a word, I turned and set off for Hannah's.

The following morning, I lay staring at Hannah's ceiling. By then, my thoughts of home had all but vanished from my mind. I looked at my watch. It was five o'clock. I did a quick calculation; I'd been lying awake for over three hours. I was exhausted, and just reaching the level of tiredness where imagination and reality start to blur. In this confused state, my mind allowed me to think that it hadn't happened. Tentatively, I looked towards the floor.

They were still there.

If Dan had walked into the room right then and glanced at the ground, he'd have been delighted with what he saw. But I had no reason to feel proud; the sea of condoms that covered the carpet didn't signify a night of passion. Rather, each one recalled a moment of frustration the evening before, a moment in which some minor swelling had tricked me into thinking I was ready for love, only to vanish in the moment that rubber met skin.

That was pretty much the story of the last week. Our lives had become entirely scheduled around my desperate quest for love. With each failure, I'd become increasingly frustrated. Hannah had become increasingly bored.

I rolled over to face Hannah and sighed dramatically. She didn't stir. I sighed dramatically again.

'What is it, James?' she asked, without moving. She was curled up tight into her blanket, her head tucked away from the light so that only her ear and the white of her neck were showing.

'Will you break up with me if this sex thing doesn't get better?'

She tutted. 'Come on, you *know* I love you more than that.'

I knew that, but I enjoyed the reassurances.

Hannah rubbed her eyes lazily, rolled over to face me. 'Anyway,' she said, 'it's not like it's going to last forever.'

'You don't know that,' I said, despondently. 'Maybe I'm doomed to fail at this.'

I looked up and noticed that Hannah was trying hard not to laugh. 'James, you're just stressed,' she said. 'That's all. You've been under pressure for years. It's understandable your body's reacting to that.'

I narrowed my eyes towards Hannah. 'How do you know that?'

Hannah shrugged. 'I read a lot of girly magazines,' she said. 'Listen, we'll just give things a little time. If they're still no better in a week or two, we can go see a doctor.'

I recoiled in horror. 'A *doctor*?' I said. 'Oh, god no!'

Hannah laughed. 'Why not?'

I looked away, embarrassed. 'Well,' I said under my breath. 'They might ask to see it.'

Hannah rolled her eyes, still smiling. 'Okay,' she said. 'So, no doctors.' She stared at me thoughtfully for a few seconds. 'Well, maybe there are things I can do to help.'

'Things?' I said.

'Yeah,' Hannah said, kicking the thin blanket from our bed. 'Things.' Sitting up on the bed, she placed her warm legs on each side of me and slipped her nightgown over her head. 'Little things,' she said. 'To help you relax.' Her hair was hanging forward, hiding her face, except for her eyes, which she held against mine.

She lightly bit my ear, brushing her breasts across my face. 'Am I helping you relax?' she whispered. She laid a hand on my chest and let it fall slowly down my body, down, down, until, 'Oh!' she said. 'There he is.' She ran her fingers along the soft underside and a noise escaped me, an embarrassingly low-pitched moan. I felt myself growing harder by the second, the competing muscles of anxiety having finally relaxed. Hannah grinned. 'Looks like he's interested,' she said.

'I think perhaps he is.'

'Maybe, then, we could try again. Perhaps it'll be better this time. What do you think?'

I thought it was a tremendous idea.

And so, we did.

And it was.

AUGUST 30 2005

The doctors say that it will take me a long time to get over this illness. But I don't want to get over it. I want to turn the clocks back to a time before it, when all the future was sunny. Then I could do it all again, but do it right. There'd be no illness, no need to find the courage it takes to recover. For I know I don't have that courage within me, and I know I never will.

The doctors disagree, of course. They tell me I don't need to go back to move forward, to stop dwelling on the past and concentrate on what's ahead. They make it sound so simple. But what do they know? Seriously, what do they know?

They break my heart.

13

JULY TURNED TO AUGUST, AND THE SUN CONTINUED TO SHINE on Hannah and me. Every day, we explored hidden sections of Edinburgh's Old and New Towns between shows at the summer festivals, or lost ourselves in the great beauty of the East Lothian countryside. At night, when we arrived home, we drank wine and cooked meals and burned music CDs to accompany us on our next day's adventures. There were times when our work or our family prised us away from one another's company, but for the most part we were insepara-ble. We were one thing. A whole thing. And we were happy.

And yet, there were plenty of times when the thought of Hannah leaving for home took me somewhere close to panic. I'd tried more than once in recent weeks to raise the subject of our future to Hannah, but while she'd spoken once or twice about showing me around Vienna someday, the details were always vague and failed to suggest any promise of a long-term relationship. I lay awake for hours each night sick with the thought that I was about to lose her forever.

I wasn't the only one losing sleep. For weeks, Hannah

had been disappointed by her visit to Hope Park. She felt she hadn't been confident enough, that she should have worked harder to strike up a conversation with Emma. 'I suppose it was just an off day for both of us,' she'd told me, after reflecting on the visit. But I'd told her that it had actually been a pretty good day for Emma – she'd even made an attempt at humour, albeit a wildly inappropriate one. In the few weeks since then, I'd made a number of trips to Glasgow, and on most occasions, Emma had stared trancelike at her bedroom door and ignored my efforts at conversation. Hannah had looked at me sceptically when I told her that; surely none of the visits could have been worse than the one she'd experienced.

'They were,' I said. 'Trust me.'

Whether she trusted me or not, Hannah remained determined to try again. And so, one sunny afternoon at the end of August, we set off once more for Hope Park.

I knew the moment we walked into Emma's room that we were in trouble. Despite offering one of my warmest welcomes, Emma neither moved nor looked up from her bed. I made a few attempts at small talk, but they all failed completely. I looked across at Hannah, who was perched uneasily on the edge of a chair, staring hard into a corner of the room. Clearly, she'd already seen the futility of her plan to make friends with Emma. For a very long time, none of us said a single word. I'd half made up my mind to leave when Emma finally turned to me and said, 'I can't do this anymore.'

I stared at Emma dumbly, my tongue like a stone in my mouth. I wanted desperately to say the words that would bring Emma back to me, but I was not certain what those words were. 'Emma,' I tried, finally. 'The doctors say you're doing well. Things are moving forward all the time.'

Emma scoffed. 'Yeah, sure. *Just five more weeks, Emma.* Isn't that what they're saying? Well, it wouldn't be the first promise they've broken to me. I won't hold my breath.'

'Five weeks?' I said. 'Five weeks till what?'

'Until I come home,' Emma said. Then, noticing my confusion: 'Didn't Mum tell you?'

'No,' I said. My head was spinning, my thoughts knocking into one another. 'But why... why would they let you out?'

Emma clicked her tongue impatiently. 'Uh, because I'm *fat* now?'

I shook my head, ran a trembling hand through my hair. 'That's bollocks, sis. You're not fat. For Christ's sake, you're not even *normal*.'

This wasn't the highest compliment I'd ever paid my sister, but if she was remotely offended by it, she didn't let it show. 'Well, officially it's something to do with the section or something. I don't know. Some legal shit. But what they're basically trying to say is that I'm fat.'

'Emma,' I said, slowly. 'This is horrendous.'

'No,' Emma said. 'It's good.'

I stared at her in disbelief. 'In what way is it a good thing?'

Emma leaned forward, her eyes turning hard and frosty. 'Because now, finally, I have the chance just to go home and die in peace.'

My eyes widened. I took a huge breath as if winded. 'Emma!' I said. 'You don't mean that.'

Emma nodded. 'Yes, I do.'

'No,' I said, my voice faltering. 'No. It just seems that way. As soon as –'

'James!' Emma yelled, cutting me off mid-sentence. 'I'm fucking serious! I want to *die*. All I want is to *die*. I *hate* myself, *and* my life, and everyone and everything in it. Fuck, why are none of you people able to get that through your thick fucking heads?'

Emma's eyes were blazing, her lips trembling as tears fell and panic threatened to overwhelm her. 'Emma,' I said. 'Calm down.'

Another explosion: 'I'll calm down when you start to fucking listen to me!'

'I *am* listening, Emma.' I shouted. 'Believe me, it's impossible to unhear some of the shit you say. But what do you want me to do about it? I'm your brother, not your doctor. I can't change your situation any more than you can.'

That knocked some of the wind out of Emma's sails. In the silence that followed, I turned to Hannah, who was sitting tensely on her chair. It was as though all the muscles in her body had tightened at once. 'Hannah?' I said. 'Hannah! Go on to the car, okay? I'll be with you in a minute.'

It took Hannah so long to move that I began to wonder if she'd heard me at all. But then, eventually, she shut her mouth with a snap, rose slowly from her chair and just sort of shuffled out the room. I waited until she was safely outside, then turned back to Emma, who met my gaze and held it defiantly. 'Are you happy?' I asked.

Emma snickered. 'I'm fucking delirious.'

I closed my eyes, forced myself to stay calm. 'Emma, that wasn't fair. You can't talk like that. I know things are shit right now, but we have to try and stay positive.'

Emma shot me a reproachful look. 'That's easy for you to say,' she grumbled.

'Suddenly, my own anger spilled over. 'Don't you dare do that,' I said. 'Don't you dare think you're the only one who's suffering here. This is a fucking nightmare for us all. Do you hear me?'

All the rage went out of Emma then. Defeated, she let out a long, sad breath and fell back against her pillow. I looked down at her hands, tensed against her chest. Her fingernails were bitten to shreds, dried blood in the cuticles. As I looked at them, I sensed my own anger begin to dissolve. Choking back tears, I reached out and took Emma's cold hand in mine. 'I know it's hard, sis, but I really need you to try and stay positive. Just try. Please. I can't do it without you.'

Emma smiled wearily, allowed her eyes to close. 'I'm sorry, James,' she said. Her voice was soft. Barely a breath. I remained with her until she was asleep. Then, pressing my lips to her forehead, I struggled to my feet and made my way from the room.

I stepped outside to find Hannah leaning against the bonnet of my car, her eyes closed against the afternoon sun that was spreading its warmth across the hospital's elegant driveway. It was a beautiful deception, I thought, as I glanced around the grounds. Hope Park could do that to you. Make you forget the heartbreak that lay within its graceful borders, that behind every pretty picture you could find an ugly story.

I joined Hannah on the car bonnet, and for a minute or more we sat in silence, feeling thoroughly miserable even as the sun warmed our faces. I was searching desperately for something to say when, suddenly, Hannah picked up her bag and marched away from the car. I began to march away too.

'*Don't* follow me,' she said, sharply.

I sat back down.

Hannah continued stamping until she reached the hospital gardens. Then, feeling the softness of grass beneath her feet, she slipped off her shoes and continued the journey barefoot. There was no apparent pattern to her travels, no obvious direction. She simply walked until she ran out of grass, then turned on her heels and carried on at another random angle across the lawn. It was a strange kind of behaviour, and on another day, I suppose I'd have taken a moment to question it. But right then I was too tired to care. Sighing deeply, I leaned back heavily against the car and set about trying to erase the past sixty minutes from my mind and memory.

A full half hour passed before Hannah made her way back to the car. When she reached me, she said nothing, just bumped her head softly against my shoulder.

'I'm sorry,' I said. 'I'm so sorry. Even by Emma's standards that was truly horrendous. I never heard her talk like that before.'

Hannah sighed into my chest. 'It's not just your sister,' she said. 'I just wish I knew where we go from here, you know?'

For the first time that day I felt a flutter of hope in my chest. 'God, yes,' I said. 'Absolutely.'

I felt Hannah's brow furrow against my breast. 'Really?'

'Of course,' I said. 'I mean, you're leaving here in less than a month. It's natural that I'd want to talk about it.'

Hannah lifted her head from my shoulder, looked at me above her dark sunglasses. 'James,' she said. 'I meant *we* as in *everybody*. I didn't want to talk about us.'

'Oh,' I said, as my own brow creased. 'But... why not? Isn't it important?'

'I suppose so,' Hannah said. 'But it's too early. For God's sake, James, I just got out of a relationship.'

'You *got out* of a relationship? Hannah, you talk about it like it was a prison sentence.'

Hannah shook her head. 'You know that's not what I meant.'

'And yet, you're still against continuing *this* relationship after you leave Scotland.'

'Don't say it like that,' Hannah said, with a touch of anger. 'You know I'm not against *anything*. But I want to travel. I want to see the world, to experience all the things it has to offer. I always told you that, James. I told you that the first night we met.'

'Things have changed since then,' I said.

'Yes, they have,' Hannah said. 'And I love you. But I still want to travel, as far and widely as I can. I need to understand why I'm here, find my place in the world. And that won't leave much time for us.'

'So, what do we do?' I asked.

'We make the most of the time we have left together.'

'And after that?'

'We can see,' Hannah said. 'We'll... we'll be friends.'

'Oh Christ, Hannah,' I said, my eyes wide with anger. 'Whatever you do, spare me the fucking F-word!'

'Okay, I'm sorry,' Hannah said. She fell quiet for a moment, searching for some words that might spare my feelings. In the end, she just dropped her eyes to the ground and sighed.

Breathing hard, I shook my head. 'This is all so *fucking* complicated.'

Hannah shrugged. 'But that's just life, isn't it?'

My shoulders dropped. Perhaps it was.

14

THE RUMOURS TURNED OUT TO BE TRUE. ONLY THREE DAYS after I visited Hope Park with Hannah, Emma's doctors confirmed that she was to be released on the tenth of October. I couldn't believe it. It would have been enough to learn that my suicidal, manically depressed, sickeningly thin sister had been allowed to leave hospital at all, but fate had also seen fit to deliver her to Myreton on the very day Hannah was to leave for home. It seemed unbearably cruel that the two events were to happen simultaneously. After months of relative peace, I began counting the days until the world returned to shit.

It wasn't that I felt sorry for myself. Truly, I didn't. I knew that countless other people were forced to endure adversity. I knew that, if confronted properly, adversity would help me to grow as a person. The problem was that overcoming adversity required patience and perseverance, and I really wasn't sure I possessed enough of either to get through this latest set of crises.

Two weeks before D-day, Hannah and Elisabeth invited a few friends round to their apartment to help celebrate

Elisabeth's final evening in Scotland. With the lease on the flat set to run out the following morning, the party was also our final chance to say farewell to a home that had played host to some truly remarkable adventures.

I spent the first two hours of the evening alone on the living room sofa. With the exception of Elisabeth, everyone else had spent their time smoking weed in Hannah's kitchen, and those who weren't still smoking were now behaving very oddly in various corners of the apartment. Three of Hannah's colleagues were intently studying a light switch by the hallway door. A fourth was holding a conversation with a fly that had landed on her arm. A man I'd never seen before had been trying for several minutes to text a friend from his wallet. And Hannah, bless her, had thrown off her shirt and was dancing to an old Bruce Springsteen record, her body nothing but the hard, pulsing beat of the track.

I'd been watching Hannah for some minutes when Elisabeth sat down beside me and laid a hand on my shoulder. 'You okay?' she asked.

'I'm going to miss this place,' I said. 'After everything that's happened here, it's started to feel a bit like home to me, too.'

Elisabeth cast her eyes across the room. I suppose she wanted to agree with me, but in the end, she just sort of wrinkled her nose and shrugged. 'Bloody hell,' I said. 'It seems like you're more ready to leave than me.'

Elisabeth smiled. 'You should remember that I haven't been riding the rollercoaster with you and Hannah. I've enjoyed my time here, but there haven't been any crazy love affairs or midnight adventures. I'm ready to go home. I've been ready for some time now.'

Having convinced us that he had indeed been born to

run, Bruce made way for the White Stripes, who just didn't know what to do with themselves. Hannah stepped off the dancefloor and sat down on the sofa, where she began to examine herself in a compact mirror she'd stolen from Elisabeth's handbag.

'She's going to miss you when you leave, you know,' I told Elisabeth.

Elisabeth shook her head. 'In a couple of days, she won't even notice I'm gone.'

'You know Sofia Coppola directed the video for this song,' Hannah said, dreamily.

'That's not true at all,' I told Elisabeth.

'It is,' Hannah said. 'The one with Kate Moss pole dancing.'

Elisabeth and I both looked towards Hannah; she was trying to kiss her eyes in the mirror's reflection.

'You do love her, don't you?' Elisabeth asked, turning back to me. When I nodded, she relaxed against the sofa. 'That's good,' she said, with obvious relief. 'Because she's not as strong as she thinks she is, you know. She's going to need someone there to help keep her feet on the ground.'

The song was reaching its crescendo now. Hannah threw down the mirror and burst into the final chorus, raising her arms and bobbing her head frantically as she belted out the lyrics. 'I just don't know what to do with myself, doo doo-doo doo. Just don't know what to do with myself, doo doo-doo doo…'

'You know she's given no guarantee she even wants to be with me after she leaves for home,' I told Elisabeth.

'But she does,' Elisabeth said. 'She just hasn't figured it out yet.'

'You think so?'

Elisabeth gave a half-smile. 'You get to know a person

when you find yourselves in a strange place together.' We both looked towards Hannah, who was studying a loose thread on her bra with deep fascination. 'Just promise you'll look after her,' Elisabeth told me. 'Promise you'll make her happy.'

'Sure,' I said. 'Of course.'

Elisabeth, still looking at Hannah, raised a hand and patted my cheek. Then she got to her feet and wandered off to the kitchen, leaving me alone with the unenviable task of somehow coaxing Hannah back down to earth.

Hannah was in pieces as she hugged Elisabeth goodbye at the airport the following morning. I couldn't see her face, which was buried in Elisabeth's hair, but it was obvious from the violent heaving of her shoulders that she was crying harder than I'd ever seen her cry before. Elisabeth stayed with her for as long as she could, stroking her hair, whispering reassurances, before making her way towards security. Hannah remained rooted to the spot long after Elisabeth had disappeared from sight. Walking up to her, I placed a hand on her shoulder. 'It's going to be okay,' I said. 'I'm going to make this fortnight so special for you. We're going to have such a wonderful time.'

Hannah nodded, faking a smile, and I hugged her, pulling her into me, where she cried some more, soaking the shoulder of my T-shirt. After a moment, she wiped the snot from her nose and took a deep, trembling breath. 'I didn't think all of this would bother me so much,' she said.

'I'm glad it finally *is* bothering you. I was starting to think you were made of stone.'

Hannah snorted. 'If only.' She took another deep breath

and then, after glancing back sadly to the spot where she'd said her last goodbye to Elisabeth, she grabbed my hand and led me outside of the airport.

15

MUM TREATED HANNAH'S ARRIVAL TO THE HOUSE LIKE A ROYAL visit. The house was tidier than it had ever been, and we started eating dinner at the table for the first time in a decade. Serviettes were served with meals instead of kitchen roll, and the menu was expanded to include prawn cocktail, Quiche Lorraine and a host of other dishes that Mum considered to be the very epitome of haute cuisine.

It's little wonder that Mum was so excited. Hannah had brought a cheer to a house that had long been engulfed in sadness and kept her company while I worked at the County. One night, I arrived home from work to find Mum and Hannah sitting cross-legged on the living room floor beside a bottle of rosé wine and a pile of glossy magazines. On the television, Carrie Bradshaw was sitting in Starbucks, talking at high volume about anal sex and dildos.

'Oh, James!' Mum cried, when I appeared by the living room door. 'We've had such a lovely evening! We painted each other's nails and found this wonderful program on the television. You just missed the part where the sex instructor ejaculated in Miranda's hair!'

I looked enquiringly towards Hannah. 'Is this your first bottle or your fifth?'

Mum narrowed her eyes. 'I know what you're implying, James,' she said, with exaggerated enunciation. 'But I assure you I'm cone sold stober.'

Hannah smiled. 'Sort of.'

'Yes,' Mum said, breaking into a grin. 'Almost.'

'Tell him about tomorrow,' Hannah said.

'Tomorrow?' Mum said. 'Oh yes! The alarms are set – Pilates starts at 8am!'

I forced back a smile. 'There's no way you'll make it to the gym that early.'

'Yes, there is,' Mum said. 'We'll sweat our hangovers away and come home feeling wonderful.'

'Well,' I said. 'I look forward to hearing about it. But for now, I'm off to bed. I'll see you pair of crazy cats in the morning.'

'Not if we see you first,' Mum shouted, which absolutely slayed both her and Hannah. Shaking my head, I turned and made my way to my room. Another two hours passed before Hannah and Mum turned in, too. They did not make it to Pilates the following morning.

Even more surprising than the bond Hannah shared with Mum were the changes she wrought in Dad. Almost as soon as Hannah arrived in Myreton, Dad began to spend a little less time in his workshop, involve himself a little more in conversations. At first, I assumed he was being polite, but pretty soon I realised that he actually enjoyed having her around.

There was no reason he shouldn't. Hannah laughed at all of his jokes and seemed sincerely interested in his opinions about modern pop culture and Hibernian's chances in the league. When he made a grumpy comment, she sailed over it entirely and brought the conversation back into more positive waters. She told him all of her funniest stories and asked for his views on everything from world politics to the clothes she wore. There was no way she could have eliminated his sadness, but she certainly helped make him feel a little calmer and a little lighter for the duration of her stay.

Our final Sunday together found Hannah and I in Edinburgh, first seeking out treasures in the city's second-hand bookstores and then at an exhibition of vintage travel photography that Hannah had been dying to see. The photographs were brilliant, but as usual my attention quickly drifted towards Hannah, to the way she studied every image from every angle before allowing herself to move on to the next. It always amazed me, her ability to be fascinated by things. Life, it seemed, was just that little bit more interesting and beautiful to her than it was to regular people. I supposed that was why she never got bored – because every day, every interaction was different to the last.

It took Hannah nearly two hours to make her way around the small gallery, and when she was done, she bought postcards of more than half the pictures. After the gallery, we ordered coffee and cakes at a nearby café. I turned my attention to the street outside, while Hannah took her postcards from her bag and became instantly absorbed by them all over again. 'My god,' she said, after some time. 'Don't they just make you want to *be* there?'

'Where? 1926?'

Hannah rolled her eyes and let out a huff of air. 'No,' she said, spinning the postcards round to face me. 'There! In

Paris and Madrid and Chicago and Cape Town and... everywhere!'

I shrugged. 'You'll be able to go soon enough, won't you. Another few days and the world's your oyster.'

Hannah gathered the postcards together and cleared her throat. 'Actually,' she said, with unnatural shyness. 'Rose Glen asked me to come back for a week or two next month, to help the new volunteers settle in. I was hoping maybe you'd put me up again.'

My mouth dropped open. 'You're shitting me,' I said. When Hannah shook her head, I burst out laughing. 'Hannah, that's... that's brilliant! It's wonderful! Now we'll be able to see that exhibition at the Portrait Gallery together. And, oh! Rufus Wainwright's playing the Usher Hall in December. I could get us tickets.'

'Okay,' Hannah said. 'If I'm here while he's playing.'

'Oh sure, yeah. Well, if that doesn't work, we can always see someone else.'

'Or,' Hannah said, looking up from the table, meeting my eyes, 'there's always next time. Or, you know, the time after that.'

I stared back at Hannah. Then snickered.

Hannah's brow furrowed. 'Why are you laughing?'

I shook my head. 'Doesn't matter,' I said. I snickered again.

'No, tell me,' Hannah said. 'Why are you laughing?'

'Hannah,' I said, 'you're talking as though we have some kind of future together.'

'That's right,' Hannah said, all seriousness.

My head was still shaking. Apparently, there was no way to stop it. 'Fine,' I said. 'If you say so.'

Hannah's mouth set in a hard line. 'Yes, I do.'

'Okay,' I said. 'I mean, you'll be travelling for a year here, studying for a year there. But yeah, sure, there'll be plenty of time for us to be together.'

Hannah threw up her hands in exasperation. 'Oh my god, James – just listen to me. I'll find the fucking time to see you. Alright?'

Hannah had made this last point rather too loudly. I turned and smiled apologetically at the rest of the diners, fearing some of them might have overheard. None of them had; they stared back at me, trying to understand why I was suddenly so eager to make friends with them.

'Fine,' I said, more quietly now. 'Tell me how you're so certain we can keep things going.'

A blush crept up Hannah's neck towards her face. 'Because I love you, James. I made my plans, but love's standing in my way now.'

'But what about your travelling?'

Hannah's blush deepened. 'I thought maybe you could come with me.'

There was a long pause. Then I said, 'You're serious, aren't you?'

Hannah nodded. 'As a heart attack.'

I leaned forward in my chair and stared at Hannah in disbelief. 'I don't know what to say.'

'Really?' Hannah asked. 'So, the conversation's over now?' She laid a hand against her chest. 'Oh, that's good. All that talk of commitment was starting to make me dizzy.'

Whether Hannah really meant that or not, I broke into an absurdly goofy smile. Reaching out for my cup, I raised it in a toast to our future, took a sip of coffee and leaned back in my chair, and as I looked back out of the window a great flood of relief washed over me because everything looked just a little bit brighter than it had a few minutes before.

OCTOBER 9 2005

'Sometimes the only way to stay sane is to go a little crazy.' That's what they say. But what happens if you venture too far into crazy-land and find yourself lost there, in a place where sanity isn't an option? It's happened to me, I think. I'm stuck in crazy, and it's killing me. Everything is a struggle. I'm becoming increasingly anxious, increasingly obsessive. I can't think or concentrate or string words together. My thoughts no longer belong to me. There's a devil inside my head.

I can't cope with feeling like I do now. I'm nuts, I've really gone mad. I don't want to keep going, but everyone seems to have other ideas, including my body, which seems to be so FUCKING INVINCIBLE that I fear I'll be stuck living in this hell for all eternity. Just imagining that makes me desperate. I struggle to go on.

16

HANNAH AND I WERE EATING A LATE BREAKFAST IN OUR pyjamas when we heard Mum's car turn into the street. She was an hour earlier than scheduled, and for one guilty moment I found myself pleading that some clerical error had prevented Emma from being discharged as planned. But when I reached the front porch I found Emma already standing in the driveway, looking overwhelmed and frightened. I threw open the front door and walked quickly towards her, my arms outstretched. She stiffened the instant I touched her and did not relax again until the moment I let her go. As Mum led her indoors, I realised that the rough ride we'd all predicted had already begun.

Sighing, I turned and walked towards the car. In the back seat, there was a suitcase and a thick binder full of papers. I grabbed the suitcase, and Hannah, who'd been following close behind me, reached for the file. When she caught the full weight of it, she exhaled sharply. 'My god,' she said. 'What the hell do they keep in this thing?'

I cast a bitter glance at the folder, the source of a thousand family arguments in the past few years. 'That, in there, is all the stuff they pretend to agree on before allowing Emma to come home.'

'What sort of stuff?'

I shrugged. 'Meal plans. Appointments. Rules and regulations. All the fun shit.'

Hannah looked at the folder, wrinkled her nose. 'Does she follow any of it?'

'Nope,' I said, heaving the suitcase past Hannah and towards the front door. 'Not a single fucking word.'

We arrived back inside to find Emma sobbing quietly against Mum's shoulder in the hallway. 'It's just a wee bit overwhelming,' Mum said, when she saw me and Hannah staring. 'No need to worry, though. It always takes a few days to readjust. Doesn't it, sweetie?'

This time Emma did answer, but her face was pressed so hard into Mum's shoulder that it came out sounding something like 'Hannph'. Mum shut her eyes for half a second, gathering her strength. 'And what about you two?' she asked. 'You'll be celebrating your last day together, I hope.'

Call it strange, but right at that moment I wasn't in the most festive of moods. Still, I smiled and nodded dutifully. Then, with Hannah still in close pursuit, I made my way to my room to prepare for the day ahead.

Half the day was gone by the time Hannah and I left Myreton, and with tomorrow already looming large, we tried to stuff ourselves as full as we could of our remaining time together. We took a final walk along Cranston beach, before moving onto Edinburgh, where we watched a movie and ate a final meal of nachos at the Filmhouse. I wanted none of those hours to end, but the clock kept ticking, the seconds kept passing by, and before we knew it the sun was setting and we were making our way home.

Neither of us said a word as we wound our way along the narrow country roads towards Myreton. While I stared stoically ahead of me, Hannah sat with her hand out of the window, and then put her head out, feeling her hair blowing behind her and the cool autumn wind against her face. The silence between us had grown so intense that I started visibly when, two miles from Myreton, Hannah suddenly grabbed hold of my arm and yelled for me to stop.

'What?' I asked.

'Stop the car,' she said. 'Please. I'm not ready to go home yet.'

I pulled into the side of the road and turned questioningly towards Hannah. But she was out of the car before I even had the handbrake on, and by the time I clambered outside myself she'd already leaped a fence and begun running at full speed across a stubbly field. 'What are you doing?' I shouted.

'Come over here and find out,' Hannah said, breathless.

Self-consciously, I climbed over the fence and began to tramp after Hannah. I'd completely lost sight of her in the darkness, but she continued to call to me, her voice growing louder and louder until finally I found her standing by a huge pile of freshly cut straw bales. 'You wanna play?' she asked, patting the straw.

'Oh, come on,' I said. 'How old are you?'

Hannah's lips set in a hard line. 'Humour me here, Mister,' she said, before turning and swinging a leg up to the top of the nearest bale. 'I don't get to do this sort of stuff in the city.'

So, I climbed up alongside Hannah and together we jumped around the bales, howling and laughing beneath the light of the partial moon. We did that until our energy was spent, then lay down side by side on the hay to catch our breath. Bats swooped through the inky darkness above our heads. An owl hooted its lonely call from a nearby tree.

'I'm not ready to go home yet,' Hannah said again, more quietly this time.

'I know,' I said. I found her hand and held it tight, and with tears in our eyes and an ache in our hearts, we gazed out once more into the glowing Milky Way.

Edinburgh Airport was as chaotic as ever the following morning. All around us, a sea of travellers moved like an unseen current, flowing like a wide river through the terminal. Here and there, small groups had stopped to study plasma screens showing arrival and departure times, causing a small eddy, but those who followed simply swept around them and continued on their way. Hannah and I stumbled through the crowds to check in our suitcase, then made our way to departures, where we turned to face one another in mournful silence.

'So, I guess this is it,' Hannah said.

I threw a sleeve across my eyes, coughed self-consciously as my lip began to tremble. I hadn't meant to cry. 'Ah shit,' I said.

Hannah shook her head, kissed me hard on the mouth. 'It's not so long,' she told me. 'Six weeks isn't so long.'

I nodded, though I already suspected that our time apart would stretch on for an eternity.

Hannah glanced at the clock above our heads. 'I have to go, okay?' she said. She squeezed my hand, then began to tiptoe backwards in the direction of security, smiling gently the whole time. And in that moment, in that final moment before she turned and vanished into the crowd, I was reassured. In that moment, I believed the smile. I believed that we could carry on as normal, that nothing between us had to change.

I should have known that fate wasn't done with me yet.

PART III

NOVEMBER 17 2005

It's time.

I can't stand this pain any longer. Things have just got too messy.

It would have happened soon enough anyway. I've only been delaying the inevitable. But I'm seeing things more clearly now. I'm finally ready to do the right thing.

I hope it won't cause too much pain. I hope they'll understand why I needed to do it. If they don't understand, I hope at least that they'll forgive me.

1

I WAS WATCHING *PORRIDGE* IN THE LIVING ROOM WITH DAD when the sound came. It was a strange sound, one I was unable to place over the canned laughter that exploded from the television. Had I imagined it? I sat up straight, pricked up my ears. In the same moment, the television screen went blank. I turned my eyes to Dad. He was holding the remote control in his hand, his entire body tense with concentration. I glanced nervously at him. He glanced nervously back at me.

We listened.

After a moment it came again, louder this time – a wounded howl. Dad and I threw ourselves off our chairs and raced through to Emma's room. There, we found Mum crouched down over a small pile on the floor. I studied it for a moment, and then a hot wave of nausea washed over me. The something had legs. Mum threw her head around to face us, her eyes wild. 'Call an ambulance, John!' she cried. Dad ran from the room and I grabbed the pair of legs and together Mum and I raised Emma onto her bed. Her face was ghostly, her mouth hanging open. 'Oh god,' Mum said.

'Please, no.' She held the middle two fingers of her left hand to Emma's neck, held them there for so long I thought something in me might burst. Then, finally, relief broke in her face and I knew that Emma was still there. Mum pulled Emma close into her, looked down at the face below her where the breath laboured in and out. 'Oh, baby,' she said. 'It's alright. It's going to be alright.'

I started to sob until Mum turned to me and said, 'Darling, I need you to put some of Emma's clothes together in a bag. Could you do that for me?' Blinking away tears, I nodded, and forced my eyes from Emma. That's when I saw the two pill boxes sitting empty on Emma's bedside table. Shock flashed through me, then, and I stumbled back a step. Actually stumbled.

'James?' Mum said. 'Don't think about that now. Do you hear me? Just go and sort the bag.'

I hardly remember the hour that followed. Sometime after I staggered from the room the ambulance showed at the corner of our street, its bright blue light cutting through the darkness. I hurried the paramedics inside and watched numbly as they shone lights and made tests and dispensed medicine. Then I was outside again, watching as Emma and Mum were driven off in the back of the ambulance, not even noticing the cold winter wind as it bit at my face.

Then Dad and I were in the car, and I was driving, fast and reckless, towards Edinburgh, my mind a million miles from the road ahead of me. There was no conversation. A couple of times Dad threw a hand over his face and mumbled some words, but they were addressed to no one. I didn't say a single thing.

At the hospital, Dad and I ran into the waiting room to find Mum sitting, pale and exhausted, in a hard, plastic chair. At the sound of our footsteps she turned her head heavily towards us, then struggled to her feet. 'She's still with the doctors,' she said. 'They haven't told me anything yet.'

'Was she awake when you got here?' Dad asked.

Mum shook her head. 'Not even close.'

I sat down to the right of Mum, who in turn patted the seat to her left, motioning for Dad to join us. But he shook his head, choosing instead to pace up and down, his hands clasped tightly in front of him, his head hung forward grimly. Now and then Mum reached over and squeezed my knee with a shaking hand, told me that I wasn't to worry. She meant to reassure me, but her voice betrayed her fear.

Dad was still pacing an hour later, when a doctor, a young female with a thin nose and a pulled-back ponytail, entered the waiting room. At the sound of her footsteps, he swung round to face her. 'How is she?' he said, his voice trembling.

'She's awake now,' the doctor said. 'She's very tired and woozy, but she's awake. Fortunately, the pills she took weren't able to take full effect before you found her.'

Dad swallowed hard before asking the next question. 'She'll be okay?'

The doctor nodded. 'From what we've seen so far, she's going to be fine.'

Dad's face fell into his hands and he began to cry. I turned and stared at him, shocked by his tears.

'The therapist's speaking with Emma now,' the doctor continued. 'But you'll be able to see her as soon as the consultation's over.' And with that, she smiled sympathetically and turned back towards the ward.

Dad continued to sob. When Mum reached out and laid her hand on his arm, he pulled away without even looking at her. But Mum wasn't to be discouraged; she took him by the forearm and drew him down into a chair. 'John,' she said, quietly. 'It's alright. She's going to be alright.'

'If anything had happened to her...'

'Shh,' Mum said, rubbing his shoulder gently. 'It wasn't your fault. It's not your fault.'

Dad shook his head, his face contorting angrily as he fought back the tears. 'I should have been there,' he said. Mum took his face in her hands and kissed the tears from his cheeks before resting her forehead against his. 'Our little baby,' he said. 'Our beautiful baby girl.'

I walked across the room and fixed my own tear-stained gaze on the darkened car park that lay outside the window.

Sometime past two in the morning, a nurse arrived to take us to Emma. We were desperately tired by then, so it took real effort to pull ourselves from our chairs and follow her down the ward. When we arrived outside the room, we were met at the door by a doctor, fresh from his conversation with Emma.

'I'm Doctor Steel,' he said, shaking each of our hands in turn. 'I thought I should speak with you before you went in to see Emma.' He took a deep, almost nervous, breath. 'Now, Emma's going to be fine. However, from what she's told me, it seems that this was an entirely serious attempt on her life.'

We all nodded wearily. None of us had even considered it might have been anything else.

'I know it's been a difficult night,' the doctor said, pushing the door to Emma's room open. 'But she's still very tired. Be patient with her.'

We stepped gingerly into the room to find Emma lying beneath a thick blanket on a cold, unwelcoming hospital bed. Her eyes were open but fixed on the ceiling directly above her. It took longer than it should have for her to register that we'd arrived. Dad had stopped crying after the nurse had led him from the waiting room, but in the second he saw Emma again his face crumbled and the tears fell once more.

'Don't cry, Dad,' Emma said, her voice small. 'Please don't cry. I didn't mean to.' Then she turned to Mum. 'I didn't mean to,' she said again, an exhausted tear creeping down her cheek. Mum moved forward and crouched by the bed, stroking and kissing Emma's face. 'It was mistake,' Emma said. 'It won't happen again.'

Mum nodded, kissed Emma again. But she knew. We all knew. There was a chance that Emma would give it another try. From now on, every time she came home from hospital, we'd spend our lives in a state of constant vigilance, watching for changes in her attitude that might hint at another attempt, keeping an eye out for any potential weapons, any possible poisons, that she might use to finish the job.

'Hey, Jamie,' Emma said, looking around Mum's shoulder. Her voice was hardly more than a whisper.

'Hey, baby sis,' I said. 'You doing okay?'

Emma nodded slowly, but her eyes were drooping. Moments later, her head fell back and she gave a faint snore.

For some time, we remained in silence in our plastic chairs, watching Emma sleep. Then, finally, when our own heads started to drop, we gathered our coats and made our way to the car. By the time we reached the hospital car park, the sun had already begun to rise.

I shucked off my shoes and fell, fully clothed, into bed as soon as we arrived back in Myreton. We'd arranged to visit Emma again in the early evening, and my plan was to sleep until then, but the sleep I got was fitful and restless, and when I awoke it was still only the middle of the afternoon. The thought of skulking around the house for four more hours seemed unbearable, and I knew I'd find no peace at all until I saw Emma again. So, as quietly as I could, I scribbled a note to my sleeping parents, grabbed the keys to my car, and set off once more for Edinburgh.

Back at the hospital, Emma was lying in bed, her head propped up by a mountain of pillows. She'd been dozing, but when she heard me hovering by the doorway her eyes opened and she patted the bed, beckoning me to her. She looked a good deal better than she had that morning, but I felt no less nervous as I crossed the room and sat down by her side. For the first time in over a month, the two of us were alone.

'How's it going?' I asked.

Emma's bottom lip trembled. 'It's going,' she said.

'As good as that?'

Emma rolled her head away from me and towards the window. 'They found a bed for me at Hope Park. I'm going back tomorrow.'

'They said that might happen,' I said, trying to hide my relief at hearing the news. 'I guess it's for the best. I mean, I know it won't be easy, but the doctors said –'

Emma whipped her head back around to face me. 'The doctors know shit!' she shouted. 'I'm not getting *any*where, and it's *killing* me. Do you hear? I have no motivation to get better. I'm too fucking scared to get better. Christ, Jamie, those fuckers are filling you full of hope, and I *hate* them for it.'

I stared at Emma, shocked. I probably could have counted on one hand the number of times she'd acknowledged her illness like that, when she hadn't taken the attitude that she was the reasonable one and the rest of us were crazy. Mum always welcomed those moments, when Emma seemed to accept that it was her own fucked up head and not everyone else that had led her to ruin. To me, though, they were almost worse than the usual insanity, because they forced me to see the person who was trapped inside.

'I'm so sorry, Jamie,' Emma said, tearfully. 'I wish I could find the person in me that everyone else seems to see. I know I must seem like such a failure next to her.'

'No,' I said. 'You don't. Not remotely.'

If Emma heard that, she chose to ignore it. 'Don't think I didn't try,' she said. 'I wanted so much to be normal. Really, I did. I've dreamed a thousand times of living an ordinary life, but it's just not possible.' She fell silent, catching her breath. 'Oh, Jamie,' she sighed. 'Who'd have imagined that food could be such a hassle? I know it shouldn't be a big deal but, by god, it's ruined me.'

I swallowed hard, my Adam's apple bobbing. 'Was it really worth killing yourself over, though?'

Emma's eyes fell to the ground. 'At the time it was. I'm sorry that I hurt you. I didn't want to do that.'

'Emma, what did you expect? That we'd dance the conga around your corpse?'

'I don't know,' Emma said. 'I wasn't exactly thinking straight at the time.'

'I just don't get it. Why on earth would you want to die?'

'I don't,' Emma said. 'I've never wanted that for a moment.'

'Then why?' I said, my lips trembling with emotion. 'Why did you do it?'

'Because I needed to stop the *pain*, Jamie.'

The trickle of blood in my ears turned to a roar. I pressed a palm against each of my temples, tried to ease some of the tension there. 'You have to promise you won't try any of that shit again.'

Emma tried to hold my gaze but couldn't. 'Can we just not talk about that?'

I fixed her with a stern look. 'You can't even promise?'

'No!' Emma said. 'I can't. I can't make a promise that big.'

I looked away, shaking my head in frustration. It must have hit a nerve with Emma, because she offered a rare concession. 'I'll try,' she said, more softly than before. 'I'll try to be good, try not to let you down. I can promise you that much. At least, I think I can. But I just... oh, I don't know. Oh, Jamie, can't we just change the subject?'

And so, I did. As usual, I did whatever the fuck Emma told me to do.

2

MUM AND DAD HAD BEEN EATING DINNER BEFORE I ARRIVED
back to Myreton, but as soon as I walked through the door,
they laid down their cutlery and began to bombard me with
questions. 'How was she?' they asked. 'Was she sitting up in
bed? Had she said anything? Did she seem any better than
before?'

'Yeah,' I told them. 'She was less than cheery, but definitely better.'

Mum and Dad immediately shed some of the weight
they'd been carrying for the past twenty-four hours. I blew
out a shaky sigh and started towards my room, but I hadn't
moved a yard when Mum put a hand on my arm. 'Are you
feeling the cold, darling?'

'No,' I said. 'Why?'

'You're wearing your jacket.'

'Oh,' I said. 'No, no. I just forgot to take it off at the door.'

A line appeared between Mum's brows. 'Well, we're
leaving for Edinburgh in a few minutes. We should be back
around ten. Is that okay?'

I shrugged. 'I'll see you when I see you.'

Mum smiled gently and patted me on the shoulder. And I moved away once more, grateful as hell that she hadn't touched me on the chest instead, because that's exactly where I'd hidden the half bottle of whisky I'd bought for myself on the journey home.

I hadn't meant to start drinking again, but there'd been days recently when I'd hardly had the energy to get out of bed. I needed something to help me undertake the painful operation of living, and alcohol, I knew, was the perfect remedy. Since Mum had found me doing battle with the hallway furniture at the beginning of the year, I'd been careful not to drink more than a glass or two of wine in the company of my parents. My real drinking, I did in secret. I always kept a bottle of something beneath my bed, along with a packet of mints to hide the smell of alcohol on my breath. I never got stupid-drunk, just maintained a nice, warm glow in the evenings and, when times were particularly bad, the hours after lunch.

That said, the evening that followed Emma's overdose had called for something more than usually extreme. I'd hoped the whisky would be enough, but within two hours it was all gone and I found myself trapped in some middling stage of drunkenness that had left me even more depressed than I might have been if I hadn't partaken at all. I made my way through the house in search of something else to drink, but stopped short when I passed an old framed photo of me and Emma on the dining room cabinet. Suddenly, all the wind was knocked out of me, and I slumped to the ground like a broken doll.

Oh, Emma. Why had she done it? How could she have done it? Was life really so painful? Was the world really so cruel? I'd heard her speak of suicide a hundred times, but never once had I imagined she'd reach a point where living truly seemed worse than dying.

I wouldn't be able to cope if she tried again. It wouldn't be fair, for her to leave completely, to feel nothing at all while I was left behind to pick up the pieces of my broken self. If she was ever to leave... If I ever had to say goodbye...

But no. It didn't do to have these thoughts. I couldn't let them get me. I had to distract myself. I wiped the tears from my face, then pulled my phone out of my pocket and called Hannah. I was almost relieved when she didn't answer. After all, what could she have done from such a distance away anyway? No, I needed a drink. This night called for drink. I looked at my watch – it wasn't yet ten. The County would close soon enough, but the Grange would be open until midnight. If I left now, there'd be just enough time to catch the last bus to Cranston. I grabbed my phone again and sent a text to Holly:

So, are you going to meet me for a drink tonight, or do I have to get drunk alone?

When I reached Cranston a half hour later, Holly and Steve were waiting for me at the bus stop, shivering inside their coats. 'What the hell, Jamie?' Holly asked, as I stepped out onto the pavement. 'Where's your jacket?'

Actually, I'd left it behind in my haste to get to the bar, but I wasn't about to admit that. 'It's not so cold,' I said, clenching my jaw to stop my teeth from chattering.

'James, I can't feel my hands,' Holly said. 'And Steve here's been farting snowflakes for the past ten minutes.'

I shrugged. 'All the more reason for us get a move on, then,' I said, marching past them.

We sat down at the bar and I bought a round of drinks. Holly and Steve supped their pints slowly, glancing nervously at one another as I attempted to inhale my own.

When my glass was empty, I slapped a hand down on the bar and set about re-establishing eye contact with the barman.

'Oh, no you don't,' said Holly, grabbing my hand, pushing it into my lap. 'You're not having another sip until you tell us what the fuck is going on.'

I looked towards my knees. My eyes were stinging like I was going to cry, and my hands, I now realised, were shaking beyond my control. Taking a deep breath, I told them everything that had happened in the past twenty-four hours.

When I was finished talking, there was a long silence. Holly and Steve sat tensely in their stools, staring hard at their drinks. Things were just starting to get awkward when, finally, Holly cleared her throat. 'I don't understand,' she said. 'Why would she want to die?'

'She didn't,' I said. 'She just got tired of living.'

Holly sat back in her chair and stared at me. 'I don't get it.'

'Yeah.' I ran a hand through my hair and felt very tired as I said, 'Welcome to the club.'

'You, too?' Holly asked, genuinely confused. 'Even after all these years?'

I nodded. 'Which is a shame, because at least then I'd have some chance of making things better. As things are, I'm just tired. And frightened. And really fucking angry.'

'James,' Steve said, laying a hand on my shoulder. 'Everything will be okay.'

'No, it won't,' I told him. 'I mean, yeah, it might be, but what the fuck? I'm supposed to leave here in two months. What the hell am I supposed to do if something happens while I'm away?' I looked imploringly at my two friends, but neither was able to answer. I shook my head irritably, the heat of tears suddenly in my eyes.

Steve squeezed my shoulder again. 'Things *will* get easier,' he said.

I nodded, not quite believing him, then turned to Holly and said, 'Do you think I could get that drink now?'

For the next hour, both Holly and Steve attempted to cheer me with sentimental talk of our school days but I didn't listen, having chosen instead to drink myself as subtly as possible into oblivion. By the time last orders were called I'd managed to force down three more pints of beer and two shots of whisky. I stood up and started towards the toilet, but my legs refused to cooperate and before I knew it they'd begun to stumble backwards towards the exit. Too surprised to change course, I simply whipped my head around to face my feet and carried on through the door.

The cold air hit my face like a slap as I lurched out of the bar. I stood still for a moment, allowing the wind to wash over me, then unfastened my trousers and took a piss against my shoe. I was so drunk fastening my fly that I stumbled and had to catch myself on the front wall of the hotel. Chuckling, I decided it was time to go home and turned resolutely in the direction of Myreton. I'd taken three steps when I fell sideways into a rhododendron bush.

I'd been thrashing around for some time before I heard muffled voices coming from somewhere above my head. I felt a tug on my feet, then a terrible dizziness as I was brought back to standing. When the world around me stopped spinning, I found Holly and Steve staring at me with very obvious concern. I shook myself free of their grip, teetering slightly as I battled to maintain my balance, and kicked the rhododendron hard, twice.

Holly put a hand on my arm to settle me. 'Would you calm down?' she said.

I looked angrily towards her. 'Why should I?' I shouted,

practically trembling with rage. 'Everything's so fucking shit, Hols.'

Holly nodded, her eyes filled with pity. 'I know,' she said.

I allowed my chin to fall tipsily to my chest. 'Why'd she have to do it?' I asked, my words coming out sluggish. 'What'd I've done if she'd succeeded?'

Holly and Steve's jaws tightened. 'Just... try not to think about that,' Steve said.

'Know what I think?' I said, ignoring the advice. 'If she ever *does* manage? I think I might just follow on right behind her.'

'Jamie!' Holly said, putting a hand over her mouth. 'Don't talk like that. It's crazy.'

'Oh, shush,' I said. 'I'm not talking about killing myself.' I leaned heavily against the wall of the hotel for a moment. My head was fuzzy, and I was having a hard time putting my words together. 'It's just I'd miss her too much,' I added, eventually, 'I'd try to go on, but soon enough I think I'd just sort of... cease to exist.'

I looked towards Holly, who turned away, too late to hide the tears that had come to her eyes. Standing next to her, Steve set his mouth in a hard line. 'You can't think like that, James,' he said. 'It's too dangerous.'

'Can't help how I feel,' I said, stubbornly.

'It's how you feel tonight, with a bellyful of alcohol. Things will seem better in the morning. For now, I'll get you a taxi home. Okay?'

'Don't wanna taxi,' I said, shaking myself from his grip. 'Wanna walk.'

'You want to walk home?'

I nodded.

'In the freezing cold?'

'Yes.'

'Drunk, and without a jacket?'

I nodded hard, almost falling over with the effort.

Steve smiled. 'Okay then.'

I looked at him with one half-closed eye. 'What'sa problem?'

'I can see the headlines already.'

'No headlines for me,' I said. 'I'm fine and dandy.'

'James,' Steve said, his tone sterner now. 'Just come here, would you.' He made a grab for my arm, but I stumbled outside of his grasp, and before I knew what I was doing I'd broken into an unsteady zigzag along the street, bouncing along walls and hedges as I went.

I woke up the following morning on death's door. My head throbbed like a bitch, my mouth felt like a carpet, and I was plagued by a desperate thirst that my increasingly exasperated dream-self had worked in vain to quench throughout the night. Cautiously, I opened my eyes. The daylight that poured through the window entered my eyeballs like thick needles to the brain. Immediately, I closed my eyes again, then cursed myself for having forgotten to close my curtains the night before.

Except they weren't my curtains. Were they? Very carefully, I levered up my right eyelid and peeked once more around the room. The mystery deepened. Not only were the curtains not mine, the bed didn't belong to me either. Neither did the wardrobe, nor the wallpaper, nor the pyjamas. *Oh god*, I thought, *I've been kidnapped*. A mild wave of panic passed through me, but I was too wretched to act upon it in any way except to lift the sheet above my head, close my eyes and fall back into unconsciousness.

I awoke two hours later to find Holly reading a magazine by the foot of the bed. 'Well, well,' she said, laying down her magazine. 'He's alive.'

'Oh god,' I said, grimacing. 'If that's true, then kill me now. There's not one bit of me that doesn't hurt.'

Holly's mouth twitched. 'Oh, sweetie,' she said. 'That's just your body reminding you that you're a fucking idiot.'

'Was I really awful?'

Holly nodded. 'And then some.'

I wrinkled my nose, thought hard, which hurt. 'I remember leaving the bar and, uh...'

'And then you ran off into the centre of town, where you proceeded to beat on the door of the co-op, demanding more beer.'

'Ah,' I said.

'Indeed,' Holly said. 'The neighbours were not impressed. After that, you had us chase you across the putting green to the end of town. It was ten past one when you finally collapsed outside the chip shop. We'd been chasing you for an hour.'

I stared hard at my hands, said nothing. Holly shuffled up to the top of the bed and flopped down next to me, her head against mine on the pillow. 'Jamie,' she said. 'Some of the things you said last night really freaked me out.'

'I'm so, so sorry.'

'I know,' Holly said. 'But please, don't ever, ever do it again. I don't want to go through that a second time.' Those words gave me such a bad case of the guilts that tears sprang to my eyes. Holly clicked her tongue in sympathy and pressed a hand to my chest. 'Jamie, listen to me. Things aren't always going to be so hard. You know that, don't you?'

'I have my doubts,' I said, my voice shaking.

'Hey!' Holly grabbed my chin and forced me to look at

her. 'Listen to me. Things are going to get easier for you. I know they are. Okay?'

I sniffed hard, gave a small nod. Holly let go of my face. 'You know,' she said, after a moment. 'I hate to admit it, but maybe this trip with Hannah will be good for you. Maybe you do need to get away from this place for a while, even if it does mean breaking my poor little heart.' Raising herself up on an elbow, she pressed her forehead against mine and looked at me through smiling eyes. 'We really do love you, you know.'

'I don't see why you should,' I said.

'Well, perhaps not. But it's true.' Patting me playfully on the cheek, she kissed my forehead, then laid my head against her chest. That seemed to be exactly what my body needed. Listening to the steady beat of Holly's heart, I felt peaceful for the first time in days. Sleep crept over me like a warm blanket.

3

I GRINNED STUPIDLY THE SECOND I SAW HANNAH WALK through the packed arrivals gate at Edinburgh Airport. When she spotted me a moment later, she wove quickly through the crowds and hurled herself into me with such force that I almost lost my balance. I closed my eyes, taking in her warmth, her smell, the taste of her mouth. After six weeks apart, I felt almost drunk in her company.

We spent the next five days walking the same streets and admiring the same shores that had acted as the setting for our first great adventure. Just as she had throughout those early months, Hannah packed our days with activities. She spent hours flicking through magazines or gazing at websites, keeping her eyes peeled for things we'd want to do. When she found something, she would add it to the list she kept of things that needed to be done. She was deeply proud of that list and took great satisfaction in crossing things off it. Sometimes I watched her write things she'd already done – 'coffee with James,' 'exhibition at the Dean Gallery' – just to score them out again.

So far, I'd managed to fend off Hannah's attempts to

discuss the trip we were to take the following month, but Hannah awoke on Friday determined to spend the evening planning our journey, and no matter how many exciting alternatives I offered over the course of the day she refused to be distracted any longer. So, it was with enormous trepidation that I joined Hannah and my laptop on my bed that night to talk – really talk – for the first time about where on Earth we were headed.

'So, this is only a rough plan,' Hannah said, once we were settled. 'But I thought Dubai would be a good place for us to start. Then maybe Thailand and Vietnam. New Zealand, Australia, Fiji, the Cook Islands, Hawaii, Mexico, Costa Rica, Cuba, New York. And, to finish, maybe Paris?' Hannah chuckled. 'Can you believe I'm twenty years old and I've still never been to Paris?'

I didn't answer her, just stared at my laptop screen, trying to comprehend the list of countries she'd mentioned, shocked by the ease with which it had rolled off her tongue. I waited until I could speak, then said, 'Are you sure we can afford all that?' As if money was the real cause for concern.

Hannah nodded happily. 'We can get a round-the-world pass for a couple of thousand Euro. If we live cheaply while we're away, there's no reason for us to spend more than we've saved.'

'Okay,' I said, trying to sound calm. 'But that list... I mean, wow, that's a lot of places. I think we'd struggle a bit for time.'

Hannah shook her head, grinning broadly. 'The passes last for a year,' she said. 'If you book Vienna on a separate ticket, we can spend a couple of weeks there, then start travelling properly around the end of January. If we do that, we'll be good to go all the way into 2007.'

I stopped listening then. A feeling of disbelief had taken

over me, and although I kept going through the motions, nodding when I was supposed to nod, smiling when I was supposed to smile, I wasn't really there at all. I stayed that way until Hannah dug me in the ribs. When I came around, she was smiling at me expectantly.

'Pardon?' I asked.

Hannah rolled her eyes. 'I said, it's tricky, isn't it, deciding a route. But, like I say, we don't need to confirm anything yet. So long as we keep moving clockwise, we'll never even need to plan our next stop till we're ready to book the flight. That's the beauty of these tickets.'

'Hmm,' I said, nodding. Beads of sweat were forming on my brow. 'Beauty.'

'So, shall we do that, then? Book your flight to Vienna tonight, then concentrate on the big trip when you get to Austria?' When I nodded, Hannah clapped her hands, gave an excited squeal. Taking my face in her hands, she kissed me hard on the mouth. 'My god, James. This adventure's going to rock our fucking world.'

I forced a smile but tried not to think any more about the future. My world had been rocked quite enough for one cold, December night already.

The following evening, Mum and Dad headed off to visit Emma, leaving Hannah and I with the house to ourselves. We'd been out earlier in the day to buy the ingredients for a curry and were in the kitchen preparing it when Hannah's phone vibrated in her pocket. I looked around just in time to watch the colour drain from her face as she read the message.

'Uh oh,' I said. 'Bad news?'

Hannah took a moment to collect herself, then shook her head. 'No,' she said. 'It's nothing.'

'You look as though you've seen a ghost.'

'James,' Hannah said, shaking her head impatiently. 'Just... just give me a minute, okay?' Then, before I could say anything more, she turned and made her way into my room, shutting the door quietly behind her.

Two hours later, Hannah still hadn't reappeared and I was growing nervous. I hated to bother her when she was in one of her moods, but we'd agreed to spend the evening at the Grange and were already running late. I walked towards my room, but as soon as I reached the door I lost my nerve. I stood stupidly in front of it for a full two minutes until the spectacle of my own cowardice became impossible to bear. I knocked softly, and when there was no answer stepped timidly inside.

Hannah was sitting on the side of my bed with her back to the door and gave no indication that she'd heard it open. I flicked the light switch and walked over to get a better look at her. She was wearing a look of infinite sadness and was nowhere near ready to leave. I took a deep breath. Then I threw on my best fake smile and clapped my hands together. 'Well, come on. Let's get you up and ready for tonight, shall we?'

At the sound of my voice, Hannah turned to me and met my eyes. Her own were entirely without feeling. 'James,' she said. 'You can stop talking to me like a child. There's really no need to patronise me.'

I sat down next to Hannah. 'I'm sorry,' I said. 'I get nervous when you're like this.'

'Well, you shouldn't,' Hannah said. 'I know you're worried we're running late for the Grange, but I've no intention of letting anybody down. This is hardly my first attempt at meeting up with friends, you know.'

Wow. That was a bit harsh, but, 'Okay, point taken. I'm sorry I bothered you. I'll leave you in peace.'

'Oh, sit still,' Hannah said, unnecessarily, since I'd made no attempt to get up. 'Let's face it, I've already spent enough time in my own company tonight. Can you pass me my make-up bag?'

I picked up the bag from my chest of drawers and threw it down beside her on the bed. 'I don't understand,' I said. 'You seemed just fine, and then suddenly you were gone.'

Hannah glanced at me, broke into a little smile. 'James, we've known each other for nearly a year now. That should have been long enough for you to realise I'm a little peculiar.'

I smiled teasingly. 'Just a little?'

Hannah grinned, and punched me playfully on the arm. It hurt a bit, but I didn't tell her.

'So, are you going to tell me what's bothering you?' I asked.

Hannah sighed. It was a long sigh, weary and worldly-wise. 'Lots of things,' she said. 'But it's Christian today. He's started sending me texts, telling me he misses me and loves me. He wants to try again, he says.'

'Oh,' I said. 'What did you write back?'

Hannah grabbed her favourite cherry-red lipstick from her bag. 'What do you think?' she said. 'That I'd moved on, that there was no chance for us. The truth, basically. I just feel terrible. It was hard enough to break his heart once. I didn't think I'd have to do it again.'

She blew her nose, then stood up and checked herself in the mirror. Happy with what she saw, she laid down her lipstick and walked to the window, where she spent a couple of minutes staring out into the street. By the time she returned to the bed, I saw that some of the colour had returned to her face. Smiling, she grabbed her suitcase, and began to throw an assortment of dresses onto the bed next to me. 'Now,' she said, 'if you don't mind, I'd like a little privacy while I make myself look beautiful. Just give me five minutes. Then I'll be good to go.'

She wasn't good to go for another hour. When, around nine o'clock, we finally arrived at the Grange, we were quickly joined at the bar by Holly. 'It's good to see you,' she said, kissing us both. 'Wow, Hannah, I *love* the necklace.'

The bad feeling between the Hannah and Holly had healed in the past couple of months, on the surface at least, though there was still something incredibly stiff about their conversation, about the way they acted around one another. Hannah returned Holly's smile and thanked her for the compliment before making her way to the opposite end of the room, where she quickly fell into conversation with Will.

'So, how *is* Mad Mary?' Holly asked, the coast now clear.

'She's fine, thank you,' I said. Then, after a moment's reflection: 'Still a bit mad.'

'No kidding,' Holly said, dryly. 'You still in love?'

'Yep,' I said, grinning. 'You jealous?'

Holly shook her head. 'She's not my type.'

I'd usually have laughed then, but I had some news to break to Holly, and no idea how to let it be broken. I'd planned the entire conversation an hour before, but now, standing by Holly's side, I was almost too afraid to speak. It wasn't that I was frightened of upsetting Holly. It was just that saying the words out loud would make everything seem so much more real. Still, what else was there to do? I took a deep breath and told her everything all at once.

When I was finished talking, Holly's face was slack with

amazement. She shook her head slowly and said, 'Well. A year's a good deal longer than I bargained for.'

I told her the feeling was mutual.

'And it's definitely happening?' she asked. When I nodded, she studied her drink, thinking hard, before looking back towards me. 'Well,' she said, 'like I said, it certainly won't do you any harm to get away from things for a while. And I truly hope you'll have a magical time. It's just...'

'Just what?' I asked.

'Well, Christ, Jamie, I can't believe you're going to spend a whole year travelling with *her*.'

I followed Holly's eyes towards Hannah, who was in fits of giggles at something Will was saying. It was almost impossible to believe she was the same girl who'd been staring so hopelessly at the darkened wall of my bedroom only a couple of hours earlier. It seemed as though there was no level resting-place for her. All the time, she was either terribly down or else soaring. Holly was right – life with Hannah could be difficult. But it could also be wonderful, and as I watched her there, laughing by the bar, I experienced a shudder of happiness. *It's true*, I thought. *When I'm with her, I am living a life.*

4

By the middle of December, Emma had been in Hope Park for a month, and had long since passed her breaking point. I'd visited her twice a week since her readmission, and on every occasion, I'd spent an exasperating hour attempting, unsuccessfully, to coax her out from under her blankets, where she'd lain in wretched silence since breakfast.

It was a shock, then, when I visited Emma with Mum and Hannah to find her not only out of bed but also busy writing at her desk. Then, instead of racing back under her blankets at the sight of us, Emma stood up from her desk and ushered the three of us good-naturedly onto her bed. I looked at her questioningly, but she made no effort to explain herself, just waited until we were all comfortable before sitting back down on her chair.

Mum and I looked towards one another. This was very unusual. Nothing like it had happened in years. Was it for real? Had Emma somehow staged some kind of freak recovery? We held a little unspoken conversation with one another from across the mattress but found no answer to our questions. I decided to ask one of my own directly. 'Aren't you going to close your door?' As a rule, Emma always kept her door closed during visits in order to escape the watchful eyes of the Hope Park staff.

'No, no,' Emma said, with something approaching good cheer. 'Better to let some fresh air in.'

Mum and I glanced at one another again, then gave a shrug. *Fine*, we were saying. *Just go with it*. After all, it beat anything else we'd faced in the past few years. Maybe we were finally being rewarded for our patience. I lay back on the bed, while Mum crossed her legs and set about filling us in on news about friends we'd never met or couldn't remember meeting. Normally, Emma lost interest in Mum's gossip within seconds, but today she nodded dutifully as each story unfolded. Once or twice, I think, she even smiled.

I should have guessed that something was up. I should have wondered why Emma was suddenly so keen to abandon routines that were years in the making, why her attention was so firmly fixed on a corridor she'd always worked so hard to ignore. Later, I'd wonder how I could have been so stupid, so given over to carelessness, despite all the signs. At the time, however, I suspected nothing until an hour into the visit, when Emma stood up and began to creep quietly across her bedroom carpet.

Mum was first to notice. 'Off to the loo?' she asked. But Emma gave no answer, just continued to prowl towards her door like a leopard to its prey.

I looked out into the corridor but saw nothing that she might be waiting to pounce upon. 'What are you up to, Ems?' I asked, laughing nervously.

'I, uh...' Emma said, before tailing off. She poked her head outside of the door and looked cautiously around.

'Emma,' I said. 'You're being weird.'

But she wasn't. She was biding her time. In the next second, she leapt out of the room. A cry went up from the three staff members at the nurses' station as she crashed through the exit door of the ward and into the building's main corridor. Yelling desperately, I leapt off the bed and sprinted after her.

Two of Emma's nurses had given chase before me, but for a pair of health professionals they were profoundly unhealthy, and I caught up with them both before they even left the building. Together, we burst through the door just in time to watch Emma dart around a corner fifty yards away. I raced off ahead of the nurses, and soon left them trailing behind.

By the time I reached the corner, Emma was obviously tiring. I ran as hard as I could and quickly began to bridge the gap between us. By the time we were ten yards from one another, Emma's pace had slowed to a crawl, though she still clearly held some vague hope of escape. 'Jesus, Emma,' I shouted. 'Would you just stop for a minute?'

She wouldn't. Her whole body was tense with effort as she pushed herself forwards. 'Emma, this is crazy,' I yelled.

'I'm not going back, Jamie,' Emma said, breathlessly. 'You can't make me go back.'

'Emma,' I shouted. 'Please!'

'You don't know what it's like in there,' Emma said. 'I can't stand it anymore.' She stumbled slightly, threw out a hand against a wall to steady herself.

'This isn't the way to change things.'

'They won't make me better, you know,' Emma said. 'I swear. They can hold me in there for as long as they like, but they'll never make me better.' She reached a lamppost and hugged herself against it, desperate to keep herself upright. 'Oh god. My chest hurts, Jamie.'

'Emma,' I said, taking a step towards her. 'You need to see a doctor.'

Emma looked at me desperately. 'You could tell them you couldn't find me,' she said. 'Tell them you lost me on the High Street. You'd do that much for me, wouldn't you?'

'There's nowhere for you to go, Emma. You have to come with me...' But Emma had stopped listening. Her eyes suddenly widened as they moved from my own to a space above my left shoulder. I looked around to see the two nurses stumbling breathlessly towards us. Desperately, I held up a hand to them. 'Wait,' I shouted. 'Please, just give us a minute.' But their pace didn't change. I looked back towards Emma, who glanced at me, her eyes glistening with tears, before turning to run. But she was too exhausted to make a second attempt at escape. She collapsed against the pavement before she'd even taken a step.

Dizzy with fear, I threw myself upon Emma and pressed myself against her, keeping her warm against the biting cold. In a few seconds, the two nurses were by my side, followed quickly by Mum and Hannah. I leaned away from Emma, inviting the nurses to take over, but Emma wouldn't let them near. 'Please, Jamie,' she said, looking at me pleadingly. 'You do it. If I have to go back there, I'd rather it was you who took me.' She raised her arms to be lifted up, and I wrapped mine around her. As I picked her up, I could feel her body like sticks in a bag, her ribs like some fragile bird-cage beneath my hands.

Emma sobbed quietly as I carried her back to Hope Park. Mum stayed by our side the whole way, squeezing Emma's hand but saying nothing, while behind us the two nurses dabbed their sweating faces with handkerchiefs and worked desperately to find their breath. Bringing up the rear was Hannah, silent and sombre and staring numbly at the ground beneath her feet. Not one person failed to stop and stare at our odd little procession as we traipsed back to the hospital.

Back at the ward, I lay Emma down on her bed and then joined Mum and Hannah by the nurses' station while Emma was checked over by a couple of doctors. Hannah remained silent and expressionless in her chair, her head turned to watch the rain falling outside the window. Mum, meanwhile, was crouched on the edge of her seat, a clenched fist on each knee, glaring into the middle distance. Her normally calm face had given way to a look of fury, her nostrils flaring and her eyes narrowed. Save for a few fleeting moments when she shook her head and mumbled some angry thought beneath her breath, she remained completely still.

When the doctor came out of the room and gave his permission for us to see Emma, Mum was ready. Before I'd even thought to move, she jumped to her feet and stormed past the doctor into Emma's room. Emma was lying miserably on her bed, but this didn't seem to bother Mum in the slightest. 'You selfish little shit,' she said. 'How could you even *dream* of doing that to us?'

Emma didn't answer. Her face was pressed against her pillow. I started to say something placating, but Mum only glowered at me before continuing.

'Tell me, Emma,' she demanded. 'I want to know. What the hell were you up to?'

Still no answer.

'Where were you even going to go?' Mum asked. 'Come on, you can tell me that much, at least.'

Emma peeled her face from her pillow, just far enough for her to speak. 'I wanted to go to London,' she said.

Mum breathed very deeply, trying hard to maintain her

composure. 'But you don't know a single person down there,' she said.

Emma shifted to look straight into Mum's eyes. 'That's why I wanted to go. I wanted to disappear for a while, go somewhere I could just blend in.'

Mum's cheeks flushed, but her voice remained steady as she continued. 'And how exactly did you plan on blending in?' she asked. 'You left the ward in your pyjamas, Emma. You had no money. You had nowhere to go. And you look like shit. For god's sake, they wouldn't even have let you on the train.'

'I'd have managed fine,' Emma said, stubbornly.

Mum studied Emma for a moment and crossed her arms over her chest. 'Darling, if you truly believe that, then you're even more sick than I thought.'

Emma glared at Mum, her teeth gritted. 'No, I just want *out* of here.'

Mum glared back. 'Well in that case, you'd better start behaving yourself, hadn't you?'

And there it was; the final straw. Emma sprang onto her knees. 'You don't *want* me to get out,' she snarled. 'You *like* it when I'm in here. You're no fucking better than those stupid fucking doctors out there.' She leapt onto the carpet, bawling, kicking, flipping her bedside table. 'It's not FAIR!' she yelled. 'You have to get me out of this FUCKING PLACE. I MEAN IT! Get me the FUCK OUT OF HERE!' She kicked her bed, took off her glasses, and smashed them – literally smashed them – against her wall.

Mum stared for a moment at the broken glasses on Emma's floor. Then, without raising her eyes, she left the room without a word. A second later, Emma limped back to bed, where she crouched down with her knees against her chest. Hannah had backed herself against a wall and was staring, pale-faced, at the debris on the carpet. I tried to offer her a reassuring smile but found I couldn't, so I turned to Emma and, nodding towards the broken lenses on her floor, said, 'You know it'll take a week or more to replace those, don't you?'

'I don't care,' Emma said. 'I just want to get out of here.'

'So that you can starve yourself again?'

'Oh, fuck off, James,' Emma said.

I closed my eyes, sighed heavily. 'I don't understand it,' I said. 'I can't understand how you can hold so much against these people. They're only trying to make your life better, Emma. They only want to help you, for Christ's sake.'

Emma found my eyes and held them. 'Well, like I said, James, you can fuck off.'

I don't know if it was rage or grief that began to fill my chest right then, but whatever it was I swallowed the feeling down. It wasn't an act of surrender – I just knew it would do no good to argue any further. I was tempted to follow Emma's example, to lie down and rock myself into oblivion, but now wasn't the time. Crossing the room, I sat down next to Emma on the bed and placed a hand on her bony shoulder. Emma flinched at the touch, then surprised me by falling into my arms. 'It's going to get better,' I whispered, as softly as I could. But Emma said nothing, just stared at her bed sheets, sobbing quietly into my chest and feeling sorry for herself and the whole world.

Hannah remained distant in the hours after we left Glasgow, so that evening I decided to cheer her up by cooking us dinner while Mum and Dad visited Emma. I made a real effort, trying out a recipe from one of Mum's *Good House-*

keeping magazines and decorating the table with a lighted candle and some fancy napkins folded into swans. The whole thing was supposed to look romantic, but with just the two of us at the table we looked more like one of those royal couples in an old movie, where the king and queen are sat so far apart they can't hear one another speak. Ironically, it was an arrangement perfectly suited to the occasion, as Hannah seemed determined to continue her silence through the entire meal. I'd only taken a few bites when I finally lost patience and asked her what was wrong.

Hannah stared deeply into her pasta bake and said, 'I don't like to talk badly about anybody, but I really hated how cruel Emma was to you today.'

'She wasn't being cruel to *me*,' I told her. 'She was being cruel to her doctors. And to Mum. Besides, she wasn't being cruel.'

'James, she told you to fuck off. Twice.'

'Yes,' I said. 'Because she was upset. She didn't mean anything by it. And anyway, I told her off for that.'

'No, you didn't,' Hannah said. 'You never have, not once in all the time I've seen the two of you together. You're always too eager to please, too desperate to spare her feelings. She takes advantage of that.'

I laid my fork down on the table. 'It sounds like you're holding something against her,' I said.

'Can you blame me?' Hannah said. 'After all, I see what it does to you and your parents. It breaks my heart to watch you all struggling like you do. And yes, I know it's not Emma's *fault* as such, but on some level, at least, she picks the words she uses, she decides on the actions she takes.'

'It's not true,' I said. 'For god's sake, Hannah, *try* to understand.'

'Oh, I do try,' Hannah said. 'Believe me, I do.'

I grabbed hold of my napkin and pressed it to my face, swallowing back my anger. 'Look, I feel bad talking about Emma like this. She's really struggling with her illness at the moment. She'll always struggle.'

'Will she always be an asshole?'

The room fell silent, save for the pounding of my heart. Very slowly, I lowered the napkin from my face until Hannah appeared from over it. 'What did you say?' I asked.

Hannah squared her shoulders defiantly. 'You heard me,' she said.

'Emma's a very sick girl, Hannah.'

'Yes, I know. But that doesn't give her the right to make life so difficult for others, too.'

Maybe there was some truth to that, but I was far too angry to concede the point. 'You're being unfair,' I said.

Hannah glared at me from across the table. I stared right back, my fingers curled tightly around my glass of wine. This continued for some time until, finally, Hannah shook her head in frustration and snatched up her fork. 'For goodness' sake,' she said. 'Let's just shut up and eat before we drive each other crazy.'

But I was too far gone to return quietly to my meal. 'It's fine,' I said, standing up and grabbing my coat. 'You enjoy your dinner.'

Hannah looked up at me, with an expression at once disdainful and imploring. 'James, you don't have to be like this.'

'It's fine,' I said again, struggling into my shoes. 'I'm going for a walk, okay?'

'James, please!' Hannah said. 'We need to talk about this!'

But I'd already reached the door, and without looking back I stormed off into the night.

My breath left me the moment I stepped outside. The air was painfully cold, and the few others who'd braved the night were wearing heavy coats and gloves and scarves draped up to their chins. As I walked past them, my hands in my pockets and my teeth chattering, I began to wish I'd put as much care into covering up before storming outside.

My first thought on leaving the house had been to drink, but all the shops in the village were closed for the evening and I was feeling far too antisocial to join other drinkers in one of the local bars, and so I walked to the end of the main street and continued up Myreton Hill, where I sat, shivering furiously, on one of the benches that bordered the golf course. Below me lay the North Sea, the water shining in the faint moonlight that crept through the clouds. In the distance, there were lights from a few houses but it was very dark where I sat. There'd been a time when I was afraid of the dark. As a child, I would lie awake at night, listening for danger, my bedroom door open so I could hear the voices of my parents. But it was a different story these days. These days, the darkness was one of the few things that helped me relax.

As my mind began to settle, I was able to reflect on my argument with Hannah. Already, part of me knew I'd been too quick to lose my temper. I always tried to remain reasonable when the subject of Emma came up, but the last few years had left me battered and bruised, and my patience had been exhausted. Nowadays, a person only had to look at Emma the wrong way and I'd begin to fantasise hitting them with something heavy. Like a freight train.

I remained on the bench until I could stand the cold no longer, then groaned to my feet, my legs having stiffened in the few minutes I'd been sitting, and began the short walk home. Hannah had been crouched on my bed reading while

I'd been away, but in the moment I returned, she placed her book down and crept wordlessly under the blankets. Flicking off the light, I climbed into bed and found her head with my hands. It was turned away from me, so I leaned forward and kissed her gently on the back of the ear before bidding her goodnight.

She made no attempt to answer.

5
_____

ALTHOUGH OUR ARGUMENT LEFT SOMETHING OF A BAD TASTE in our mouths, Hannah and I recovered our tempers well enough to enjoy her final three days in Scotland. And if the farewell, when it came, was less dramatic than before, it was only because our second separation was to be half as long as our first.

No, the real drama resumed the evening after Hannah left, with a quiet knock on my bedroom door. It was Mum who knocked, and when she stepped inside, she crossed my room and sat down on the end of my bed without once making eye contact with me. She was trying to smile, trying to look calm, but her face was rigid with tension. 'Are you okay?' I asked.

Mum's arms were folded tightly across her chest, her foot tapping furiously against my carpet. It was some time before she spoke. 'It would appear that changes are afoot,' she said. 'For some reason, Emma's doctors seem to be coming around to her argument that hospital isn't helping her.'

My stomach turned. I felt my insides grow warm in an unpleasant way. 'What do you mean?'

'I mean that they may start looking for alternatives to hospital.'

'But... but there aren't any alternatives to hospital, are there? No doctor in his right mind would consider letting Emma loose in the real world.' I looked desperately towards Mum, pleading with her to say something, anything that might reassure me, but no words came. 'They're just humouring her,' I said. 'They're just trying to keep her spirits up. They'd have to be crazy to –'

'James,' Mum said, laying a hand gently on my knee. 'They've set up a meeting for the middle of next month.'

I tried to take a deep breath, tried to relax, but the air around me had grown heavier. Everything had grown heavier. I felt buried, as beneath an avalanche, by the weight of Mum's news. I closed my eyes tightly, waited until I could speak again. 'How long before she gets out of hospital?' I finally managed to ask.

'I don't know.'

'Yeah, but are we talking about weeks or months or what?'

'I don't know, James.'

'But they'll at least give us plenty notice, won't they?'

'James!' Mum snapped. 'I don't *know*. You try calling the hospital if you want to know more. But I doubt you'll have any more luck gathering information than I've had in the past week.'

'Okay,' I said. 'I'm sorry. I didn't mean...' Then Mum's words sank in. 'The past *week*? Hang on, this has been arranged for a week? Why didn't you tell me before?'

Mum bit down on her lower lip. 'I thought you might leave for Vienna before the meeting.'

'You thought –'

'I mean, I hoped you might.'

Groaning, I pressed a thumb down hard against each temple. 'In other words, you were going to let me leave without telling me.'

Mum looked at me, her eyes glistening. 'I didn't want to worry you,' she said.

I gave a frustrated sigh. 'You can't keep this sort of stuff from me. I'm not a child anymore.'

'There was no point in ruining your trip,' Mum said.

I shook my head. 'It would have been ruined far more if I'd learned all this from an Internet café in Viet-fucking-nam,' I told her.

Mum swivelled her neck to meet my gaze. Her expression hadn't changed, but I saw hurt in her eyes. I'd wounded her. 'Try to understand,' she said, after a long pause. 'I only want to protect you.'

I opened my mouth to reply but found I couldn't. Dropping my head, I took a few deep breaths, trying to relieve some of the weight that was pressing down on my chest. I couldn't tell if the pain was anger or panic, but it didn't matter. There was no way the conversation could end positively from here. I was relieved when Mum used the silence that had fallen between us to stand from my bed and leave the room.

I spent some time gathering my senses, then called Hannah, only to be told over a messy background of music and laughter that she was too busy to talk, and to call again the next evening. The day that followed was a write-off, the hours dragging as I waited impatiently to find some solace in Hannah's words of comfort. But on that second evening exactly the same thing happened, and it happened again the evening after that. My feelings were beyond hurt. I couldn't believe how much Hannah was relishing her newfound independence from me. It began to feel like some sort of punishment, as though she was slapping me across the face with her contentment.

While Hannah embraced Vienna society, I sank into a little bubble all of my own making. For the first time since I'd met Hannah, the old feeling of fear and panic had well and truly returned. I woke up with it and carried it around with me all day. The agony wore me out, and, whenever I was alone, I simply gave out and fell fast asleep. Christmas came and went, and a week later 2005 came to a close, but I hardly noticed any of it. I made an occasional trip to see my friends in Cranston, but my heart was no longer in the visits at all. For the most part, I spent my evenings drinking in the comfort of my room or, if I became overwhelmingly bored of my own company, at the County.

The night before the meeting I tried to call Hannah, but there was no answer, and no answer when I tried again. I left a message, asking her to ring me when she got home, then grabbed the TV remote and slumped onto the sofa to await her call.

I was deep asleep when the phone rang. At first, I thought it was the alarm clock and threw out a hand to hit the snooze button, but the clock wasn't there and neither was my bedside table. I forced my eyes open and realised I was still on the couch, shivering wildly and aching all over. Groaning loudly, I reached inside my pocket and grabbed my phone.

'Hey, Mister!'

I looked at my watch. It was seven thirty in the morning.

'Why are you calling so early?' I asked. Then, remembering my message to her the night before, added, 'Or so late. You were supposed to ring when... Wait, did you just get home now?'

'Yes!' Hannah said. 'I had the most wonderful time. We ate some amazing food at a little café around the corner from Stephansdom, and then danced the whole night at Flex. I caught the train home this morning just in time to watch the sun rise over the Danube. It was so beautiful.'

'Wow,' I said. 'And to think you'd planned to spend last night at home.'

'Yes, well, it all happened at the last minute. Sue called to let me know that...' She stopped talking then, suddenly aware of my tone. 'Are you okay?'

I breathed out through my nose, audibly. 'You don't remember, do you? It's Emma's big meeting today, the one I've been trying to tell you about for the past three weeks. You promised to be there last night to talk with me. To help me... prepare, or whatever.'

'Oh. I'm sorry. I forgot. I was –'

'Having too much fun,' I said. I let the accusation hang in the air.

'James,' Hannah said, after a moment. 'You're putting too much pressure on me. I'm your girlfriend, not your counsellor.'

'What are you talking about?' I said, incredulous. 'For God's sake, I'm not asking you to lie me down on some leather sofa. Just... be there.'

'I told you I was sorry,' Hannah said. She didn't sound sorry, though; just angry and hurt.

'I really needed you last night,' I said.

Hannah exhaled slowly. 'I'm too young for this shit,' she said, just loud enough for me to hear.

'Well, if it's too much fucking trouble –'

I stopped talking then, and so did Hannah, but we made it clear to one another that we were still on the other end of the line by throwing out a series of disgusted snorts and exaggerated sighs. After considering my position, I decided that I'd talk with Hannah some more *if* she offered some sort of apology for the way she'd acted. One thousand miles away, Hannah had reached exactly the same conclusion. We realised this in the same moment, and the snorts and sighs subsided as we began to consider an alternative plan of action. There was only one real alternative, of course...

'Look, I have to go.'

'Yeah, fine. Me too.'

'Bye.'

'Mmph.'

Click.

I was shaking when I got off the phone, shivering violently as if I were standing in a freezing gale. I sat down as still as I could, waited for the shaking to pass. It felt like fury, but it also felt like a panic. For weeks, I'd felt less and less in control of my fate, but now things were getting messier by the day. Hannah and I were arguing, and events at home were spinning entirely out of control. And yet, in less than a week, I was due to leave for Vienna. For the first time in months, I had absolutely no idea what to do. And I was completely terrified.

6

A FEW HOURS AFTER HANNAH'S CALL, I FOUND MYSELF, bleary-eyed and exhausted, in the Hope Park waiting room. I was practically running on empty, and yet I could hardly stay still. I kept fidgeting, crossing one leg and then the other. I wanted desperately to bite my nails, but in the past few days I'd chewed them all to the quick and just looking at them was painful. I tried biting a couple anyway, but they still hadn't healed from the previous evening. Soon the taste of blood was in my mouth.

Mum and Dad were sitting to either side of me. Dad, like me, was shifting impatiently in his chair, his sweaty palms clenched like pale starfish against his knees. Mum, meanwhile, had set her gaze outside the room's sole window. Her face, rigid with tension, looked tired and frightened. Both seemed to have aged a decade in the past few hours.

We'd been sitting in silence for ten minutes or more when Emma arrived, her face pale, her eyes edged sharply in red. Mum, as usual, was first to her side, offering words of reassurance, trying to make her sit down, but Emma couldn't rest and spent her time pacing the small waiting room as though determined to wear a trail in the carpet. I was ready to run screaming from the room by the time a junior doctor finally arrived to usher us into the meeting.

Inside the room, the significance of the meeting was clear. An ensemble of doctors and other professionals were all sitting in a great circle of chairs. I already knew Rosa and Elaine from their regular trips to Myreton, and both of them smiled and waved when I looked over. Apart from them, the only other person I'd ever met was Doctor Bell, the head consultant. A giant of a man, he was one of the few professionals that Emma had remotely liked since her spells in hospital had begun. He said a quick hello, and then invited his colleagues to tell us their names. I forgot all of them instantly.

'I think it's only fair to start with you, Emma,' Doctor Bell said, once the introductions were over. 'After all, you're the reason we're all here today. So, tell us, how do you feel? How do you think things are going?'

On entering the room, Emma had immediately fixed her gaze on the floor. It had remained there throughout the introductions, and it remained there now. Had it not been for the tiny shrug that followed Doctor Bell's question, I might have wondered whether she was even awake.

'Do you fancy elaborating on that shrug?' Doctor Bell said, smiling gently.

'It's not good,' Emma said. After such a long silence, her voice was hoarse. She cleared her throat before continuing. 'I know I'm not the ideal patient, but this mess isn't my entire fault. Yes, I fight, but only because you people don't listen to me. For years, you've been telling me what to do, forcing me again and again to follow some stupid recovery plan that I just can't stick to. You've never once stopped to ask what I think about all of this.'

Doctor Bell brought his hands together into a steeple near the middle of his chest and leaned forward on his chair. 'Okay,' he said. 'What do you think about it?'

Emma took a deep breath. 'When I first got here, you told me the road to recovery was about more than the numbers on the scales, but since then you've become obsessed with those numbers yourselves. The focus has shifted from my head to my body, even though we all know my head's the real problem here. Your entire treatment plan has become nothing more than a pointless weight-gaining exercise.'

'So, what do you want to happen?' Doctor Bell asked.

'I want a break,' Emma said. 'I want a break from all this shit, from all this pressure you put on me all the time. I'm tired of spending my life fighting people who are trying to change parts of me I'm not ready to change. Please, let me have some say in how I can be helped. Give me a chance for once to work with someone who's actually willing to listen to me. Give me a chance to get away from hospital, from all this stress. I need to clear my mind a little. I need you to give me a little of my life back. Because at the moment I'm not living – I'm only existing. And I'm tired. I'm just so fucking tired.'

Doctor Bell's eyes were fixed on Emma. Like the rest of us, he was clearly surprised to hear her speaking so openly. We'd all been to plenty of these meetings before, and in each of them Emma had shrunk inside herself as soon as her company had begun discussing and debating her health. She'd occasionally spoken, but only when she'd been asked a question, and, so long as she held her temper, she'd only ever said the things she knew we all wanted to hear.

When Emma finished speaking, Doctor Bell smiled gently at her. 'To a large extent, I agree with what you're saying,' he said. 'Hope Park's treatment plans are suited to those who are ready to try and recover, who want to try to live a normal life. I understand you're not ready for these things, and that the time's come for us to start looking at alternatives. The doctors and I have spoken at length, and we've agreed to make some compromises, to work with you in building a new treatment plan that we *all* feel comfortable with.'

Emma sighed, and for the first time in as long as I could remember a weight seemed to life from her shoulders.

'Before you get too excited, though, you should know that there *will* still be boundaries. You *will* be required to work with us on agreed terms. Unfortunately, weight loss will not be one of these.'

Emma smiled at this – whatever the situation, there was always time for a spot of gallows humour.

The rest of us did not smile. 'So, what are these boundaries?' Mum said, sceptically.

'With our assistance, we expect Emma to maintain her weight at an agreed safe level and to control her anorexic behaviours.'

Mum swallowed, trying hard to remain calm. 'These boundaries were in place the first time Emma was released from hospital,' he said. 'Why would you think she'll be any more willing to stick to them this time around?'

'Well, the agreed level will be closer to the one she wishes to see herself at.'

'That doesn't sound like a safe level,' I said, struggling to keep the frustration from my voice. 'It sounds as though you're asking us to watch her weight drop from dangerously low to critical. She already had a collapse that almost killed her, and she was heavier back then than she is now.'

I saw Emma wince at my use of the word 'heavier' and felt guilty.

'Actually' Doctor Bell said, 'the evidence suggests that Emma's collapse was caused by the speed of her weight loss rather than her weight itself. Our bodies simply aren't built to cope with such enormous changes over short periods of time. The critical thing is to prevent Emma from exposing her body to these risks in future. One way to do this is to break the pattern of hospital admissions, which has been the main cause of her fluctuating weight.'

Mum shifted uneasily in her chair. 'Will the care team at least be continuing their visits to Emma in Myreton?'

Doctor Bell laid down the pen he'd been holding and sat a little straighter in his chair. 'Actually, we don't expect you to look after Emma after she's discharged. We don't think it's in her best interests to return home.'

Mum's face was fixed in place for a good second or two. Then, in a trembling voice, she asked Doctor Bell to repeat the last thing he'd said.

In the past few minutes the room had been pervaded by an air of deep and hopeless gloom, but if Dr Bell had lost any of his composure, he refused to show it. 'We think it would be a more positive step, and less pressure for you all, if she were to live outside the family home,' he said. 'Many of our patients have benefited from a change in environment, away from the old associations and memories that might previously have held them back. We want to offer Emma this same opportunity.'

Dad's mouth fell open. Mum sobbed and stuffed her face into the hankie she'd been fussing with since the meeting had begun. Emma's eyes finally moved from the carpet and began gaping at Doctor Bell instead.

'But I want to go home,' she croaked, bringing an end to a deeply unpleasant silence.

Doctor Bell took in some breath and leaned back, hands flat on his knees. 'It's your ticket out of here, Emma,' he said, softly. 'It won't be easy at first, I grant you that, but I assure you it'll be a great deal more enjoyable than Room 25.'

'Won't it also give her a great deal more opportunity to try and kill herself again?' I said, suddenly. The words were out before I even knew I was going to speak.

Emma stiffened, fixed me with a fierce stare. 'James, I told you not to speak about that.'

'I'm sorry if I felt it was worth a mention.'

Emma shook her head huffily. 'It wasn't even so bad.'

'I thought you were fucking dead, Emma!'

Emma began to cry, then. Forcing back tears of my own, I turned to Doctor Bell, more angrily than I meant to, and said, 'I'm sorry, but this sounds fucking crazy to me. Setting Emma loose in the big wide world, alone at last with her anorexia? I mean, what, have you exhausted every other possibility? Because it really looks like this is some kind of last ditch attempt to set things straight. Truth be told, it seems pretty fucking desperate.'

Doctor Bell held out an appeasing hand. 'I understand your concern, James,' he said. 'And yes, we have to accept there'll be risks involved here. But the fact is that we need to give Emma every chance possible to remain outside of hospital. The longer she's out, the more chance there is that she'll find a new focus. In the meantime, of course, we'll work as hard as possible to keep her out of harm's way and following her release the Edinburgh team will be at least as active as they are now in offering help and support. I can promise you, James, we're in no way giving up on your sister.'

I remember nothing of the meeting from this point. Unable to listen to anything more, I fell into a kind of daze, aware of nothing but a faint set of echoes in the corner of my mind. By the time Mum shook me back into the present, the doctors were shuffling papers and starting to head out of the room, and Emma was standing by her seat, looking lost and frightened amidst all the hustle and bustle, her eyes red and swollen. Instinctively, I walked over to her and put an arm around her shoulder. 'Are you okay?' I asked.

'I don't know yet,' Emma said. 'It's a lot to take in, isn't it?'

I nodded. 'I'm a bit scared, to be honest.'

'Honestly? You're not the only one. Do you really think it'll take them three months to sort everything out for me in Edinburgh?'

'Three months?' I asked. 'Is that what they said? And you'll be staying in Edinburgh?'

Emma rolled her eyes. 'You switched off for a bit back there, huh?'

I lowered my chin. 'Is that terrible?'

Emma shrugged. 'I should have done the same.'

Rosa and Elaine arrived by our side then, their smiles as warm and positive as always. 'Guess who got permission to chum you back to your room?' Rosa asked Emma, wiggling her eyebrows. Emma smiled before turning to kiss my cheek. Then, with a quick wave towards a corner of the room, she made her way out into the corridor towards the ward.

With Emma gone, I looked in the direction she'd waved to find Mum and Dad talking with Doctor Bell. Doctor Bell was listening intently and continued to nod solemnly until the end of their conversation, when he was visibly startled by something Dad said. He took a moment to regain his composure, then gave a final, resolute nod and shook both Mum and Dad firmly by the hand. When Dad turned around, I thought I detected a small spring in his step, but he gave me no opportunity to confirm this. 'Come on,' he said, marching quickly past me. 'It's time to go home.'

7

I HADN'T PLANNED TO LEAVE THE HOUSE FOR AT LEAST A DAY after the meeting was held, but I felt so lonely that evening that I decided to make a quick trip to the County. I arrived to find Sharon standing at her usual spot behind the bar, looking very bored indeed.

'Where is everybody?' I asked her, as she began pouring me a drink.

Sharon shrugged. 'What do you expect for a Tuesday evening? The place has been dead since the weekend.'

All but one of the tables were empty. In a far corner, Mervyn and Norrie, two of our older regulars were nursing pints of beer and studying the week's racing cards in one of the papers. Both met my eyes across the room and nodded their heads in greeting. Then Sharon handed me my glass and together we settled down to watch the second half of *Coronation Street* on the telly.

An hour later I was on my seventh, or maybe my eighth, vodka when Barry Kemp arrived and the evening was pretty much ruined. Though I should had grown used to his presence by now, it still surprised me every time Barry walked into the County. Loose cannons generally stayed clear of the County, preferring to spend their time in the unrulier bars of Cranston, where there was at least a chance they'd find the trouble they were in search of. Barry, though, seemed to feel quite at home in Myreton, though the other customers did not feel nearly so warmly towards him.

After shaking the rain from his coat, Barry took the seat two down from mine and barked his order to Sharon, before turning to me. Though only a few years separated us, Barry could easily have passed for forty. He had a stocky build, bad teeth and a nose that looked like it had been broken more than once. 'This place a gay bar now?' he sneered. 'Someone should have told me.'

'I wouldn't worry,' I said. 'You haven't missed much.'

I'd imagined we'd been exchanging banter, but as soon as I made my joke, I saw something flash in Barry's eyes and realised his comment had been made solely to offend. Barry Kemp, I remembered, did not participate in friendly conversation, because to do so would distract from the larger goal of his life: to one day become Scotland's most notorious bell-end.

Barry lifted the shot glass Sharon had laid down in front of him and, closing his eyes, drank it off. When he opened his eyes again, he noticed Sharon looking at him. 'You got a fuckin' problem?' he asked. Sharon sniffed and went back to watching the telly. It clearly wasn't the reaction Barry had hoped for. Mumbling something beneath his breath, he grabbed a bag of tobacco from his pocket and set about rolling himself a cigarette. 'This shithole never gets any more interesting, does it?'

'It's usually bouncing in here on Tuesdays,' Sharon said. 'Somebody must have put the word out that you were coming.'

Barry glared at Sharon. 'You're a funny fucker, eh?' he said, without laughing. Then, clamping a cigarette between his teeth, he took a box of matches from his pocket and readied himself to light it.

Sharon rolled her eyes wearily. 'Barry,' she said. 'how many more times are we going to go through this? You are not. Allowed. To smoke. In the bar.'

'Who says?' Barry said, the cigarette bouncing on his bottom lip as he spoke. 'The manager? Far as I can see, the old bastard's not here. So, I'll do as I fuckin' please.'

'Barry,' Sharon said. 'I'm telling you. You'll take that cigarette outside right now.'

'Or what?' Barry said. Holding Sharon's gaze carefully, he took a match and struck it against the box.

'For Christ sake, Barry,' I said. 'For once in your life, just do as you're told.'

Barry froze in place, the burning match flickering an inch from his cigarette. Very slowly, he turned towards me, his eyes wild and red with booze, and said, 'The fuck you say?'

'I said, I think you –'

'No, no, no,' said Barry, who clearly didn't believe in allowing other people to finish their sentences so long as he had any kind of thought whatsoever floating around in his head. 'You don't tell me what to do, faggot. I'm a paying customer, and I'll do whatever I want.'

'Outside, Barry,' Sharon said, warningly. 'Now!'

Barry slid from his stool and walked towards me. He stopped only a few inches from my side, watching me. I, in turn, watched his right hand, the one that wasn't holding his cigarette. Noticing this, he made his hand into a fist and jerked it towards me. Without wanting to, I winced. He liked that. He made me wince again, then turned back to Sharon.

'I need some fresh air anyway,' he said, moving towards the exit. 'Get another drink ready for me.'

I should have kept my mouth shut then, but the events of the day and the drink inside me had weakened my defences. I hated Barry in that moment, hated his sneering and his arrogance and his stupid, angry fucking face. Most of all, I hated that he was winning. Why was it always the strong who won? Why was it never the ones who were good but not strong? Suddenly, my anger was too great to contain. So, I said, 'Go find somewhere else to drink.'

Barry turned back to face me. 'The fuck you just say?'

'You heard me,' I said. 'Go get drunk somewhere else if you hate this place so much.'

'It's not the place I hate,' Barry said, walking back towards me. 'It's the fuckin' faggots they've got working here.'

I shook my head, frowning, and said, 'Go fuck yourself.'

Instantly, Barry grabbed me by the neck and slammed me into the back wall of the bar. I felt a sharp pain in my shoulders and fell to the ground. Then he was shouting above me, his face a bright, steaming red. In a panic, I tried scrambling to my feet, but a kick to the ribs sent me sprawling again. In another second his shoe was against my cheek, grinding my face into the carpet.

That was as far as he got before Mervyn and Norrie arrived. Grabbing him by the arms, they dragged him across the room and spun him out of the front door into the street, before hopping back inside in time for Sharon to lock the door behind them.

'My god, James,' Sharon said, turning a pale face towards me. 'Are you okay?'

I looked back at her helplessly. 'Barry pushed me over,' I said.

Sharon breathed a heavy sigh of relief, stifled a smile. 'Yes, he did,' she said. 'And he made your lip bleed. Let me get something for it.' She turned to gather the first aid kit from behind the bar but had taken only a few steps when she caught sight of a figure stumbling towards the hotel's back entrance. 'Oh god,' she said, her voice trembling. 'He's coming back.'

I looked at her stupidly. 'What?'

'He's coming back in! Someone lock the door, quick!'

But it was too late. Heavy footsteps had already begun to sound along the back corridor of the hotel. A moment later, Barry appeared from around the corner and made his way towards me. Sharon began pulling frantically at the back of his jumper in a bid to stall his progress, but Barry hardly seemed to notice. Within seconds, he was face to face with me.

'I don't. Take orders. From faggots,' Barry shouted, then delivered a punch to the side of my head that sent me spinning to the ground. He stood over me, sneering. 'Soft mother *fucker*,' he shouted, chords standing out on his neck. 'Get the fuck back up.'

I struggled back to my feet, tasting blood in my mouth for the second time that day. 'You miserable bastard,' I growled. 'You really enjoy this shit, don't you? Don't you think people have enough to worry about without you turning up and making things worse for them?'

'I know you do,' Barry said, with a smirk. 'I know all about that little sister of yours. Yeah, I hear her mentioned all over town. Tell me, how is she? You see her recently, or is she already dead?'

The punch I delivered caught Barry flush on the nose. His head went backward and returned red, the baseball cap he'd been wearing landing upside down on a nearby chair. I grabbed straight for his neck, but he ducked to the side and I ended up instead with a handful of his sweat-stained shirt. Then I was back on the ground, trying frantically to divert the barrage of blows that Barry was delivering to my face. Mervyn and Norrie were tugging at his arms, their eyes wide and panicked, yelling for him to stop, but he wouldn't, just kept punching and snarling, and when I looked up all I could see were his blood-soaked, tobacco-stained teeth, and the fist he brought down on my face, an inch from my eye, and right then I realised that despite all the pain and the horror of it all this felt good, like some kind of release, an emptying of anxiety, a chance to finally breathe, and it didn't stop feeling like that, even when Barry raised his fist once more and brought it crashing down on the top of my head.

Then the room fell very quiet. I was lying, closed-eyed and half-smiling, when a strong hand gripped my right shoulder and I was pulled upwards, away from the melee, into the relative peace of a nearby sofa. Then Norrie was in front of me, studying my face, and his hand appeared, and he asked how many fingers he was holding up and I counted and said 'three' and he smiled and patted my cheek and was gone. Propping myself up on an elbow, I peered over the sofa towards the scene of the fight to find Barry squirming on the carpet, grasping his balls and gasping for breath. Above him, Sharon stood clutching the baseball bat we kept behind the bar for emergencies. 'Barry,' she said. 'You're an arse. I'm calling you a taxi, do you hear? You can either accept the ride or else you'll enjoy another night in the cells.'

Shaking her head wearily, she made her way to the phone, leaving Mervyn and Norrie to take a seat and watch as the colour began to return to Barry's face. His breath was coming back to him now, but every so often he let out a strange whimpering noise, like a frightened puppy. It was fascinating and disturbing in equal measure.

Norrie shook his head pityingly. 'Poor sod'll no' ken whether to puke or shit himself.'

Mervyn nodded his agreement. 'Aye,' he said. 'Happened to me just the once, but I'll never forget it. It was like one of them ice cream headaches. But in my balls.'

I fell asleep then. By the time Sharon shook me awake half an hour later, the others had left and the hotel was in darkness. Sharon offered me a lift, which I gratefully accepted. My head was hurting worse than before, and I felt a little woozy, either from the punch to my face or the booze I'd drunk. I sat the whole way home with my head pressed against Sharon's dashboard, praying for the awfulness to pass, but it didn't. When the car stopped and I raised my head, Sharon reached out and squeezed my arm. 'He's a dick, James,' she said. 'Don't let the things he said bring you down. Go inside and get some rest and wake up happy tomorrow. Please.'

I nodded, then made my way into the house, where Mum and Dad were already asleep. I washed my face, the cuts on my lips and forehead stinging, then lay down in the darkness of my room and cried harder than I had in years.

My bruises turned surprisingly ugly overnight. As I studied them in the bathroom mirror the following morning I concluded that, while I wasn't quite Ed Norton in *Fight Club*, I could probably at least have made it on set as an extra. Dad, I knew, was already out working, but I could hear Mum clattering around in the kitchen. And so, to prevent questions being asked, I threw on a pair of sunglasses before making my way to grab a coffee.

Mum had been about to take a sip of tea when I walked into the kitchen, but when she saw my face the cup's journey ended an inch short of her mouth, which she used instead to mutter something undecipherable.

'Pardon?' I asked.

Mum sucked an invisible crumb from her teeth. 'I can only presume those stupid sunglasses you're wearing, indoors on a cloudy day, in the middle of January, are meant to hide that ridiculous black eye.'

Feeling silly, I took off the glasses and placed them by the toaster. 'I fell down. On the... pub. Ground,' I said, by way of explanation.

'What a ridiculous lie,' Mum said, which was true. 'Tell me, is the County carpet also responsible for your split lip and thick ear?' When I didn't answer, Mum shook her head, then clicked her tongue and sighed, a rare hat-trick of disappointment. 'James,' she said, 'I know you're stressed at the moment, but this behaviour has to stop.'

'What behaviour?' I asked

'The drinking mostly,' Mum said, placing her cup of tea by the kettle. 'But generally, I'd feel a lot more comfortable if you'd just stop acting like such an arse. It was bad enough having to unearth you from the hallway furniture last winter. I thought meeting Hannah had put a stop to all that, but then last month you vanished off on that boozy all-nighter in Cranston. Now, it seems, you're involving yourself in... well, what was it? Some sort of –' she hesitated before tasting the words '– bar room brawl?'

'Barry Kemp hit me,' I told her.

Mum crossed her arms across her chest. 'Why?'

'Because he's a dick.'

'Barry Kemp never hit you before. Why last night?'

'It wasn't my fault.'

'But you had been drinking.'

It was not a question. I dropped my eyes to the ground.

'And you were the only person he hit.'

A statement, again, though Mum was clearly disappointed when I didn't contradict it. She fell quiet for a moment, then asked, 'Did you hit him back?'

I took a deep breath. 'He said something terrible.'

Another shake, click and sigh. A double hat-trick. 'What did I always tell you about sticks and stones.'

'It's not always true,' I said.

Mum looked at me, gave another sigh. I sighed, too, and we fell into silence. Then something occurred to me. 'Hold on, how did you know what happened in Cranston last month? Have you been speaking with Holly?'

Mum shot me a dry look. 'For goodness' sake, James, I put two and two together when you arrived back home a day late and looking like shit. I *was* young once, too, you know. I just never acted like such a fucking idiot.'

I winced like Mum had slapped me. I wasn't used to hearing her swear, though I guessed sometimes 'gosh darn' and 'silly billy' just didn't cover it.

Mum walked the few steps towards me and placed a hand on my shoulder. 'This isn't you, James,' she said, forcing her gaze upon me. 'You're too good. Your *life* is too good. I know some things are far from perfect, but you have so many other things to be thankful for. Don't become so bitter that you forget to appreciate them. Please, try, try, *try* to be happy.'

'I am happy,' I said, which was sort of true, but mostly not. 'I'm going to go through to my room now.'

'Okay,' Mum said. 'Well, maybe in that case you could

make a start with your packing. Do something positive with your day.'

I stifled a shudder at Mum's mention of packing. Despite what she believed, preparing for the trip would not fill my head with happy dreams of future adventures, but with the painful thought that in only three days' time I'd be forced to abandon Emma. So, while I knew that I *could* start packing, I also knew that I wouldn't. I knew I'd spend the morning sleeping off my hangover and pointedly ignoring the chaos that was life, and that I'd wake up panicked, and that my suitcase would remain empty for the remainder of the day, and the following day, and quite probably the day after that.

I didn't say any of this to Mum, though. Instead, I swallowed back my terror, declared her idea to be a very brilliant one indeed, and set off for my room with an artificial spring in my step.

8

I STILL CAN'T TELL IF IT WAS SENTIMENTALITY OR PANIC THAT drove me to heave the old leather suitcase down from the attic the following evening, but I clearly remember the looks of surprise that Mum and Dad adopted as I dragged it past them to the centre of the living room floor. It had been years since any of us had thought of the suitcase, and longer still since its rusted clasps had been snapped open. But think of it I had, and snap its clasps I did, and whether they wanted to admit or not, Mum and Dad were both intrigued.

The suitcase was home to our collection of old family photographs. Mum and Dad had rarely been without a camera during my childhood, snapping away happily at every birthday, every holiday, and every party we'd ever been part of. Emma and I had always insisted we keep every single photo that came back from the chemist, and this had left us with a huge collection of blurred or grainy images. Looking at them now it was difficult to understand why we'd been so insistent. Smiling, I picked up one of the duds, a deeply unfocussed image of a mountain – or perhaps it was a dog – and tore it in half.

Until then, Dad had been pointedly ignoring the photos, but when he heard the tearing of paper he suddenly jumped to his feet and turned to me with a murderous look in his eyes. 'Don't you dare do that!' he growled.

I looked at him helplessly. 'Dad,' I said, 'I wasn't doing anything.'

Dad squared his shoulders and took a step towards me. 'Put. The paper. Down,' he said.

I put the paper down.

It did not help. Dad continued to glare at me in silent fury. Then, after the best part of an eternity, he marched across the room and out the back door, slamming it behind him.

I looked towards Mum. 'Did I do something wrong?' I asked.

Mum looked towards me, smiled sadly. 'It's hard to know these days,' she said. 'But it's probably best to put the photographs away for tonight.' Still wearing her half-smile, she stood up from her chair, gave my hair a playful rub, and made her way to bed. Left alone, I tried to turn my attention back to the photos, but the pleasure had gone out of the whole thing. I threw the pictures back in the suitcase and crept off to my room.

I've never understood people who sleep easily. How do they ever manage to clear their brain of its messiness, to sweep all the day's nagging doubts and worries far enough aside to allow space for a full eight hours of untroubled rest? My nights were built on a series of fitful naps sprinkled with long waking spells of regret and self-loathing, and depending on how well my brain was behaving, a single night could last for anything between a day and a lifetime.

After tossing and turning for about a month after Dad's tantrum, I finally resigned myself to another sleepless night and left my room to get a drink of water. I imagined that Mum and Dad would both be in bed, but the light was still on in the living room, and when I reached the door I saw Dad crouched on the carpet with the suitcase open in front of him. The torn photo was standing on the mantelpiece. Dad had taped its pieces together and left it there, presumably as a challenge against my earlier act of destruction. I stood by the door and waited for him to notice me, waited for him to start up again, but when he turned around he didn't look angry any more, just tired, weary to his bones.

'Do you remember this one?' he asked, offering me the photo in his hand.

I looked at the picture and nodded. It showed Emma and me, aged around four and six, on a beach during a family holiday in the north of Scotland. I was skimming stones across the water next to Emma, who gazed carefully at the pebbles below her feet. In those days, Emma always collected the shiniest stones from the beach, pleaded with Dad to let her take them home. Dad always told her to leave them, that they never looked the same when they dried out, but she could never resist.

This day, the day the photograph was taken, we'd showed our stones and shells to Dad on the way back to the caravan and asked the scientific name of each. He made deliberately stupid guesses like *Tyrannosaurus Crabbus* and *Norman*. It wasn't even funny, but he made it funny. Emma and I had howled with laughter.

I handed the photograph back to Dad. 'We had some good times back then, didn't we?' I said.

'The best times,' Dad said, his voice small. He picked another picture from the suitcase, one of him sitting with a chubby, blue-eyed baby Emma in the garden. He looked at it for a moment, then turned away quickly, hoping that I hadn't seen the film of water that had glazed his eyes. I picked up a few photos and began shuffling through them, but I wasn't paying any attention to the pictures. I simply didn't know what to say.

It was Dad who broke the silence. 'They should never have kept her in hospital after she was out of danger. All those months they spent forcing that food down her throat. All they did was make her angry at us all. I tried to tell them, but they wouldn't listen. Those doctors have ignored me for years, told me not to say this or that, to leave things to them. Well, look where it's got us. Your sister's right, you know. They don't have the answer to everything.'

'They only want to help her, Dad.'

'At least they've had the chance to try,' Dad said, a touch of anger returning to his voice. 'And meanwhile we've been left to pick up the pieces each time they sent her home. It's been the hardest thing in the world to sit around and watch others taking charge of her life. All I want is to help her, to make her see some sense. I only ever wanted to help her.'

'I know that, Dad.' I said. 'We all do.'

Dad took up another bundle of photographs but set them down without even looking at them. 'I'm sorry I lost my temper tonight,' he said. 'I shouldn't have done that. I know you don't deserve it.'

'It's okay.'

'It's just,' he said, and he paused, and he looked away from me, and his face crumpled.

'Dad?' I said.

'It's just so hard,' he said. 'It's so terribly, terribly hard.'

'It's okay, Dad,' I said. 'Really it is. You don't have to explain.'

Dad rubbed his forehead, all of his weariness seeming to

pour out of the gesture. 'Do you think this new idea of theirs will work?' he asked.

'I don't know,' I said. 'I suppose it's worth a shot if Emma starts warming to the idea.'

Dad nodded, dragged a hand across his eyes. 'That's what I think, too.'

'Dad,' I said. 'I saw you whisper something to Doctor Bell after Emma's meeting. What did you say?'

Dad stifled a grin as he turned to look at me. 'I told him not to fuck it up this time.'

'You did not!' I gasped.

'I did, too,' Dad said. He started to laugh, and so did I.

We'd been talking in hushed tones, but our laughter must have woken Mum because we soon heard her pad through to the kitchen for a glass of milk. After another few seconds she appeared at the door. 'What are you two giggling about?' she asked, clearly delighted that Dad and I were somehow getting along. Sighing contentedly, she sank into the sofa and took a sip of her milk. 'Well, James,' she said. 'Two more days and you'll be in Vienna. You must be getting excited.'

I cleared my throat self-consciously. 'Not so much,' I said. 'Actually, I don't think I'm going to go.'

Mum started so violently that the milk in her glass made a little *plop* sound. '*What?*' she said, her voice raising several octaves. 'But *why*? Has something happened with Hannah?'

'No,' I said.

'Did you break up?'

'No, Mum.'

'Don't you love her anymore?'

'Of course, I do,' I said.

'So, you should go, then.'

I put my head in my hands. 'Mum, you don't

understand.'

Dad hadn't said a word since Mum's arrival, but I'd felt his eyes on me throughout our conversation. Now, as silence took over, he finally took his turn to speak. 'It's your sister, isn't it,' he said, softly.

'It's just... after the meeting yesterday, I... I'm not sure I can abandon her.'

'James, you're not *abandoning* her,' Mum shouted. 'For goodness sake, you have a life to live. I've been trying to tell you this for years. Will you please start *listening* to me?'

Dad placed his hand on Mum's shoulder. She threw her head around to face him, and he smiled at her reassuringly. She took some time to wipe her eyes before relaxing slightly. Then Dad turned to me. 'Your mother's right, son,' he said, quietly. 'You have to stop trying to be Emma's big saviour. You can't sacrifice your own happiness just to try and make her well.'

'But she *needs* me,' I said, my eyes tearing over.

'She needs her *family*, James, and that includes me and your mother. It's *our* job to look after your sister, not yours. It would break our hearts to watch you just sitting around, waiting for things to get better. And that's all you'd be doing, you know – sitting around and waiting – because nothing you do or say is going to make any difference to Emma's chances of recovery. You have to start making the most of your life, son. You have to start taking care of yourself.'

I was really crying now. 'I'm just so scared,' I said. 'I just want my little sister back.'

'And we just want our little baby,' Dad said, swallowing hard. 'I know how you feel. It's the hardest thing in the world to watch her suffering. But you can't let that suffering define you. You need to go, without guilt, and find yourself, find the person you're meant to be.'

'But I don't know how,' I said.

'It's simple,' Dad said. 'Go to Vienna. Take the trip you've planned with Hannah. Try not to worry every moment what might be happening here. And wherever the journey leads you, whatever comes of your relationship, never stop living your life to the absolute fullest.'

I gaped at Dad in stunned silence. I'd long suspected the father I'd once known was still there somewhere, but it had seemed impossible to think that I'd ever find him again, that he'd ever manage to break through the seemingly impenetrable wall of anger that had built up around him. But on that night, he did exactly that, and he was once again the father who'd loved and cherished me as a baby. For the first time in years, I was my father's little boy. I remembered how he'd always been there for me, how he'd bounced me on his knee and kissed the tears from my face. I remembered how he'd held me close to him when I was afraid, how he'd told me that everything was alright, that I mustn't be scared, that Daddy was there.

Dad must have been surprised by his speech, too. As soon as he stopped talking his confidence faded and his eyes dropped to the floor. Reaching out, I laid a hand gently on his shoulder. 'Dad?' I said, my voice trembling. 'I love you, Dad.'

Dad's head shot upwards, his eyes wide. He looked first to Mum, who was beaming at him through her tears, and then towards me. He started to speak, found a frog in his throat, cleared it, and said in a strained voice, 'Aye, well, I love you, too.' He wiped a hand across his eyes, cleared his throat again. 'You're a good lad,' he said. 'You're a good lad.'

I'd never loved my father more than I did in that moment.

9

EMMA WAS DELIGHTED WHEN I ARRIVED AT HOPE PARK THE following morning. She kissed my cheek, held me tightly for a moment and said, 'Thank goodness I was able to see you again before you headed off. Monday afternoon was hardly an ideal farewell. Do you want to watch some telly?'

'Actually, I thought maybe we could do something a bit more interesting. Maybe even go out somewhere, if you like.'

Emma's eyes widened. 'Just the two of us?'

I nodded. 'We've got a three-hour pass. But you have to promise to behave. I'll drag you back here by your hair if you decide to make any more spontaneous trips to London.'

'I promise I'll be good,' Emma said, and I think she nearly smiled.

Five minutes later we were out of doors together for the first time since Emma's dash for freedom. As usual, she began to shiver as soon as the cold air hit her, so I drove to the Kelvingrove Gallery, where we wandered indoors through random galleries, studying everything from art to animals, Ancient Rome to the Victorians. We spoke very little during the first hour, but for once the silence was comfortable rather than strained. Walking around, Emma seemed almost peaceful, and I was given a rare glimpse of the girl I'd once known, the girl who'd been so fascinated by things, who'd been so content with life, before her illness had arrived to claim her happiness.

After a while, Emma sighed contentedly and sat down in front of a large canvas, a landscape by Sisley, which she'd already picked out as her favourite. I sat down next to her. 'So,' she said, 'a little bird told me that you'd thought about cancelling your trip to Vienna.'

'Was that little bird called 'Mummy', by any chance?'

Emma turned from the painting towards me. 'Don't be upset with her. I already suspected pretty much everything she told me in any case, so it's not like she gave away any secrets.' There was a pause as she looked down. 'So, I take it it's true, what she said?'

'I've had some doubts.'

Emma sighed. 'You're an idiot, do you know that?' When I said nothing, she took my hand and squeezed it. 'Jamie, do you remember that summer Daryll Cockburn kept turning up outside our house to call us names as we played on the street? We learned so many new words that summer, but we never paid the slightest bit of attention to him. I guess it bothered him, the way we managed to ignore him, because that final day of the holidays he jumped off his bike and began to throw pine cones at us.'

'He clocked you on the head with one,' I said.

'Yeah, he did, square on the temple, the nasty little shit. I wasn't bleeding or anything – it didn't even hurt that much – but I'll never forget how frightened you looked as I fell to the pavement. Then, it was like something had possessed you. None of us could believe how quickly you ran at Paul, how hard you kicked him. He must have been nearly twice your size, but he was terrified, and the friends he'd brought with him did nothing to help, not even when you threw that punch at his head. I've never seen you as angry as you were then. You looked as though you were ready to kill him for what he'd done.'

'I was,' I said. 'And I'd do the same thing now if he tried it again.'

'I'm sure you would,' Emma said. 'But here's the thing; you can't save me anymore. You can't rescue me like you did that day. My life's so much more complicated now than it was all those years ago, and nothing you do is going to help us get back to the way we were. I wish it was as simple as spending time with you until some little switch flicked on at the back of my head, but it's not.

'I love you, Jamie. I always did and I always will. But there was always going to come a time for you to move on, to take a step back from the sister you've spent your life protecting. You need to start living your life. Seriously, you've missed so much these past few years by hanging around waiting for me to get better. You can't afford to keep doing that.'

'Emma,' I said. 'I –'

'No, I mean it, Jamie. You have to stop thinking about *me*. It's time for you to be selfish. Whatever decisions you make, make for yourself. Whatever things you do, do for yourself. And, most importantly, do not DARE to feel guilty for leaving me. Because I won't blame you for a single thing.'

I looked towards the ground. 'But what if something happens to you?' I said. My voice was little more than a whisper.

'It won't, James.'

'Because I'm not sure I could stand that,' I said. 'I couldn't ever bear to lose you.'

Emma exhaled slowly, nodded her head as if she were coming to some kind of decision. 'Okay,' she said. She took a deep breath. 'Jamie, I know I said last month that I wouldn't make any promises to you. I wasn't trying to be mean. It's just that there's nothing I hate more than making promises, nothing that scares me more than the thought I might break one, even by accident.'

'It's alright, Emma,' I said. 'I understand.'

'Maybe,' Emma said. 'But it's hardly fair to send you off feeling like this, is it.'

'It's not perfect,' I said, 'but I'll be okay.'

Emma clicked her tongue. 'Jamie, if you'd shut up for a minute, you'd realise I'm trying to say something here. And I've been thinking on this for days, so don't think this is just some stupid attempt to make you feel better.'

'Okay.' I said, trying to keep my voice level.

'I'm ready to make an exception,' Emma said. 'I promise you, from the bottom of my heart, that I won't do anything stupid while you're away.'

My jaw dropped. I stared at my sister. 'How can you be so sure?'

'Because, Jamie, my life's finally about to change. You heard it yourself at the meeting. For the first time in years, I'm being given the chance to save myself, to make my own choices and decisions. I'm finally going to be in charge of my own destiny.'

'Do you think you can do it?' I asked.

'What?'

'Turn some things around.'

'I don't know,' Emma said. 'I mean, there's no such thing as a magic cure for anorexia, no making it all go away forever. But there's always some small step I can take towards a better day, some minor victory I can win. Yes, it'll be frightening, and I'll panic a thousand times before things start to come together, but I think I'm finally ready to make some changes. I think I finally want to be happy.'

I was looking at Emma in amazement. 'I don't know what to say.'

'Good,' Emma said. 'Because talking like this is fucking exhausting.' She looked down to her watch. 'Also, we need to get going before they send out a search party. Again.'

Back in Hope Park, Emma immediately lay down on her bed, dog-tired from her adventure. I sat down by her side and searched for some final words, but none came. Emma looked up at me and smiled, laid a hand on my cheek and swept away a tear that I hadn't even known was there. Then, very softly, she said, 'Go now. Go, and remember what I told you – don't worry. Enjoy your journey. And remember; no matter where you are, I'll be thinking of you, and hoping with all my heart that you're happy.'

I kissed her, and hugged her, and then made my way to the door. 'I love you so much, Emma.'

Emma shrugged. 'Of course, you do. You'd never have stood me for this long if you didn't.' She smiled, though she was trying hard not to cry. 'Now go. Please.'

Without another word, I turned and made my way from the room.

'You stopped drinking?' Dan asked, wincing as he tasted the phrase on his lips. 'But why? It's not like you're not an alcoholic. Alcoholics go to meetings. You go to parties.'

'At worst, you're a drinking enthusiast,' Will said. 'Which is actually a positive thing, when you think about it. It's nice to have hobbies.'

'Precisely,' Dan said. 'Come on, James. You can't come to the Grange and not drink. It's like hiring a hooker that just wants to cuddle. Am I right guys?' A cheer erupted around us as Dan raised his hand for an apparently well-earned round of high-fives.

'Hilarious, guys,' Holly said, who'd been standing listening by my side. 'Last time I heard those jokes, I laughed so hard I fell off my dinosaur.'

Immediately, the laughter faded and eyes began falling to the floor. 'We were just saying,' Dan mumbled.

'Well, if you're done just saying, then shut up and go get the boy an apple juice.'

Dan shook his head, gazed at his boys. 'Can you believe this?' he said. They couldn't, of course.

Holly turned to me and smiled, patted a hand against my cheek 'Very impressive, Mr Barnes,' she said. 'Very impressive indeed.'

Holly and I found a table, and for the next couple of hours we sat with Steve, reminiscing fondly about school friends we'd never really liked, and fun we'd never really had, and whether Mr Bevan the PE teacher had really shagged Katie Smith at the school leavers' dance, and whether Mark Johnstone really was spending time in prison. Then, at around eleven, the bar staff called last orders. I wasn't remotely prepared to leave, but before I found time to panic my phone began to vibrate in my pocket. I stepped quickly outside and answered the call. It was Hannah.

'So,' she said, after a few horrible moments of silence. 'It turns out that I'm sorry for how I acted on Tuesday. Very sorry. I don't know why I got so defensive. I know I should have been there for you. I guess I was just... being...'

'A dick?' I suggested.

'Actually, I was going to go with twat.'

I considered that. 'Okay,' I said. 'Also, true.'

Hannah sighed. 'I'm just not used to being this close to another person,' she said. 'I've never known anything like this before. Which isn't to say I'm unhappy, because I'm not. It's just... this whole thing's so incredibly intense.'

'Is intensity such a bad thing?'

'No,' Hannah said, 'but it still scares me. I mean, I'm not even twenty-one yet. There are so many things I want to do, so many places I want to see. I can't afford to take things easy. Not yet.'

'But I'd never expect you to take things easy.' I said. 'I wouldn't want you to.'

'So, what do you want?'

'I want you to be happy. And I want me to be happy. And I want us to find that happiness together.'

Hannah fell silent for a moment. 'Well,' she said, 'I guess we're in with a chance, then. Because I want exactly those same things. I love you James. I love you so much. Life's going to be good to us. I just know it.'

'I hope so,' I told her. 'I guess we'll find out tomorrow.'

Hannah gave a little squeak of excitement. 'Yes! You'll see me tomorrow. So, go now, and have fun, and make sure your friends don't hate me too much for stealing you away.'

I said I would, and we both said goodnight, and as I hung up the phone, I realised how grateful I was to find myself with Hannah. I mean, she wasn't perfect. She wasn't a fairy princess or anything like that. She was challenging, and crazy, and frequently frustrating. But she loved life with a passion that made all of those things seem worthwhile. She had her own unique vision of the world, and she wanted to find her place in it, to test life's limits and boundaries. And in allowing me to be with her, she was showing me a life far beyond the limits I had set for myself.

Standing alone in the car park, I suddenly realised how tired I was. I stole a look through the hotel window to find Holly and Steve falling about laughing at the punchline to one of Dan's jokes. I wanted to hear it, too, but I knew I wouldn't, not that night at least. After saying goodbye to Emma earlier that day, the thought of another round of farewells was too much to bear. I whispered a silent adieu to my friends, then turned on my heels and made my way home.

10

I GOT OUT OF BED AT FIVE O'CLOCK THE FOLLOWING MORNING and peered out through my curtains to find the street blanketed in darkness, the stars hidden behind a wall of cloud. The ground was laid white with frost, and a light drizzle danced in the wind against the street's solitary lamppost. I quickly took a shower and got dressed and when I returned to the window a taxi was idling a few yards from the front door. I threw on my coat and shoes and picked up the suitcase I'd finally got around to packing the previous evening. Then I crept through the house, past the bedroom of my sleeping parents, and went out into the cold winter morning.

As I climbed into the taxi, I hoped my parents would understand why I was setting out on my journey alone. Mum had been eager to drive me to the airport and wave me off at departures, but after leaving the Grange I'd realised that I had to leave in the fastest way I could, and with the least possible fanfare, if I was to find the courage I needed to set off on my adventure. I'd call Mum and Dad when I arrived in Vienna to check they'd found the note I'd left them, to check they'd forgiven my decision.

When I arrived at the airport, the butterflies in my stomach began beating their wings so hard that I thought I might puke. I checked in my bags as quickly as I could, and then made my way to the airport café. When I sat down, I noticed my hands were shaking. Small ripples appeared on the surface of my coffee each time I lifted the cup to my mouth. At the next table, an overweight baggage handler was making his way through a huge plate of scrambled eggs. The sight of it made my legs wobble.

I felt relieved when my flight was finally announced on the loudspeaker. Grabbing my backpack, I hurried towards the gate and waited impatiently to board the plane. Fifteen minutes later I'd found my seat, and as the cabin crew prepared for take-off, I took my phone out of my pocket and saw that, in all the excitement, I'd missed a text from Emma. Nervously, I opened the message and began to read:

You'll be all set to fly by now, I suppose. I hope Mum didn't cry too hard as she waved you off at the gate. No matter – she'll be happy as Larry when she realises how much she's saving on food. In any case, don't worry. Just enjoy your time with Hannah. Enjoy the city, the friends you meet, the food you eat. Treat every day as a new chance to change your life. And remember, at all times, that your sister is safe and everything will be fine.

Staring hard at my phone, I lingered over those last words. *Everything will be fine*. It was so long since I'd thought that, since I could even have imagined myself thinking it. And now here it was. Everything would be fine! Life, the future, the universe – they were all going to be fine!

Smiling, I closed my eyes and leant back in my seat and allowed myself to be carried away by dreams of the future. I stayed that way for a long time and when I roused myself and looked out of the window the plane was flying above the clouds, away from Scotland, away from Myreton, and for the first time in as long as I could remember I knew I was headed in the right direction.

ACKNOWLEDGMENTS

A special thank you to my wife and beautiful daughters, for their love, support and general excellence.

To Marya Hornbacher, for her essential guidance and endless encouragement.

To Pete Davies, Steve Hales, Natalie Herdman, Ellen Maloney, Roberto Rodriguez, David Sodergren and Maria for their faith and hard work and good advice.

To Kate Maré and Janetta Klemensová, for making my book look so pretty.

And a final thank you to Mum and Dad, for always being there. You are the two bravest human beings I will ever know, and I love you.

ABOUT THE AUTHOR

After finishing university, Andy Marr took a job in a bank, but he hated it, so he stopped and became a writer instead. *Hunger for Life* is his first novel, and is closely based on the life he shared with his amazing little sister, Seonaid. He lives in Edinburgh with his wife and two daughters, where he spends his days writing and his nights fantasising the downfall of Boris Johnson.

You can visit him online at the following locations:

 twitter.com/androomarr

 instagram.com/andy_the_actual_author

Printed in Great Britain
by Amazon

29470413R00175